Ghost of The Past

BRIDGET AKANBIEMU

Ghost of the Past

Copyright © Bridget Akanbiemu 2023

All rights reserved.

No part of this publication may be reproduced, distributed, or transmitted in any form or by any means, including photocopying, recording, or any other electronic or mechanical method, without the prior written permission of the author, except in the case of brief quotations embodied in critical reviews and certain other non-commercial uses permitted by copyright law.

ISBN: 979-8-3789-8507-4

Book Cover Design by TDBB STUDIOS
Published by TDBB STUDIOS | hello@thedigitalbrandboss.com

Acknowledgements

I have always wanted to write a book and writing this acknowledgement gives me great joy because it only means that my dream is finally becoming a reality. Although I wrote this book myself, I couldn't have done it without the support of God, my family, and my friends.

To my father, Dr Francis Adegoke Akanbiemu, I cherish and love you. Thank you for always believing in me. Thank you for supporting my dreams and being the biggest cheerleader in my life.

To my mother, Mrs Ngozi Clara Akanbiemu, you are the best mother anyone could ever ask for. You brought me up and taught me things I would never forget. Your prayers for me are deeply appreciated and I love you wholeheartedly.

To my sister, Janefrances Ifeoluwa Akanbiemu, I love you. Thank you for being my best friend, you are beyond amazing. My other sisters, Mojirayo and Tofunmi, you both are still so young but knowing that I have you ladies is more than enough encouragement for me to keep going. I love you both.

Mayowa Sanusi, my best friend, I love you and there is no way I would have written this acknowledgement without mentioning you. You mean the world to me. Thank you for giving me the courage to do this. Tise Alokan, I adore you. Thank you for being my best friend and supporting me.

Isioma Ezinwa, thank you for being there for me. You are beyond beautiful and amazing, and I love and adore you. Toyin

Aduwo, I'm proud to call you my friend because you are the sweetest and most supportive friend ever and I truly love you.

Ifunanya Ezechukwu, thank you for being you. You are a friend that I will always want to have, and I hope you never forget that. I love you. Mabel Mac-Harry, thank you for your support in this journey, I love you to pieces.

My dear friend, Shifra, you were the first person to read my manuscript. Thank you for that. I love you. Aisha, thank you for helping me in this journey despite your busy schedule, you are loved.

To my publisher, The Sarah Ari of TDBB STUDIOS, thank you for your help in this journey. You are beyond amazing.

To everyone else that has supported me, I remember you all and I'm truly thankful.

To my future readers, I hope you enjoy this book of mine. Thank you.

Contents

Prologue

When it Happened

Have you ever felt so frightened that your life is being taken away from you right under your nose? So paralysed that you couldn't speak, scream, or even fight back. It's like your breath is shortened, and the words are stolen from your mouth. Everything is in a haze, your eyelids insignificant because you cannot seem to comprehend the little things you see right in front of you. It gets worse when you get pushed to your front. You try to feel the hands holding you, as you feel your skirt being lifted so forcefully like they were not yours in the first place. Rough calloused hands grasp your breasts as if they belong to him. Your underwear is ripped away from your body like you're a ram yet to be slaughtered.

You try as much as you can to resist, but you feel numb all over. All you can think about is how much you want it to end - how much you want it to be just a dream or a horror story from your imagination. You don't want it to be your reality, story, or tale. It's not what you would want to tell, and not what you would be proud of. It's your worst moment, the worst day of your life. And as reality hits you in the face, the tears begin to pour in big drops, you begin to choke, and you try to push the tyrant away. But the sound of his guffaws fills your ears, 'You think you can resist me? Don't bother' Those words are followed by a sharp squeeze to your nipple and you feel the tears pouring rapidly. 'Please' you try to talk, but he chuckles loudly. 'Can you hear yourself? You are definitely enjoying this, so just keep quiet or I will stop being gentle.' He tweaks your nipples more forcefully this time for emphasis and that shuts you up. 'That's a good girl,' he says, his voice hoarse. You try to push him away again but the more you push, the more force is used, and you feel the worst pain ever; your virginity is being taken away from you, right in your home, your comfort zone. All you want is to get as far away from there as possible, to leave this horrifying setting because it's not more your domicile, it's your worst nightmare.

As you hear the voice whispering into your ear telling you your body is his to take, you belong to him, you have no right to resist, you deserve this unforgivable thing that's being done to you, all you want to do is run. But what do you do when you can't? You continue to feel the constraint on your body as he pushes in and out of you, for long seconds, minute upon minute, till you feel him flagging on you. You hear his low growl, you don't know if you should feel relieved that it has ended or just find a way to take your own life because the deed has been done. When he turns you back to him and you see your blood befouled all over the cheap wool rug you got after your first paycheque, all you want to do is scream.
But you don't, you watch him buckle himself up. Then he moves to touch your hair and as much as you want to resist, you feel handcuffed, chained. 'Why are you looking at me like that wasn't the best moment of your life? Because for me, it was,' he says in hushed tones.

You try to look at him but you can't see his face as he's wearing a mask. You have no idea who this is and it's at that revolving moment you realise that you don't have a face to hate. You are a lost soul with nowhere to direct your pain to, and your voice comes back, not in whispers, nor hushed tones, but in a piercing cry.

Chapter One

What is Life Really?

THEY SAY LIFE IS ORDINARY, extraordinary, unexpected, scary, vast, practical, miserable, and so on. Everyone has their own opinion on what it truly is. But for me, life is melancholy, bleak, depressing, a cage, if not my prison. I know there's a curiosity about how someone can live so negatively, but most of life has been tragic. I have lost more than I have gained, I have cried more than I have laughed. I have felt helpless more than I have felt grateful.

The only thing that keeps me going is my mother's last words,

'I want you to be stronger than me, never give up no matter what. I see strength in you.'

Those words were like a wake-up call, a silent prayer, they gave more pump to the blood in my veins. They gave me a new intendment, a reason to live, to make me not give a damn about my haunted memories, my horror story. I held on to those words because without them I had no reason to fight.

I never knew my birth parents, all I knew was I was found by my adopted mother at the gate of her house. She said it was like God had answered her silent prayers. She was not married, and never wanted to be, especially after escaping an abusive relationship that she had endured for years. She had just had a miscarriage from an attack with her ex-boyfriend when she saw me on her way back home. She said we connected instantly; my small palms had fitted into her warm ones, and they had held onto hers like they needed the shield. Now that I think about it, I'm sure they did because she was my protector, my mother, father, sister, and brother. She was everything till she lost her battle with cancer.

I remember when her case got serious. 'I feel myself getting worse, and my immune system is weakening. Tiwa, get ready for the worst please.'

Her words had been in soft mutters. She was weak. It was evident in the thin lines of her face, her agonising short breaths, the beads of sweat on her forehead, the bony structure of her face, and her dry lips.

'What do you mean? How am I supposed to get ready? Can anyone ever be ready for this? Mum, please you need to fight this,' I had pleaded, if only it was that easy. I usually tried to keep my tears in check, to be the strong one for once, since she was always the resilient one, but at that moment I couldn't. I was losing her - my only family, my best friend.

'Find love around you, make friends, meet someone, get away from this city, go somewhere else, find your birth parents if you can. Just do everything you can to stay happy, Tiwa. That is my last wish, that's all I ask.'

As she spoke, I recalled all the times we would both sit down and repine about how much people had hurt us; my birth parents for dumping me like I was a curse, and her ex for using her as a punching bag. But listening to her talk about me finding love was too much of an irony.

'I thought you said there was nothing like love' I queried as I moved to help her sit up. She coughed loudly, and I moved to give her the leftover water on the table.

'Trust me, there is. You just have to find it. You have a lovable spirit, no one could want to hurt you,' she continued.

Oh, how much faith she had in me, so much credence in me living a good life. Who could blame her? She had to say those words to give me hope. But as I looked at myself in the broken mirror of my room, relieving the most traumatic moment of my life, I envisioned how wrong those words were. Someone did hurt me, and it was the worst kind of hurt.

***

'Life can get you down, so I just numb the way it feels, I drown it with a drink and out-of-date subscriptions, and all the ones that love me, they just left me on the shelf.'

I sang along to Ed Sheeran's *Save Myself* as I struggled to close my already tattered door. I had complained about the little hole in it to my new landlord and he said he would have it fixed. But that was the third time he had made the espousal and I would be really lucky if he heeded my pleadings this time. I was ready to leave to find somewhere else if he refused because of how perturbed I had become, especially after what happened.

Following my late mother's advice, I left Lagos for Calabar, a quieter city, and just as beautiful, especially because of the splendid landscape, considering it was a tourist city in Nigeria. No one knew me there, and neither did I know anyone. The few friends I had ever kept in my pathetic life were never really close to me, but I would blame myself for that. Opening up to people was a chore on my part and not everyone had the time to fight their way in. One did try hard though, Chioma. She called me a lot and was with me while I grieved when I lost my mum. She stayed back in Lagos and was in full support of me leaving there despite not knowing the real reason behind my flight. This points to the fact that I'm indeed alone here, and to be honest I don't feel abysmal about it. If anything, it paves way for less disappointment.

My quest for a new life involved me finding a new job, especially if I wanted to be able to continue to afford my new place and fend for myself. I had an interview appointment with Adebanjo Publishing and Co, a well-known publishing company in Nigeria and I couldn't remember ever being that nervous. Of course, I had good credits, considering that I graduated with first-class honours in Public Relations and Advertising at the University of Lagos. Having friends that I could count on the fingers of one hand was beneficial as it gave me more time to study and less time to worry about drama. My life was easy, just me and my mum, till it got shattered by life's tragedy.

The sound of a loud horn stopped me in my tracks as I came to a halt in front of a black Mercedes. I wasn't current on cars, but the looks of the one right in front of me hid no indication that it was beyond expensive or at least one of the latest models. I wasn't sure of my surroundings till I saw a dark man in a black three-piece suit and a blue tie walk out of the car. He probably wasn't a male model, but he should have been. He was tall and masculine, he carried an imperious nose well, and his angular cheekbones carved down towards a flinty jaw. He walked forward and it was then that I noticed his eyes, they looked somewhat brown from where I stood, and they darted constantly as they gaped at me in what first seemed like awe, then confusion, and maybe anger. I couldn't tell.

'What the hell are you doing walking across the road like that? Do you want to get killed?' His voice wasn't exactly different from his looks, it sounded too cold and hard for someone who wore a three-piece suit. Well, what did I expect?

'I'm sorry, I didn't mean to. I was distract...'

'Please don't say you were distracted because that would make you more stupid. What in the world is a grown-ass woman like you doing crossing the road like a three-year-old? Do you even drive? Do you know how much trouble I would have gotten into if I had hit you?'

His voice was louder and I looked around me nervously, thankful that it was a barren road. His face was shaped in a frown and it took everything in me not to slap it off him, especially when he still looked beyond handsome. The one reason why I hated people was to avoid getting annoyed because I had a hell of a temper and this man here was going to bring the worst out of me if he kept going on like a barbarian.

'Who the hell do you think you are to talk to me that way? How dare you?' I held on to my handbag tightly in anger as I pointed my right finger at him, glad to see the surprise on his face as he glared at me. It was obvious he wasn't used to people talking back to him. Well, he was in for a treat.

'Do you know who I am at all?' He crossed his arms across his chest, as he waited for my response. I wasn't sure of what drama or show he was trying to put on here, but I had an interview to hurry to and I wasn't going to let one stupid rich man make me go late.

'I don't know if you're crazy or just jobless but as you mentioned earlier, I'm a grown-ass woman and I have somewhere to be. You can keep standing here wondering who remembers you while I leave,'

I said quickly, as I moved to walk past him, without looking back, ignoring the few glances I got from passers-by. I could feel his eyes on me as I walked away but all I could think about was how his eyes had looked at me that first second. It was like he savoured what he saw, but I couldn't be too sure since they changed to something else. I shook my head at myself as I hurried along. This wasn't good. For me, men were bad, and they always would be. I had to shut down this deadly attraction because that's what men were to me - deadly!

Chapter Two

Hired or Not

I WAS ONCE TOLD BY my mother that being positive was a way of having hope in your life. Maybe that's why she also named me Hope because I was hers. I went more with my maiden name Tiwalade because that was what she called me anyway. She only called me the other when she had a bad day or had no sales in her small store behind the house. I was her reassurance that all was well in the world, her saving grace. I didn't have many people around me to call me names. I would hear from Chioma that her dad called her Angela, while her brother called her skinny pumpkin. It was hilarious but also sweet. No one called me nicknames. I had been called a nerd, a statue, by my few friends because I hardly went anywhere. But no family setting. My grandma already died before I was born. My mum never even knew her father, she was raised by a single mum too and that's why she felt that I was God-sent.

'Aunty, *we don reach o*,' the bike man's voice resonated through my thoughts as I held onto his shoulder while getting off the motorcycle.

I heard the sudden sound of my skirt tearing slightly and I gave out a loud gasp. I knew I shouldn't have worn this skirt. I wanted to look very professional and I figured that this would do. It was obvious that bad luck was after me this morning, who did I offend?

'Na small tear, make you no bother yourself. Abeg people don dey born for back,' he gestured to the cars waiting behind us and I grabbed my handbag as I asked him how much the fare was.

After paying him, I tried to adjust my skirt by pushing the slightly torn part to the side, making it look more like a slit. It was a black skirt coupled with a blue cotton blouse. My hair was braided and it was packed up as the hot weather discouraged me from pouring my hair. I had no makeup on, except for transparent lip gloss, not because I didn't wear makeup as a custom but because I decided to just come as I was, and I would have been late anyway.

There were cars parked outside, people going in and out, and co-workers, sharply dressed were chattering behind the opened doors of the building. I could tell that they worked here because of the similar badges on their chest. As I walked closer to the building, I took in my breath sharply and stopped. The magnificence of the place hit me. It was a glass building and from where I stood, I could see the piles of books from what I would assume to be the third floor.

The thought of publishing my first book and seeing it there gave me goose bumps.

'Show me your ID, please,' one of the security guards asked me.

I showed him the email that was sent to me instead and he let me through. Inside the building was more beautiful. It smelt heavenly and I could see different opened offices vaguely from where I stood. Some were empty, while others had people inside. I smiled as I thought of myself sitting in mine. Working here would be a dream come true, it was something I had continuously longed for and now it was within my grasp.

'Hey there, can I help you?' The receptionist asked me politely. As I tried to bring my phone out, she stopped me.

'You applied for a job here, didn't you?' I nodded my head in affirmation as she held out her hand to check my phone.

'I was told to show that email when I get here.'

She nodded as she pressed something that looked like a bell, but it made no sound.

'Please, hold on,' she said courteously.

I looked at her badge more closely and saw her name, Damilola Akinwale. She noticed me staring because she held it up for me to see clearly.

'I'm Dami. You're Tiwa, right?'

I nodded pleasantly, glad that everyone appeared to be nice here, at least the only person I had met.

'Are you the new girl?'

I turned around to another lady behind us who was smiling so sweetly that it felt weird.

'I don't have the job yet,' I responded.

She was a bit on the big side, with a shapely figure. She had glossy skin, and her slender eyebrows were more obvious through her smile. 'Well, you must, because I need a new friend here,' she retorted. She held my arm as we both waved at Damilola before moving to the elevator.

'I'm Zainab, what's your name?' She asked as she pushed the button for the floor. She had an infectious smile on, as she studied me closely.

'Tiwa,' I said, unsure of how to react to this delightful spirit in front of me.

I had met nice people, but I still never felt used to it. I had tried to make myself unassailable, as a protective mechanism, because of how much I had been taken advantage of, and they were in the worst ways possible. Maybe that was why people being nice to me still caught me off guard.

'You seem to have a lot on your mind. Are you nervous? Don't worry, you will be fine. Mr Adebanjo isn't as scary as he looks.'

I looked at her more closely as the elevator opened. A few men in sharp suits were outside the elevator. We nodded in greeting them as they got in before turning towards the mahogany doors on the left.

'What do you mean by scary?' I asked her closely.

I could feel my heart beginning to beat faster as I walked along. A woman was sitting on a chair by the corner of a huge office with its doors closed.

'He always has a poker face on, and him being beyond handsome makes him more unapproachable' I nodded attentively as I took in her words.

As we stood in front of the elderly woman, her grey hair became more visible. She was smiling brightly at us, and it was now evident to me that everyone liked smiling here. Maybe it was part of the job qualifications.

'Good morning, ma' we both greeted her.

'Ma, please she has an interview with the boss,'

Zainab held the woman's shoulders as she spoke.

'Yes, he just finished his last meeting. You shouldn't keep him waiting, dear. Please, help me get my regular meal when you get downstairs,' she said to Zainab who nodded and whispered good luck to me before leaving.

'I'm sure when he sees you he would be glad that I insisted he gets a new assistant,' she remarked as we got closer to the doors.

From the way she spoke, it was obvious that she had a close relationship with him. My heart had already started galloping because this was it, the opportunity that would change my life and I prayed silently that it would end well.

'You can go in,' she said.

'Without knocking,' I motioned in question but she said it was fine before walking away.

I opened the door and got inside, but it wasn't the fact that it was beyond beautiful that rendered me speechless, it wasn't the velvet drapes framed around the windows, neither was it the heart-stopping view over the city or the sheer lace burgundy cotton behind the grey fabric sofa, it was the very familiar shirtless man in front of me.

***

The one thing I've never doubted in my twenty-two years of living is that there's no such thing as a coincidence. Things happen because they are supposed to, it's either they ruin you or make you. However, meeting this guy again left me addled. What was I supposed to make of it? And why would it happen in the most uncomfortable situation? It left me antsy and I loathed when someone had the capability to get into my skin this way, mainly because it was rare.

'You again? What the hell are you doing in my office?'

He moved to pick a folded shirt that was laid on his very organised table. I thought about his defined abs and how smoothly they would feel beneath my fingers. They looked like the ones you saw in movies, where you only imagined them because they seemed too unreal. My eyes were drawn to his stomach as he buttoned himself up with skilful hands, and I felt a tiny sense of disappointment when it wasn't visible to me anymore. Okay, maybe a little bit more than tiny.

'Didn't you hear me or something? Why are you in my office? Or are you going to just keep staring?'

I didn't realise I had been standing there gawking till his last words. Frankly, I wasn't sure of what I was doing here in the first place, predominantly because it was clear that I wasn't going to get the job after our disastrous encounter this morning. We had a mutual feeling of despise for each other and it was clearly not going to take us anywhere. He had already finished tucking his shirt back into his pants and it wasn't until I saw the spilled coffee at the other end of his table that I realised that he had probably stained his old shirt.

'Lady, are you deaf or something?'

It suddenly became chilly in the room and I wasn't sure if it was because of the two air conditioners or my stupid attraction to him.

My eyes rose to his instantly and I could say that I wasn't only caught up in them, but they drew me in. They had a hint of torment in them. I knew because I could see them in mine, and no matter how much I tried to conceal them, they stayed like a permanent scar.

'I came for a job interview,' I said softly, not sure why my voice sounded serene.

'You've got to be kidding me.'

He moved away from his table towards one of the shelves filled with dozens of new books and ran his hands through them softly.

I looked around the office, taking in the walnut bookcase lining the entire left-hand wall. There was a leather sofa with a fur rug over the back and an Indian blanket over the arm. I wondered if he ever slept off on them. Two antique clocks were on the right and a couple of paintings of what seemed to be the universe. There was a fancy flat-screened television on the wall to the right and in front of a shelf was an upright piano. I wondered if he played or if it was just there for decoration. The office was as classy as its owner. And I could see his suit jacket hanging on his leather seat.

'I'm very serious, I need a job', I said.

This time, I tried my best to sound as firm as I could, hoping my voice wasn't giving away the fact that I was admiring his very well-defined arms which were visible through his shirt.

'Okay, I'm very sorry but we both know this is not going to work, so let's not waste your time. I think it's...'

'Are you being serious now? So you're not going to give me a job because of the little incident this morning. I'm sorry but you're not being very professional right now.'

I wasn't sure why I was blabbing stupidly, especially when I knew how much I needed this job. I had to control myself before I let my pride get the best of me.

'That's exactly the trait I don't want in any of my employees. I'm not going to employ you if you're going to keep disrespecting me. That's not the kind of working environment I'm looking for.'

He moved to press a button as he spoke and I couldn't help but feel more agitated at the fact that he assumed he deserved respect when he lacked it himself.

'I promise to do my best to correct my attitude from now on,' I said in the most polite manner I could ever have thought of.

He was about to respond when the door opened and the elderly woman I met earlier walked in with that same smile on her face.

'What is it this time, Femi?'

From the way he sighed in response, you could tell that she meant a lot to him, and right now I was going to use it in my favour.

'We had a little incident this morning and he thinks I'm not fit for the job because of that.'

I shot her my pleading eyes and watched as she nodded as if the story was one she knew.

'Oh, so that's what has kept you in a foul mood this morning. Femi, you shouldn't allow your anger to get the best of you. Let her resume at least, you will be impressed,' she solicited.

I watched as he rubbed his temples in frustration and moved to sit down in his very huge chair. He held out his hand toward me,

'Hand it over!'

I did, careful to not let our hands get in contact because I was scared of what feelings would follow. His eyebrows rose in approval as he examined it carefully. He let out an amused scoff and I wasn't sure what to make of that.

'Well, your resume is impressive but what I'm concerned about is your attitude'

His eyes bored into mine and I looked at the woman beside me for assistance but she had her eyes on him too.

'I already said I was going to work on it,' I pleaded genuinely. I couldn't let pride get in the way of me getting this job.

'How am I supposed to be sure of that? You said I was stupid this morning?'

My face turned red quickly as I channelled my defensive side.

'But you insulted me first and I didn't even do anything wrong,' I responded.

He watched me carefully as he gave me the iciest of glares.

'You were the one who wasn't looking at the road in the first place. You were not being careful as a grown woman. I mean, what if I had hit you?'

'But you didn't,' I said louder than I intended.

'Is this a job interview or a sparring contest? You two sound like children,' the woman beside me cut in.

She was right. It was ridiculous and my legs were beginning to hurt a little from the heel of my shoes and all I wanted was for us to get this over with.

'You are a risk taker, right? You publish books without knowing if it's going to really sell or not. See me as a book you're going to try out? And if at the end of the month, you think I'm not good enough then you can let me go,' I proposed sternly.

He looked intrigued by my utterance and I prayed silently that he was considering me.

'Well, if you're not going to hire her, I will for you because your judgement is clearly clouded,' the old woman interjected.

She looked at me and held out her arm to hold mine as she said,

'Consider yourself hired, Tiwa. You can resume tomorrow.'

I didn't know I had held my breath for that long until I heard her words. 'Oh my God, thank you so much! Thank you!'

I looked at Femi who was fuming in his seat, but, surprisingly, he didn't contradict her, and I didn't want him to say something that would make this woman change her mind, so I moved to grab my resume from the table.

'You won't regret this,' I assured before turning around and walking as fast as I could.

I wondered what their relationship was that he just had to agree when she hired me. She couldn't be his mother because there was no resemblance. He cared about her deeply, that was obvious. The thought of him caring that deeply for me gave me goose bumps. Not because of how impossible that would be, but the fact that I thought of it. I never cared about men, not in any way and that wasn't going to change. I smiled as I thought to myself, mama was clearly watching over me and I knew I was going to get the job full-time because I was going to work as hard as possible. This was a new me, a new life, and I wasn't going to let an arrogant man with defined abs and a handsome face get in the way.

Chapter Three

Rules and Invitations

WAKING UP EARLY HAD NEVER been difficult for me. I had a hard time sleeping regardless of everything I tried, mostly because of the frequent nightmares that tormented my night. I kept on seeing that mask, the faceless body that was the source of my predicament, my pain, my sorrow, and my not-so-normal life. Ever since that fateful day, I got up from my bed with the usual thought that I had nothing to look forward to, but now my motto had changed. I got the job I always wanted, it was under the most uncomfortable circumstances but it was the start of something new.

This time, I made sure I wore my new black jumpsuit to work. It was long-sleeved and very fitting that it brought out my curves in a way that wasn't too uncomfortable. My hips were big enough to show even if I wore loose clothing, anyway. I am a bit on the curvy side and no matter how much I tried to cover it up, it was still obvious. I wore flat ballerina shoes this time, and I had my hair made the previous day into braids. It still ached a little, so I made sure I took some medicine before I left home for work. It took me slightly more than twenty minutes to get there on a bike. It was cheap and fast at the same time because of its capability to evade traffic. It could be dangerous, but I was at that point where I wasn't scared of dying, I was just taking life as it came.

After paying the bike man, I waited a little for my change before walking into my new workplace. The sound of that made me smile so wide that it felt like my cheeks would expand. It was somewhat early – 8:30 am – so some men were still setting up while the cleaners were tidying the place up.

'Good morning,' I greeted them warmly and they all turned to smile at me.

'Morning, Aunty,' a lady in the blue cleaning uniform greeted me nicely.

'Call me Tiwa, no need for Aunty,' I replied softly.

She smiled as she bent to pick up her cleaning brush.

'You're so beautiful,' a guy said.

He was holding a pile of new books and I don't know if I felt comfortable with the way he was staring at me. Men did that. They made me uneasy. Being around one alone in a room made me sweaty, and I tried to avoid it as much as I could. I murmured thanks to him and moved to sit in the waiting area.

I watched more people enter the building as I sat. It was probably almost 9 am now and I wasn't sure where my office would be.

'Is that Tiwa?'

I turned around to the sound of Zainab's voice. She looked pretty in her red off-shoulder dress and black heels. I let my hand out to shake her but she drew me in for a hug.

'It's so nice to see you here. I promise you, it won't be so bad' I smiled gratefully, beginning to feel more positive about the day.

'I really hope so, thank you so much,' I said gratefully as we pulled away from each other.

She turned to say hi to everyone before pulling me with her to the elevator.

'Let me show you to your office. It's close to mine, so we can gossip as much as we want,' she remarked teasingly and I began to feel more excited.

I wasn't one to easily make friends, but I came here for a new life anyway. So, I could change that about myself too.

'Am I supposed to show myself to the boss?'

I asked her nervously, not ready to face that man, especially after our previous ordeal. He was a rude human being and avoiding him was the best thing for me. She shook her head in response as we came out of the elevator.

'No need for that, you just have to settle down first,' she retorted gently and my heart leapt for joy.

It didn't take too long for us to get into an office and there were two other people there. I don't know if this was torture but I never imagined I would have to be alone with a man for long, not to talk of two. The way they looked at me wasn't encouraging as they didn't bother to hide the fact that they were ogling me in public.

'That's Dayo with the big head, while that long-legged goat is Sam. Guys, this is Tiwa,' Zainab said as she pointed at them both.

They smiled sweetly at me and I tried to hide my unease as I waved at them.

'We cleared your table for you already, we are at your service,' Dayo said as he stood up to shake my hand.

Sam did the same but not without complementing me about my beauty. I walked to my table, trying to keep my distance from them as much as possible.

'My office is next door, so feel free to tell me whenever you need anything. You can just send me an email. I left the address on your table,' Zainab said and I wished she wouldn't leave me alone with these two men.

I thanked her wholeheartedly before moving to settle down. I was just about to start reading a few instructions on my new work table when I got the notification.

'Tiwa, please I need you in my office'

I stared hard at the computer in front of me, not sure if I was ready for this. How did he know I was in the office anyway? Walking on my own this time gave me a moment to admire how splendid the building was. The outside didn't do enough justice to the beauty on the inside. The white walls and the elaborate windows gave a striking view of the outside. I couldn't help but stare at the beautiful scenery of people walking on the streets. Calabar was a beautiful city and it gave me so much hope.

The door to his office was left ajar and I walked in to find him talking to the screen in front of him.

'I have to go now, send the updates to me instead', he said before turning his eyes to me.

I stood a few meters away from him, and he gestured to the seat in front of me.

'Come sit down.'

'Thank you,' I said softly, sitting but not making myself too comfortable.

'Well, as you're on your trial stage, I wanted to tell you the things I would expect of you while you are here.'

I was irritated that he used the word 'while you are here' It was as if he really wanted me to fail this trial so I could leave. Well, I wasn't going anywhere, at least not without proving my worth.

'I'm listening,' I replied, trying my best to be professional.

'I'm just going to get into it. You have to listen to every instruction I give you. Never allow anyone to barge into my office without an appointment'.

With the way his eyes twitched as he said it, it was evident that it had happened before.

'Noted,' I said as respectfully as I could manage.

'No sleeping on your desk. As my new personal assistant, your office would have to be moved to the one outside the door. I told Dayo about it already, so he's going to assist you with moving your things.'

This last part made me feel more uneasy, not only will I have to attend to this man personally, but I will also have to look forward to knowing that he was right in front of me. This was going to be way harder than I thought. His slight chuckle drew my attention.

'I can see how much discomfort this has caused you. You are free to walk away if you can't handle it,' he offered but I was not going to give him the satisfaction that easily.

'I know what I signed up for. Is that all?' I asked him, already beginning to stand up.

'Well, for now, and you really have to reduce the way you argue with me. I believe I deserve some level of respect.'

His words drew my attention, and he stood up this time indicating how important this so-called rule of his was.

'I will sir, no more arguments,' I said as professionally as I could muster.

He nodded grimly indicating that it was all, and I managed to walk away as fast as I could.

***

People usually said no one on their deathbed ever wished they had spent more time in the office. I always contradicted that statement because to me my job was a distraction. It took me away from my despondent thoughts. That was one of the reasons for my being so hell-bent on getting the occupation I had always wanted. This was my fourth day at work and so far, it had been cooler than

I expected it to be. Especially after the bomb Femi had thrown days ago. I wondered if that was how he threw rules around to all his workers. He had a constant frown on his face especially when he looked at me.

He had made sure to avoid me ever since, at least that was what it looked like. He only responded with a morning back to my greetings whenever he passed by me to his office. He always said he would sort himself out if I asked him if he wanted a cup of coffee. To be honest, I kind of preferred it this way because I needed as much time away from him as much as possible.

Later that day, he called me to his office. This time, he was leaning back in his chair, and his eyes were focused on the computer in front of him. He rotated to face me before gesturing to one of the two leather seats in front of his desk.

'Have a seat'

I sat down abruptly and sucked in oxygen as I tried to think of what this meeting could possibly be about.

'Why am I here?' I asked him as politely as I could manage.

'I called you in to ask you about your proofreading skills'.

My smile came easily because this was something I could do without stress.

'Well, I also majored in English, so it's no problem'.

I'm sure he knew this because he looked at my CV but maybe he just wanted to hear me say it. Either way, he was in good hands because my eyes always seemed to catch typos whenever I read anything, even if it was a random newspaper and it completely drove me crazy. He nodded in approval before turning back to his computer. I watched as he swiped over his screen and admired his long tapered fingers. They were huge and they reminded me of the tales my mother would tell me about picking things from the floor. She said it would make me have longer hands and then I believed it was a disaster but now seeing his, it didn't seem so bad after all.

'I've sent you a new report that was just drafted out. It needs to be cleaned up, so that's your first job.'

'Okay, sir,' I replied before moving to stand up.

'You can send the report back to me before the end of tomorrow.'

I nodded in affirmation before leaving his office. A few hours later, my back was aching from how much I had been leaning on the table as I worked on the report Femi had sent me. It was an analysis of what should be seen as a prominent publishing company, written by someone named Zulu Hakeem. Surprisingly, there were more than enough errors and it gave me a massive headache as I considered pressing the intercom button more than necessary to ask for extra pay for this mind-blowing workload he had thrown at me.

'Hey beautiful, why do you look like your cat just died?'

I looked up to see Zainab walking towards me and it was just a relief to see that huge smile of hers. She was really God-sent and the only one I considered a friend in this new city.

'I have this report boss asked me to go through and it's stressing me out because I have seen so many errors than I have ever seen as an editor.'

Zainab chuckled softly as she patted my head and she held out a sandwich for me. 'Well, lucky you. I felt the need to bring this to you. Eat up, girl.'

I gave a loud groan as I enjoyed the savoury taste of the mixture of corn beef, sweet corn, and bread. I guess that saying that you do not know how hungry you are until you have food close to you is not a myth.

'Thank you so much for this, Zainab. You have no idea how much I was starving.'

She laughed as she watched me closely.

'You are always welcome, anyway. Feeding your empty stomach is not my only reason for coming here. I came to invite you out for a party.'

She looked at me mischievously. I waited until I was done swallowing before I responded.

'I should have known, is it not you? The thing is I'm not into parties, and besides, what am I supposed to do at a party anyway, especially when I have so much work to do?'

She halted before giving me an impatient gesture.

'I was expecting this, what else do they do at parties, Tiwa? Of course, to have fun. Please stop dulling.'

The last time I was at a party was a month after my mother's burial. My friends had convinced me to go for the birthday of someone whose name I still do not remember. It was their way of trying to get my mind off things, but it had been a huge disaster as I got vomited upon. And the uber driver had dropped us far away from our destination because we had messed up his car. That night made me feel more ineffectual than ever.

'*Whose party is it sef?*' I asked her and she giggled excitedly as if I had already agreed to go.

'One of my friends from back in the university, Isaac, is having a housewarming party and he has asked us to invite as many people as we want to come. He is pretty much excited about it and I can't blame him, it has been a long time coming.'

My usual negative self was reminding me of reasons why it would be better for me to just stay in bed like I usually did, but I promised myself that I was going to start a new life when I got here and that came with meeting new people, letting go of my dark past, and trying to find solace in this petrifying world.

'I am going to kill you if I regret this,' I uttered.

She grinned widely as she engulfed me in a tight hug.

'We are going together. I'm coming to get you at 8 pm sharp. Dress sexy,' she stressed before walking away as quickly as she came in.

I rolled my eyes as I began to think about partying after so long. This was going to be a long night.

Chapter Four

Just the Beginning

I WAS NOT SURE HOW much time had flown. As I sat there, trying to make as many rectifications as possible on the manuscript, Femi's door swung open and the man himself emerged. My gaze went straight to his sculpted forearms, then lifted as he ran one hand through his hair, something he did occasionally. He frowned down at me from his considerable height.

'What are you still doing here? Are you not supposed to be off work by five?'

I glanced at the time on the computer, it was 6:43 pm. I had been so engrossed in the editing that I had lost track of time.

'I totally forgot that I had somewhere I really need to go. Do you mind getting the report back today?' I asked him.

It was my plan all along - to be done with it as fast as possible so I could show him how much of an asset I would be to this company. He needed to see my worth and if it meant pushing myself to finish reports way earlier than they were due, then so be it. I watched his eyes grow wide in surprise as he watched me closely.

'Well, you work fast, don't you? I hope I'm impressed when I see it. You should go home, especially since you have somewhere you need to go.'

He said that sarcastically, with his eyes drawn together like he was trying to figure out where that was, but I decided to not trouble myself with it. I needed to hurry so I could figure out what to wear for the impromptu party that Zainab had committed me to.

'I will be leaving now, I hope you're satisfied with what I've done,' I asked.

He shrugged and I wondered why he was still here too, considering he owned the company and could leave anytime he wanted.

'I hope so too,' he muttered before walking away in long strides.

As I sent the edited report to his email, my phone beeped with a text from Zainab and I began to feel constant regret for agreeing to go to this party.

***

I could feel my heartbeat plummeting as I looked at the partially broken mirror in my bedroom. I met it with a very little scratch when I first moved in but as time flew by, more pieces began to fall off. I planned to get a new one but it always seemed to slip my mind whenever I got to the market. I was wearing flowery palazzo pants that encompassed my curves with a black long-sleeved bodysuit. Zainab had suggested I wore something more exposing, but that was not my thing. I hated the attention that came with it.

I decided to apply minimal makeup as I usually went with my bare face to work. I was putting on my dangling earrings when the doorbell rang, my eyes moved to the clock above the television. It was almost eight, the girl wasted no time.

'Wow, Tiwa you're gorgeous. Those eyes,' she said as she walked inside my compact apartment.

The smell of her perfume was so intense that it made me sneeze like I had a horrible cold.

'You look amazing too but *mehn*. Why is this your perfume so strong? Do you want to kill somebody?'

She laughed loudly as I watched her take in my one-bedroom apartment.

'It's my personal charm, my dear,' she pouted and I laughed.

'Everyone will know you've arrived,' I said as she collected my earrings which I was struggling with, and wore them for me.

'*Yes na*, that is my intention today. Isaac has so many fine friends and I cannot waste an opportunity like this. Who knows, we might get lucky today. Especially you. Kai, Tiwa you are fineeeee'.

I laughed loudly as I took in how beautiful she looked in her blue off-shoulder dress. It was short but in a decent way and blue braids complimented her attire alongside her blue eye shadow. Her enthusiasm made no difference because I had no plans for the night except to try to loosen up and follow my mission to start a new life. Men were the last thing on my mind. She told me that she grew up in a family where both parents were from different religions. It had been an easy task for her to choose to be on her mother's side which was Christianity because her dad was hardly ever around. In fact, only one of her five siblings was a Muslim, and it was the firstborn. Then, their father had not been in a job that required his incessant absence.

'Thank you so much. On the other hand, it is you who wants to kill us tonight. You look beautiful. Zainab, please don't abandon me for too long, I'm nervous as hell,' I said to her softly.

'I won't! Never! It's eight already, we should start leaving. My car is parked outside.'

I moved to grab my purse as I silently prayed that I wouldn't regret my decision to go out that night. The ride to the house was not as long as I expected it to be, and that made everything scarier because all I could think about was the fact that I'd not been to any party in a really long time.

'We are here, Tiwa,' Zainab said, drawing me out of my thoughts.

I looked up to realise we were at the front of a black gate. The gateman opened it immediately and I gasped at the number of cars parked in the large compound of the house.

'Wow, I thought this would be a small party, Zainab.'

She rolled her eyes at me as she followed the directions of the security who led her to park her car.

'I promise you, it will be fun. Trust me,' she assured me as she turned off the ignition.

'Time to party, girl. Let's go,' she said laughing at loud.

I moved to grab my purse, and I came out of the car. Isaac had a beautiful house. It was a duplex painted burgundy and white. The house was welcoming from the open door to the wide hallway. Upon the walls were photographs of what I presumed were Isaac's family members. Zainab's eyes were also on them.

'Those two girls beside him are his siblings and his parents are obviously the ones in the middle.'

I smiled and nodded as I admired the frame of a beautiful family. I never had that which was the one thing that I always wanted. Another photo caught my eye, it was that of Isaac and another woman. I wondered who she was.

'Don't worry, he's not married. That's his best friend, Dorcas. She's married with kids in America.'

I laughed out loud at what Zainab was insinuating.

'I don't care if he's married or not, I was just looking at it.'

She raised her eyebrows at me in disbelief and I moved to smack her arm when a man's voice came from behind us.

'I can see she's annoying you too,' a handsome man said as he walked towards us.

He was wearing a blue polo shirt, and black jeans. I looked at the picture at my side and looked back at him. The pictures didn't do him enough justice. He looked way better in person. He was more than a few inches taller than me, maybe as tall as Femi and that's when I wanted to smack my head, why was he on my mind?

'You must be Tiwa. I'm glad you made it. I'm Isaac,' he held out his hand and I moved to shake him.

'I knew you would come to get us in more than two minutes,' Zainab said grumpily and he laughed before hugging her tightly.

'I was trying to keep the guests settled', he said with his hands on her shoulder before turning towards me.

'You didn't tell me your friend was this beautiful.'

He stared at me swiftly and I smiled back, unsure of what to do.

'I wanted you to see for yourself,' she teased.

'Are those your handsome friends around already?' Zainab asked him, her eyes going around in circles.

He laughed loudly before answering.

'Well, most of them are. Let's go in.'

She gave me a knowing smile, indicating that her game was on and I chuckled softly. This girl was something else.

'So, may I?'

Isaac held out his elbow and I tried to calm my nerves as I placed my hand in it. We had just entered the party and Isaac had insisted that he introduce us to his friends. It was obvious it was because of Zainab because I wasn't keen on meeting new people anyway. I asked Isaac for the nearest bathroom so I could calm my nerves and I told Zainab not to go with me so she could meet his friends. I wasn't sure if the bathroom made any difference because seeing more people along the way didn't help. I had just come out of the bathroom when I saw a table that had a pile of bottled water. I moved to grab one and was just about to open the bottle when I heard his voice,

'I should have known it was you when Zainab said she came with a friend.'

His eyes twitched like he liked what he saw, but it was so minuscule that I could have missed it if I wasn't looking at him with so much concentration.

'I wouldn't say it's nice to see you here, because it really isn't,' I said bluntly.

'Ouch,' he said.

He had a smirk on which never failed to get me exasperated.

'You don't seem like someone that's into parties, have you been having fun so far?' He asked, and I suddenly felt less thirsty.

'It's really not your business, sir,' I said tightly, watching him nod his head like he was amused.

'You know, you really have to stop hating on me if you want the job,' his eyes were still amused, and even though his words were true, my pride fuelled my anger.

'I believe you're more professional than that. You know what I'm capable of if I'm given the job. My credentials are enough evidence and I'm going to make sure I prove it to you,' I protested suddenly feeling thirsty again. I grabbed my bottled water and took a gulp.

'I've never seen anyone like you,' he said with his eyebrows raised and his hands going into his jeans pockets.

He looked good in casual outfits. It was my first time seeing him this way, but it still didn't reduce his dominating look. I wasn't sure of what he was insinuating, and neither did I want to wait to find out.

'I need to get my friend.'

I then walked away as quickly as I could amid the throng of people. I tried to look for Zainab where I left her but she was nowhere to be found.

'Where did she go again?' I muttered to myself.

I tried to check for Isaac who was the only other face that I was familiar with. I was about to sit down on an empty chair by the fancy dining table when someone grabbed my waist.

'Hey, beautiful. Why are you alone?'

I pushed myself away from him instantly, my elbow hitting the lower part of his stomach in a way that made him lower his body in pain. I don't know how I did that, but it was mostly the effect of so much shock. It caused him to groan loudly, and I could hear light murmuring around us, despite the loud music playing in the background. Great, now I had everyone's attention.

'What the hell! Why are you so aggressive?'

He was almost the same height as me and seeing his face aggravated me more. He walked closer to me, his left hand moving to grab my arm in his attempt to bellicose.

'And who gave you the right to touch me? Do you have to touch me to talk to me?' I asked angrily.

My heart rate had gone higher. Coming to this party was a mistake. I loathed getting touched this way. It was the one thing I could not take.

'Why can't I touch you? You think you are so special because you've got a big ass, right?' He asked condescendingly.

He pushed me closer to him, and the stench of alcohol that emanated from his mouth made me want to barf.

'Let her be,' Femi's dominating voice echoed from behind me.

I was too shocked to react. I was still trying to catch my breath when he let go of my arm which stung from his tight grip.

'You know her? I didn't know she was your type,' the drunk guy said.

'You should really go if you don't want to wake up in a hospital,' Femi warned.

The guy's eyes shook from fear and I couldn't blame him, especially with how fit Femi looked.

'Geez, I was only playing with her,' the guy muttered.

His hands up in surrender, clearly scared of Femi whom I felt so grateful to right now, but I could thank him later. I was about to go when I heard another familiar voice.

'What the hell are you doing in my house, Enobong? I told you not to come.'

I turned around to see Isaac who stood tall, holding a glass of wine. A frown settled on his face.

'I thought we were past that now,' the guy countered, walking towards Isaac.

The volume of the music had gone low and all eyes were on us, which wasn't surprising. No one minded their business in Nigeria.

'How am I supposed to be past that if you keep doing the same thing? You never change. Just leave already,' Isaac demanded.

I wondered what their relationship was. Where was Zainab in all this? I wouldn't be flabbergasted if she was in a corner making out with some guy, at least she didn't come here in vain.

'Are you okay?' Femi asked.

I turned to him not knowing he had gotten that close to me. His eyes looked genuinely worried and I watched them move around me like he was checking for an injury somewhere.

'I'm okay, I just need to go home,' I shivered, wanting to leave this scenery as soon as possible.

'Do you mind me dropping you off?' He asked softly and I shook my head in disapproval.

I wasn't in the mood to be around any guy. His reaction gave me mixed feelings. It wasn't something I was used to, especially after our recent encounter.

'I'm fine thank you. I will just wait for Zainab.'

Enobong had probably gone because Isaac was the only one in front of me and he was alone this time.

'I'm sorry about that, he just left,' I nodded, not really in the mood to talk.

'I'm surprised you still talk to him,' Femi said to Isaac.

I assumed they were friends but that wasn't really my business. I was in the middle of two men who were definitely still strangers to me, and I needed to breathe.

'Finally, Tiwa. Where the hell have you been? I've been looking all over the place for you.'

I turned around in the direction of Zainab's voice and gave her my I will kill you look, but I couldn't help my loud sigh of relief.

'Well, you didn't look hard enough, did you forget that you came here with somebody?' I replied, rolling my eyes at her.
I had no strength to be mad, all I yearned for was solitude.

'I'm so sorry. I tried to look for you in the bathroom not long after you left but you were not there, and on my way out, one of the guys I told you about pulled me in for a chat, which I will tell you about later,' she whispered, her eyes going to Isaac.

Clearly confused, she asked,

'Did something happen?'

'Okay, something clearly did,' she concluded after looking at Femi who was behind me. The music had amplified and heads had been turned away from us.

'Hello, sir. It's nice to see you here,' she said to Femi as she smiled brightly.

He nodded at her in greeting before drinking me in one last time.

'You should check up on your friend. She had a rough night. It was nice seeing you both. See you on Monday,' he said before paddling across us and mingling with the small crowd.

'Tiwa, what just happened? I'm so sorry I wasn't here and why are you looking in the direction he went through like that?' Zainab asked worriedly.

'I don't really feel like talking now, but can we go home, please?' I asked her.

My bladder already felt full as if I hadn't just used the bathroom. I needed to go home.

'Okay, let's go,' she turned to Isaac whose presence I had already forgotten.

'I will call you later,' she told him and he nodded in approval, not saying anything.

When we got into the car, I let out a breath I didn't know I was holding.

'What happened in there, Tiwa?' She asked me as she buckled her seatbelt.

Her car smelt of sweet pineapples, and I wished the scent could erase the memory of that man's stench of alcohol on me.

'It's a long story, but let's just go home first'

She covered my hands with hers before moving to start the ignition. As she drove, I prayed silently that little dramas like this would end and I would just live a simple life as I'd always yearned for. But something kept playing in my head that this was just the beginning.

Chapter Five

The Ride

MY MUM ONCE TOLD ME that men were gifts and curses to the earth. They could make you wish the world had more of their gender, and at the same time lead you to pray for them to become extinct. I never understood the denotation of her words till I got raped. My hatred for men had grown a thousand folds. I vowed to never get married and promised myself that I would beware of those animals - an unbearable species. I never had a father, so no man had ever meant well to me anyway.

As time went by, my hatred for men began to feel like a fungus that irritated me. It made me full of self-hate. The social part of my life was a little bit more than pathetic, and as much as it was boring, it gave me peace of mind. I tried to contain my fear of men as much as I could knowing that men would always be around me, no matter where I went to. And it was a necessity, especially if I wanted to get my dream job. It required me to become comfortable with men whether I liked it or not.

And that's why when I got home, I tried my best not to think about the night's events. Going deeper into it would take me back to my darker place and that was what I was trying to get away from. It wasn't healthy. I couldn't bear it. I had nightmares already. I didn't need to subject myself to more torture.

I told Zainab what happened when she dropped me at home. She wanted to follow me in. I knew she meant well but I preferred to be alone. Because being with her would remind me more. I hated feeling like a victim. I wanted to just be a normal woman, and as hard as it was, the thought that my life was starting afresh gave me the capacity to close my eyes till I fell asleep.

I had gotten an email from my boss that I could take time off if I needed it.

'You don't have to come to work today, take care.'

It was short but thoughtful. That wasn't enough reason for me not to go, though. In fact, I needed to go because that was a distraction that I really needed. Also, I was trying to prove that he really needed me. It was still a trial, and although he already gave me permission, I wanted to prove to him that my personal life would never affect my work life. My job was all I had now, so I didn't reply to his email because I knew he would just try to convince me more. I just decided to show up. I didn't work to get to where I was for nothing. I needed to make my mama proud, at least. I owed her that.

***

I was seated at my desk when Mr Adebanjo saw me.

'You didn't have to come, you know.'

His face was firm and hard to read. He stood a few metres away from where I sat.

'Thank you for caring but you wouldn't have witnessed that if it happened elsewhere. So please, I'd rather just work.'

I avoided his eyes as I answered.

'Okay then, whatever floats your boat. I understand.'

It wasn't until I heard his office door shut that I knew he had left. He was being a caring employer, that was his only reason for being this way and it made me understand why co-workers were a fan of him. When we met, I had been so angry at his reaction that I felt like I couldn't bear him. But I realised that I needed to contain myself around Femi. He was my boss and as much as he got on my nerves, I needed to be civil with him, especially when he was doing that with me. We were supposed to be adults who worked together and that was what a professional would do. I took a final look at my task for the day before I stood to go to his office. Ever since the party, we hadn't spoken much. Only a couple of 'Thank you, sir, and Okay, sir,' including the few instructions he gave me occasionally.

I wouldn't describe our moments as awkward, they were more professional or that's what I would like to believe. I was about to knock on his door when I heard his loud voice.

'What do you want this time?'

I was about to answer thinking he was referring to me but he continued.

'Really? You think I'm stupid? I run a company, I don't have time for your crap.'

Definitely, he wasn't talking to me. This was where I got confused. Was I supposed to just knock and go in or wait till he calmed down? Or just email him instead?

'I didn't say I don't love you. You know I care about you. Don't put words in my mouth.'

I gasped loudly at his words.

'So, he had a girlfriend or maybe a wife. But no one mentioned that.'

'You can come in already, Tiwa,' his deep voice sounded and I couldn't have felt more embarrassed.

I had said those words out loud. I opened the door slowly like he didn't just tell me to come in.

'I can always come back later,' I replied, and tried to close the door back, but he stopped me.

'Just come in already,' he said before going back to his seat.

'I need to go now. Later,' he said before dropping his cell phone back on the table.

'Well, I wanted to hand in Peter's edited work, sir. I'm done with it already,' I said trying to avoid his eyes.

I hated looking at them. The way they drew me in scared me, it was like a spell.

'You know you can just call me Femi, and thank you, I'm sure you did a good job.'

My heart rate elevated from the way he spoke to me. He hardly complimented me, and I just had to do it, I couldn't help myself. I looked at him and his eyes were already focused on mine.

I could see a hint of pain in them, maybe it was linked to his call, but seeing them made me realise how vulnerable he was, or could be. He had feelings too. He could get hurt. Now, I was feeling sorry for him. I needed to leave.

'I hope so. It's getting late. I need to go home now, and I'm sorry for interrupting your call earlier,' I said purposely ignoring his request to call him his name.

He shrugged casually before giving me a tight smile.

'It's fine. You can go now,' he said, his eyes moving to the document I gave him.

Well, the change of mood was surprising, did I say anything wrong? I didn't waste time leaving. I turned around immediately and walked out. With him, you were never sure. I recognised that he had so much more to him than he showed. It could be good or bad but the only reason why I was able to tell was that I had more to me too.
I had stood for ten minutes outside, waiting for a bike or a cab but it was either they were full, or they weren't going in my direction. So, I decided to walk home even if it was going to be hell, especially with the kind of shoes I wore. The sound of lightning took me off guard.

'Great,' I grunted to myself as the heavy droplets of rain began to fall.

One thing I disliked about the rain here was it never gave enough signs. It just comes from nowhere and there was usually nothing like a light rain, the downpour could cause a flood. I struggled to keep my phone in my bag to avoid rain spilling on it when I heard a loud horn from behind me.

'Tiwa, is that you?'

I turned and saw Femi beside me. His car window was down as he yelled at me to get in. I really wanted to refuse but I was soaked, my pride wasn't going to let me fall sick. I rushed to open the door and got in.

'How did you know it was me? Thank you so much,' I said, feeling guilty for wetting his car and probably messing it up with my muddy shoes.

'You are hard to miss and it's fine. I can drop you off. Where do you stay?'

I turned to face him, taking in the soothing smell of his fancy Mercedes. He always drove himself, and hardly ever came with a driver which was probably what he preferred. I was unsure if I really wanted him to know my address, not that he was a kidnapper but I couldn't be too careful.

'You can just drop me wherever you are going to. I'm sure the rain would have stopped by then. I will find my way from...'

His light chuckles cut me short.

'Are you hearing how ridiculous you sound right now? I'm going home, Tiwa. Except that's your way of knowing where I live,' he said sarcastically, and I wanted to bite my tongue at how stupid I had just sounded.

'I didn't mean it that way, I....'

'It's okay for you to be worried. I promise I'm not a kidnapper. I'm just your boss, and we should really start moving now as I'm causing bad traffic.'

The sound of the horns behind us drove me back to my senses and I told him where to drive to. Well, this was going to be an eventful ride.

***

There was a lot of traffic due to the rain, as expected. Market women were slowing cars down as they pleaded for cars to stop so they could cross the road. There were loafers on the highway who mostly found their joy in trying to play traffic warden as they directed cars that sought parking spots in a quest to make easy cash. Little boys came to the windshields to clean without being asked.

'No, thank you! Just take.'

Femi said to the child who had already come to ours as he handed him a five hundred Naira note. He looked not much younger than eight years old and he was in the rain, cleaning car windshields. Not everyone was as Nobel as Femi. Some men were drivers of the cars they were in, others were probably grouchy from a bad day at work, or just indignant at being a victim of the bad Nigerian government. They wouldn't be too willing to give, but would instead yell at these unprivileged kids because they needed to let out their frustrations. It was heart-wrenching, but the sad reality.

'What's on your mind?' Femi asked as he glanced at me curiously.

'Nothing really,' I replied, unsure if I really wanted to start a conversation with him.

I preferred the stillness; it made me more comfortable.

'That answer shows there's quite more to it. I'm curious because they say the quiet ones are always capable of the worst,' he said and I rolled my eyes at him.

'You never give up, do you? How am I supposed to tell you what's on my mind when you already assume the worst?' I said, throwing my arms up.
He chuckled loudly, and as much as it made my blood boil, it was such a sweet sound to hear that I just wanted to forget how cross I was so I could listen to him.

'Okay, okay. I apologise. It's just times like this that I realise how easy it is to get on your nerves,' I turned my eyes to him trying to think of a smart comeback, but nothing came up.

'Why are you so hell-bent on starting a conversation anyway?'

I crossed my arms as I asked him and he looked at me softly before turning back to the road.

'It just seems better than being gloomy. I'm trying to keep myself distracted, but it's fine if you just want silence. I respect that.'

His face was solemn as he spoke, and I wondered if he was referring to the call he had earlier in the office, but I was definitely not going to ask.

'I was only thinking about Nigeria's sad situation but let's not talk about that. It's not really one of my best topics,' I said, hoping this would lighten his mood.

Why did I care so much anyway? Well, it didn't matter because it sure did.

'Ah, I see. So, it's either you're not into politics or you're into it and would rather not talk about it,' he remarked inquisitively, as he pressed the horn.

'I don't really see the difference between both but yes, how old are you?'

I cringed as the words left my mouth. I thought I was asking in my head. My mouth just had to fumble, why was I asking my boss for his age? I could have definitely just googled it if I was that curious.

'Are you trying to see if I'm too old for you? Don't worry, there's not much difference,' he teased and I rolled my eyes again at his capacity to turn everything into boosting his pride.

'I didn't mean to ask that. You don't have to answer. I didn't mean to ask,' I said calmly, not really having the strength to get mad.

'I'm twenty-seven, and you're twenty-two. It's not much age gap.'

He looked at me as he said it, our eyes meeting for an instant. I was not surprised he knew my age because my date of birth was on my resume.

'See, I settled it for you,' he said inclusively.

It's obvious he was enjoying this, and as much as I believed I did not have the strength to get mad, the fortitude came from above.

'I'm not interested in you, and I never will'.

It was as blunt as I could have gotten. Our eyes met and I noticed a hint of disappointment in his, but it was only for a second, not long enough to be sure, or I could have seen wrongly anyway. I knew he was joking, it was his way of lightening the mood but the slight thought that he could be right about me wanting more than a professional relationship with him made me uneasy. I needed to say it wasn't possible for any form of attraction to go.

'I assume this is the address you gave me.'

He had parked at the side of the road, a few blocks from my place as I was not ready to let him know where I lived. He already knew where I spent half of my day, he didn't need to know the other half.

'Thank you so much for the ride. I'm getting off here,' I said genuinely as I moved to open the car door. Thankfully, the rain was mizzling steadily.

'Wait! Umm... I'm sorry about how we first met. I was having a bad day, so I guess I took it out on you.'

I looked up at him as he spoke softly. His eyes looked browner than they usually did, his lips pinker, and I noticed the stubble on his face which made him look more attractive. The air was thin and I felt the pace of my heartbeat increase. I wasn't used to this. Yet, why was I still sitting here? Why wasn't I running? What was so different about him? Was it because I could recognise pain in him? Was that what drew me to this man seated right beside me? Why did I choose to sit alone with this man in his car without letting the frightening thought of him taking advantage of me cause me to flee? There were so many questions, and all of them were left unanswered.

'Tiwa!' He called me again and I struggled to grasp myself.

The way he stared at me gave me goose bumps but I couldn't look away.

'It's fine. I'm sorry too. I might have overreacted' I said, reflecting on the memories of that day.

'Sure? You don't seem fine.' He asked worriedly.

This time he was right because I needed to get as far away from this man as possible. As much as I felt safe with him, he scared me still.

'I am. Goodnight, Femi'

I didn't let the fact that I impulsively called my boss his name draw me to see his expression. It wasn't necessary. I opened the door and walked away as quickly as my legs could carry me.

Chapter Six

Out of My League

WHEN I GOT HOME, I grabbed my laptop and started researching the famous Femi Adebanjo. I had done this before. Before applying for the job, I had been more focused on his career achievements. I paid no attention to his personal life. I didn't expect to be working so close to him anyway, and neither did I ever assume that I would be in the same car with him. And the only thing my brain would have paid close attention to was how much closer I wanted us to be.

It felt like a magnetic pull. I couldn't place it, especially when I had never felt this way about any man before. Men had been villains in my life and my mother's life. Feeling this way about one was daunting and it pricked my skin. Femi was dangerous to me. He had to be, and I needed to prove it to myself.

When it came to things like this, the best place to go to was Linda Ikeji's blog, a famous blogger in Nigeria. As much as I resented her most times for trying to ridicule people's lives, all in the name of her business, I needed that now. I desperately needed to find out anything abhorrent that Femi had done. It was my only key to pushing these inarticulate feelings away. I kept trying to tell myself that it was because he apologised. Maybe I wasn't used to it. When I got raped, no one apologised to me. Instead, I was treated like I should have been thankful. My rapist believed it was his right, maybe that's why Femi's unexpected apology got to me. I checked and scrolled till I felt like my backbone was going to break from the way I sat.

'Who is this guy? Is he that low key?' I muttered to myself.

I didn't give up though. I had the willpower to ascertain that Femi wasn't for me. It was a necessity. I didn't just focus on Linda Ikeji, I checked any article, and any blog I could think of till I found something. I could have easily asked Zainab, but she would start asking questions that I couldn't answer. It was better this way. I would find something horrible, and whatever sort of attraction I felt would vanish.

'Femi Adebanjo and his siblings are not the best of friends, Mrs Adebanjo says in an interview.'

My heart skipped so fast as I clicked on it.

'It had to be his mother. He couldn't be married. No, no, no!' I kept muttering to myself.

'Femi's mother finally agreed to answer the question everyone is curious about, why is a family that's so wealthy not close knitted?' I read out loud.

I sighed in relief which made me feel stupid because I was relieved for the wrong reasons. I was happy to find out that he was not married and that was wrong because the main reason I was researching was to find something that would make these feelings go away. I kept reading as I tried to absorb everything. His parents lived in Lagos and had been married for thirty-four years.

Femi was the second child. He had an elder brother and a younger sister. None of them were close. Their mother explained that she had tried to encourage them to build a good relationship as siblings, but it was like everything changed suddenly.

Femi had been seventeen when he was rushed to the hospital from a tragic fall after his elder brother, Dapo, pushed him in a fight. This was what had raised rumours as to how much the siblings despised each other at such a young age. And three years ago, they were caught hitting each other on camera beside Femi's car at a mall. While Kikelomo, the only daughter, had begun to shut everyone out from the age of twelve, her mother said her friends stopped coming over because they complained Kike wouldn't play with them. She was her baby and her last child and all she wanted was to see her daughter happy. I teared up as I read more. It reminded me of my mum, all she wanted was to see me happy which was every mother's dream for their child. When I got to the end, I didn't find any reason for the siblings' clash. Their mother seemed to not know why either.

I was curious, and I kept reading more and more articles. Some had been with women he had previously dated. I tried to find more about his life, something more dramatic, but it was more of positivity about his achievements. He owned houses in Lagos, Abuja, Ibadan, Benin, Onitsha, Osun his hometown, and Calabar obviously.
He also had houses in the United Kingdom, the United States, Belgium, and Ghana. Just how rich was this man? He had a foundation for orphaned children and had undergone business with the famous Otedola and Aliko Dangote. He owned a shelter home in Aba, and he was building a new one in Lagos. I tried to attach the man who drove himself to all this wealth. I had the idea that he

was a prideful human being, but reading all these put a dent in that thought.

My heart melted as I read more and more. Why did I ever think that there could be more? He was out of my league. I only had a one-bedroom flat in my life, with broken windows and a door that I had to kick sometimes before it locked, coupled with my personal belongings. We were from two different worlds. I read more, but there was nothing relating to more drama in his personal life, and no more information on his relationship with his siblings. I was about to close my computer from exhaustion when something caught my eye.

'Femi Adebanjo's relationship with Amara Okolie seems to still be ongoing as the doctor revealed she moved to Nigeria for them to have more time together.'

The disappointment I felt agitated me. It wasn't supposed to be a shock, someone as popular as he was would have the attention of many women and I certainly didn't want to be one of them. I looked at the picture of them. He was in a black suit while she was in a red velvet long dress. She was beautiful and as much as I tried to find anything bad in her, I couldn't. She was a doctor. She saved lives, was rich, and fitted his class. I wondered if she was the one he was talking to on the phone as I stared at their picture together in the article.
She stayed in the United States till she moved back to Nigeria earlier this year. They were obviously getting more serious for her to have been willing to move all this way, but that was their business anyway.

As I closed my laptop, I told myself that I had been successful in this mission. I needed to find something that would

encourage me to kibosh whatever I felt for him and I did. He was taken, but why did I feel this ache in my chest?
I couldn't explain the ache I continuously felt after my rigorous research on Femi. The only way I could explain it was that I felt this way because it was new to me. I wasn't used to feeling this way about any man. They hardly got to me this way which made it more frightening.

At least, I had reasons now why I needed to let go of what I was beginning to feel. We were from two different worlds and he was in a relationship. More so, he was my boss. I came here to get my dream job, and that was what I wanted to focus on. I needed to get back to my professional self.
But why did I feel like my heart was broken when there was nothing in the first place? Maybe because, for once in my life, I felt attracted to a man. It was now apparent that I could feel this way about someone when I thought it was impossible.

I felt frightened more than disappointed. The last thing I needed was to feel vulnerable with any man. I wish I had someone to talk to. I yearned for my mother, someone whose love I could be sure of, at least. She was the only person I had. Now, who could I cry to? Who could I feel safe with? Would I ever feel whole again? Am I ever going to feel loved by someone again?

I picked up my mum's picture from my side table. I missed her so much, especially at times like this. She usually had the best advice. Her smile had a way of making you feel like all was well in the world. Her laughter was melodious. Her touch was soothing, sacred. I longed for it, even if it was just one more time. Especially when there were so many questions I had no answers to. As I grabbed my tissue to clean my snort, I picked up my Bible to read. God was the only one I could turn to. I wasn't the strongest of Christians as I questioned everything, but I tried my best to find solace in God's word during times like this. What other options did I have, anyway?

I woke up to my irksome ringtone. I chose to ignore it, but it rang repeatedly which awoke my curiosity. I finally opened my eyes, but they closed back in reflex as they got hit by the ray of sunlight from my open windows. My head was banging from me crying myself to sleep last night. The sun didn't help matters too, and that was when it began to dawn on me. I never slept with my windows open. I let out a small yawn as I scrunched my eyes with the back of my hand before checking my phone which hadn't stopped ringing. It was Zainab, but that wasn't what made me feel like I was going to have a heart attack. The time was five past eleven. I was supposed to be at work by nine. I was over two hours late.

'Oh my God, I know, I know' I said into the phone as I stood up with my pillow falling off the bed immediately I answered it.

'Where are you, Tiwa? It's past eleven,' Zainab whispered into the phone.

I wondered where she was that she had to talk to me quietly.

'I will be there soon. I don't know what happened. Is Femi there already?' I asked her and I could hear her surprised that I called him by name, but she chose to ignore it.

'You know he never comes late. He's been here since nine. The thing is, I thought you were even here already. I was so busy this morning that I couldn't come to check on you. But when I finally got my break, you were nowhere to be found, so I asked Kanayo and he said you hadn't come.'

Kanayo was the gateman and we had become friends from his usual funny greetings. He had two wives and seven children and he always said that I reminded him of one of his daughters.

'Did he ask for me?' I muffled.

I was already brushing my teeth as I asked. I just hoped she was able to pick out my words.

'Maybe, maybe not. I really don't know. I've avoided him so I wouldn't have to lie. That man can see through anything. I wonder why he hasn't asked them to call you though, but please just come here as fast as you can. Remember, we have a meeting by half past twelve except you've forgotten,' she said before ending the call.

I had forgotten that I had a business meeting today. I wondered why I hadn't gotten so many other calls yet. Except I had emails that I still needed to check. I thought yesterday was bad enough. Well, today my job was on the line. I had never dressed up as quickly as I did this morning. I had no time to sort out what to wear, so I had just worn the first thing I saw which I must say wasn't the best choice of outfit I could have gone for. My purple shirt was rumpled and the black pants I wore with it were so tight that I felt like I was going to have a huge line across my tummy and back when I finally undressed.

My hair was a mess, but that wasn't my main issue. I had first worn two different heels till I had to run back home when a child kept pointing at my feet and laughing. That had taken more of my time, but at least I was able to find a bike faster than usual after changing my shoes to black ballet flats.

'Abeg I no fit wait, don't worry,' I said as I practically ran into the building while waving at Kanayo at the gate.

I left my fifty naira change with the bike man because of how much in a haste I was. On a normal day, I would have cared to stay but my job was on the line, and I was still in trial mode.

'Jesus! Why do you look like you got robbed?' Zainab asked as she studied me from my toes all the way to my hair.

'See *ehn*, it's a long story. How many more minutes to the meeting?'

My heart was beating so rapidly that I felt like it was going to burst. 'It's ten minutes past twelve. You still have twenty minutes to go and find your way to beg Mr Adebanjo whom you supposedly now call Femi,' she said suspiciously as she crossed her arms. I rolled my eyes at her, aware of what she wanted.

'Wo, let's gist later abeg. I need to go.'

I turned to walk away but she held me still.

'At least, let me adjust your hair for you. You have no idea how bad you look. You can't go to him looking like this.'

I wanted to counter her and just go but she was right. He wouldn't take me seriously if I looked like a mad woman.
I hadn't even looked in the mirror. This was all because of my stupidity. I had cried so badly last night as if I didn't have a job to wake up early for. This was what men did. They mess up your life, but it was worse when they also had your life in their hands the way

Femi had my job in his hands and I needed to be as humble as possible. I couldn't lose my job, not because of a stupid crush.

'You can go now,' she patted my back like she was my mother before shoving me along.

After dropping my things on my table, I walked to Femi's office. The door was left ajar but thankfully, this time, he wasn't on a call. I knocked and went in without waiting for him to answer. That was how desperate I felt.

'I'm so sorry sir. I didn't mean to be late, please forgive me. I can't lose my job, please I...'
'Can you breathe first?' He answered so casually, cutting me short.

My eyes were closed before, as I was scared of seeing his glare, but he didn't look bothered when I finally opened them. If anything, he had a smirk on. Memories of last night overtook me as I stood there, and I shook my head in an attempt to get rid of them.

'I'm sorry I was so late. I didn't feel too well. I'm usually never late, I promise. I'm surprised myself,' I pleaded, unsure of what his thoughts were. He was hard to read and his face was inscrutable.

'It's fine, Tiwa. I hate tardiness and I'm keen on punctuality, so I'd appreciate it if this doesn't repeat itself. You should get ready for our meeting.'

His face was stern, but not in a mean way, it was boss-like. Since the first day I met him, he hid no indication that he took his job seriously, and I became reminded of everything I read yesterday. I was curious about his family, and the depths of his troubled relationship with his siblings. It was heartbreaking. I grew up wishing I had one at least. It would have felt less lonely. There was so much more to him than he passed across. It made him more intriguing but that didn't suppress the fact that he was a ruthless businessman who hardly failed or lost at negotiations. That elucidated how successful he was. Femi Adebanjo was my boss, and he would remain that way.

Chapter Seven

Girlfriend or Boyfriend

THE MEETING WENT WAY BETTER than I expected, at least I wasn't in trouble for coming late. I did get a few glances at probably how horrible I looked and the few friends I had made here asked questions which I answered honestly. Well, partially honest, I couldn't let them know that it was because I slept off crying which wasn't unusual. It was rare for me to go a week without my tears drying up on my pillow. I hated being so emotional, but I couldn't help it. I was like my mum and it only made it easier for me to understand why I easily forgot she wasn't my real mum.

There were so many similarities between us, and people often said we looked alike. Maybe the saying that living with someone for a while would make you guys look alike was true. My thoughts kept hanging around Femi and our encounter this morning. I expected him to have acted angrily, especially when it was my fault this time, but he was quite civil with me instead. And I had already concluded that we were not ever going to move past our employer and employee relationship. He had a girlfriend and we were from two different worlds.

I decided to pay full attention to my work, and by that, I meant doing more than I usually did in one day. It was the only way I could get him off my mind. I had been so focused that I didn't realise I was being called till someone tapped me.

'Tiwa!'

I looked up to see Sam standing and smiling at me. He held a KFC bag and the mouth-watering smell of the food made me suddenly hungry.

'Is that for me?' I asked softly and he grinned before giving it to me.

'Yes, you weren't down for lunch and Zainab said you were busy, so I decided to bring you food.'

Sam had been my friend for the past three weeks. I was wary of him and maybe I still am a little but I allowed myself to have conversations with him. He was kind and hadn't shown any signs of wanting more which made me more comfortable. He was handsome in a way that made him look very youthful.

'Thank you so much for this. I didn't realise how hungry I was. I should pay you back.'

I moved to grab my purse but he held my hand so fast that it was shocking.

'No, Tiwa. I just wanted to help. Don't pay me.'

I was about to insist when we heard the sound of Femi's door open. He stood tall as he stared at us. His eyes went to Sam's hand on mine which I instantly withdrew.

'Good afternoon, sir. I will see you later, Tiwa', Sam said as he tried to walk away.

'No, don't leave on my account,' Femi said before shutting his door so loud that I shook.

'I think he's in a bad mood. I'm paying you for your food.'

I took out the money from my purse and gave it to him despite his refusal.

'My God, you're stubborn,' he said as he shook his head as if that was new to him.

'I don't think you should be away from your office for too long,' I said and he nodded in agreement before walking in the direction of his office.

As I finished my food, thoughts of the way Femi looked at us occupied my thoughts. Why did he come out of his office in the first place? He only opened his door and went back inside. Was I supposed to ask him what he wanted as his assistant? Or I was supposed to just ignore him? How could one human being be so exhausting? I decided to just wait till he said something. I wasn't ready to see him anyway.

I had just gone to clean my hands when I saw him standing by my desk when I got back. He turned around to look at me and I couldn't make out his expression.

'Sir, do you need any help?' I asked him nervously as I folded my hands in front of me.

His eyes went to them before turning to look at me.

'Was that your boyfriend?'

My breath cut at his directness. This man really never failed to amaze me. I decided to not make it easy for him.

'And why is that your business?'

I hissed under my breath, unsure why my boss cared about my love life. I kept a friendly smile on my face in case people walked past us but that was highly impossible because this area was the last wing on this floor.

'So, he's your boyfriend then?' He snorted.

As infuriated as I was about his capacity to jump to conclusions in my life, I still wasn't going to give him an answer.

'You are my boss, yes, but I don't have to give you any answers on my personal life, Mr Adebanjo.'

I mustered a professional smile before going back to my seat.

'Yes, you don't have to. Forgive my scrutiny.'

He glanced down at me, his lips pursed in thought. Then he turned and left, and I sat frozen, an unpleasant shudder rippling through my body. I was still marvelled at today's turn of events. I had come late to work and my boss had asked if my co-worker was my boyfriend because he brought me food. The fact that he was so confusing angered me. There was so much about him that wasn't so visible except you were able to see past him.

It was past eight and almost everyone would have gone home by now except security. Femi had left over an hour ago.

'Aren't you going home?', he had blatantly asked me as he held his suit jacket on his arm.

'Not yet, sir. I still have work to do.'

My eyes had been focused on my typing in a quest to avoid looking at him. I expected him to insist that I leave like he always did, or ask me another absurd question, but he didn't. He simply nodded and left, and my disappointment flared. After packing up my things, I turned off the lights and walked out of the building. Outside was already dark but the security light was on and my eyes caught a familiar car parked there but I couldn't be too sure. I was already close to the gate when the car pulled up beside me.

'Do you want to get in?'

Femi's voice caught me off guard and I bent to see him through his windshield.

'What are you still doing here? I thought you left already,' I exclaimed, my brows arched in surprise.

'I did but came back. Just get in.'

He nodded towards the other car door and I moved to get in.

'Now that wasn't so hard, was it?' He said but his humour fell away and I couldn't ascertain why.

'Why did you come back?' I asked him, my nose scrunched up curiously but he evaded the questions.

'Let me drop you at home,' he said grimly.

As he drove me towards the direction of my place, I couldn't stop wondering why he insisted on dropping me. Was that his own way of being kind? Or his apology for earlier? I couldn't say.

'Why are you doing this?' I asked him blatantly.

He glanced at me for a minute before paying his attention back to the road.

'Doing what?' He asked like he didn't know what I meant.

'You know what I mean.'

He took his time this time but he responded,

'I saw you walking by, and it's late so I decided to help. I don't see any problem with that.'
'Right?' I acquiesced, not hiding the fact that I didn't believe his words.

'Don't you have a girlfriend to go home to?'

I bit my cheek in disgust as the words left my mouth. Femi gazed into my eyes with searing intensity before he sighed loudly as if weary.

'I see you did your research,' he said grimly and I felt embarrassed that I wasn't sure I would be able to suppress it this time.

'Well, you did ask me if someone was my boyfriend this afternoon. You can't blame me for insinuating the same.'

I looked at him this time as I said it and admired how attractive he was when focused.

'I asked according to what I saw,' he retorted.

'And so did I. I mean it was blatantly written there' I said and I watched him give an impish smile.

'I was right. You did research about me. What did you find?' He asked teasingly and I wanted to slap the stupid smile off his face.

'More than enough reasons why I shouldn't be in this car with you right now,' I said, focusing my eyes on the other cars on the highway.

'Here we are,' he taunted.

'I wouldn't mind getting off here so I don't have to endure your annoying self,' I said angrily but he held up his hand in surrender.

'I'm sorry. It's just really easy to get on your nerves. And about your question, she's not my girlfriend. She's an ex.'

His words caught my attention and as much as I hated it, I felt a sense of relief when I heard them.

'But why does it say she is?' I asked him curiously.

His eyes turned towards mine as he answered,

'We broke up three weeks ago but she's adamant about us getting together. That's why she still wants the media to believe we are. The breaking up only became more official then. Our relationship had been wrecked for longer than that, she just didn't want to end it,' he explained softly.

'Was that the morning you met me? Three weeks ago? When you were in a foul mood?' I asked him, reliving the memories of that day and how cold he had been to a stranger.

When he apologised, he said he had a bad day and it was just too much of a coincidence to not assume it was the same day he and his girlfriend broke up. His answer confirmed it,

'It was. I told her I couldn't be with her anymore before she decided to move back. But she did anyway and that morning she showed up at my house. I told her I wasn't changing my mind and we got into a bad fight. I left home really mad and I guess I also wasn't focused when driving, so I apologise again for that day.'

I took his words in as he spoke and I felt my heart ache for him. He was opening up to me little by little and he didn't seem like one to do that easily. Why he was telling me all of these, I didn't know. But I was glad. It definitely made me understand him more, and I didn't feel as awful about my feelings for him as I did when I thought he was with someone.

'Thank you for letting me know,' I said and he nodded softly, not saying a word. Neither did I.

We drove in silence till he took me to where he dropped me the other day.

'I'm guessing you don't want me to know where you live this time,' he teased and I smiled softly.

I felt safer with him than I had ever felt with any other man, but I wasn't ready for that. My new home was my comfort zone and I wasn't ready to give that away as ridiculous as it sounded.

'Not this time, but thank you really for dropping me off. It means a lot.'

He looked at me and I saw his brown eyes cloud with something fierce and wild as he stared at my lips. Unwanted desire flared through me and I felt my cheeks flush at the intensity of his gaze. My body was betraying me. As much as I felt scared, thoughts of his lips on mine didn't frighten me like they normally would.

'You should go', he said as he looked away and disappointment overtook me instantly.

For the first time in my life, I wanted a man to kiss me. At least, I felt that way even if my mind was telling me otherwise. He wanted me, I could tell, but why was he resisting so hard? What was holding him back? There was obviously something, but I couldn't ask him those questions. I wasn't that desperate. It was best this way, anyway and I needed to leave.

'Goodnight,' I said before coming out of his car.

***

Zainab kept staring at me like she had seen a ghost after I told her everything that had happened between me and Femi. She always teased me about my being in a relationship with him which made me wonder why she seemed so flabbergasted.

'Talk now,' I prompted her, curious to hear her thoughts.

'You mean he dropped you home, twice?' She held my arm as she asked and her reaction annoyed me.

'Yes, but that's not the main issue here,' I said, rolling my eyes.

Zainab could be so dramatic sometimes and I'd told her several times that she looked funny whenever she popped her eyes open that way.

'What do you mean by that? Do you know how many times this man has seen me or maybe anyone leaving the office late at night? He has never offered to drop me off anywhere. The only thing he does is maybe offer me plenty of money for bike, or a cab home, or except he tells Kunle to drop me off.'

I chuckled as she spoke, wondering if what she said was true. Kunle was his driver, but he hardly came around because Femi preferred driving himself. I could count the number of times I had seen him.

'But at least he offers you plenty of money and how are you sure he hasn't dropped someone else off?', I asked her.

I mean it wasn't a small company. There were loads of workers there and so many beautiful women. Although, I hardly saw him with any, except during our occasional meetings, and I'm sure if there was someone else I would have seen her walk past me to his office.

'Trust me, that's every woman's dream in that company. If that happens, they won't let anyone rest, especially that useless Corinne. I always teased you about him but now that it's actually very possible, it seems so surreal'

I laughed loudly recalling her fight with Corrine. They usually did projects together but never got along. Corrine was rude and a master of eye service according to her words. I hadn't had any personal encounters with her and I didn't want to based on what I had heard.

'Trust me, I'm confused', I said, as I drank from my bottle of Fanta.

'I wish you guys had kissed,' she said, extending her arms in the air, and I looked around us, wanting to ascertain that no one could hear us.

We were at a local restaurant by Zainab's place and she insisted we go out for a try. We usually just hung out inside, but the weather wasn't as hot today. It was nice to take a breath of fresh air.

'No, it's better this way. I'm not interested and I've told you that already, Zainab,' I groaned as I pressed my face to my hands.

'You're in denial, girl. From everything you've said, there could be more. I'm just saying it how I see it, and I'm sure he did hesitate because you looked like a mad woman,' she said and I moved to smack her arm.

'That man is very hard to read.'

She looked up for a second. Deep in thought, I watched her take the last gulp of her 7up.

'Yup, he really is. I'm just really scared you know? It's all new to me.'

She smiled softly as she called on the waiter.

'Don't be, I'm sure he means well. You just have to be careful because as much as I want you to be with someone, I don't want you to get your heart broken.'

I nodded attentively as I took in her words. I wasn't ready for this anyway. I felt very sane most times but when I was with him alone, everything felt different. I couldn't place it. It was all in my head. I hadn't told her much about my history and she didn't insist. It was one thing I really appreciated because I wasn't ready to let out that part of me. Talking about it would bring back distressing memories and I was trying to get past that side of my life. I needed to feel whole again.

'My change is supposed to be two hundred and fifty naira.' Zainab's words to the waiter caught my attention.

'No, ma. It's two thirty. Soft drinks are now one hundred and ten naira,' she said. I laughed as I watched Zainab's face change to her adamant one.

'*Nawa o*, something I just bought last week for hundred naira. You people can steal ehn,' she grumbled.

My laughter became louder.

'Don't worry, I will give you the twenty naira before you faint,' I joked, withdrawing from her as she rolled her eyes at me.

After spending so much time with Zainab, I got home really late, but I found it hard to sleep. There wasn't much to do. Usually, I brought my work home when I couldn't finish it at work but as I had been overworking myself lately, it was my way of getting Femi off my mind. The next day was a Friday, but that didn't excite me as it did my co-workers. I mostly spent my weekends in bed or doing more work. I hardly went out and after that party I went with Zainab, I got discouraged to want to attend more.

My mind went to Femi and my last conversation with him in his car. He wanted to kiss me, I was so sure of it. But what held him back? Did he suddenly realise that this was a mistake? Or maybe he thought that I actually looked like a mess. I hated the fact that I cared so much. I would have resisted if he tried to, but I still cared that he didn't. I couldn't understand myself. It was all complicated.

The loud sound of my phone ringing interrupted my thoughts. I moved to pick it up but it was an unknown number. Normally, I wouldn't have taken the call, but I guess I was getting less normal than I usually was.

'Hello, who's this?' I spoke immediately and I heard a loud sigh,

'It's Femi'

Chapter Eight

The Talk

I TRIED TO COME UP with any reason why he would call me but I couldn't. His voice sounded so deep over the phone that I felt myself melt immediately.

'Hello, sir. Is anything wrong?' I asked him, as I sat up, and leaned my back on the cold wall.

'Call me Femi. And no, I realised I hadn't called you before,' he said softly.

He had actually done it, though. When he needed me, he sometimes called me through the office telephone.

'But you have,' I simply mumbled and I heard him chuckle, 'Not like this.'

I heard sounds of ruffled sheets and imagined him laying his tall, magnificent built body on a fancy king-sized bed. It felt so different talking to him outside work, knowing he was at home in bed and so was I. It felt like we were almost close, as ridiculous as it seemed.

'So why did you call then?' I insisted.

Ever since I met this man, it had been a mixture of uncertainties. It was overwhelming. The effects he had on me made it seem like I had known him for years and not just weeks.

'I couldn't stop thinking about you,' he said calmly as if we were talking about the weather and not something as appalling as this.

'Um, I don't know what to say. Are you sure?'

I know it was a stupid thing to ask but my words were caught in my mouth. My heart was beating so fast as if I had just run a marathon race which I was very bad at, by the way.

'Tiwa, it's obvious that there's more than just a professional relationship between us. I don't know what to make of it but yes I do think about you even when I don't want to. I can't explain it.'

I nodded rapidly like he could see my head moving.

'This is all so new to me. I mean you're my boss, Femi.'

I only said the partial truth. My principal fear was that I was beginning to get vulnerable. This man occupied my thoughts daily. No man had ever affected me like this.

'I know I'm your boss. I tell myself that every time. I don't even know anything about you. Why does it seem like there's so much more in there? I can't place it.'

His words hit too close to home, and I wasn't sure I wanted to continue on this call.

'I think we should go to bed. I need to be at work early tomorrow so I don't lose my job,' I said, ending the call.

I held it for a few minutes hoping he would call me back. But who was I kidding? This wasn't a movie. This was real life. It was reality. No boss would easily fall for an employee, especially not me who was more or less a loner. I stood up to turn off my lights and checked that my door was locked for the last time. I had a job to wake up early for and no random night calls would get in the way.

The next day felt better than I thought it would. I was early to work, and everything was going on well. I hadn't seen Femi all day, and neither had he called me for assistance or asked me to drop anything in his office. I was being a normal working lady and it gave me a confidence boost which I needed especially after the past few days. I was packing my things up when I saw him. He had a poker face on as he walked closer to me, and I felt nervous as I recalled memories of our conversation last night.

'It's good that you're still here. I wanted to talk to you.'

His voice wasn't stern, neither was it soft. It was in between, controlled. And I wondered how he managed to maintain that level of control always.

'What do you want to talk about?' I asked him softly and he hesitated before answering. His eyes went to the pile of books I had on my table.

'We don't have to talk here. We can go somewhere more open with people around, any place of your choice,' he stated softly, as he adjusted the jacket on his arm.

It felt soothing and surprising at the same time that he asked for us to go somewhere open which was usually my preference. It was late evening and not many people were around us, so he could have just insisted we talk here instead. Sometimes, it seemed like he knew more than I thought, but that couldn't be possible. We were almost strangers to each other.

It was as if he could read in between me. He could tell that I didn't feel so secure with him yet. I yearned for his physical presence and at the same time, I evaded it. I hardly went anywhere, but I did have an idea of where we could go to. I thought about taking him to a local restaurant where Zainab and I usually hung out. It wasn't too crowded that you couldn't hear your voice, and neither was it quiet. It was the best place I could think of and I doubted he would feel comfortable going there, especially for someone as prestigious as he was. But that was his business, he was the one that requested we had a conversation.

'Lead the way,' he requested softly and I nodded before grabbing my bag.

The drive to the local restaurant wasn't unpleasant, it was quiet and my head was wrapped in thoughts on what to expect from today's ordeal. It was in the rural area of town and I looked at him, unsure of what to make of his expression. He seemed unbothered that he was in such a setting. If anything, it felt like it was something he was used to. We were already in front of the place and I showed him where to park at the side of the building.

There were loud noises emanating from the little children playing around with their tricycles. Some had wheelbarrows with someone seated in them as they drove themselves around. It reminded me of my childhood days way before I knew anything about how distressing life could be.

The smell of spicy stew filled the air and I suddenly craved the delicious taste of Ofonime's Edikang Ikong but I felt shy eating swallow in front of Femi. Especially with how messy it could become sometimes.

'Are you comfortable here?' He asked, his eyes going to the old closed door of the building.

It was amusing to see him look uneasy, and I couldn't help my smile. 'I am, except you want to go somewhere else', I teased, watching him move from one foot to another. He was clearly not used to places like this.

'No, no! It's fine really. Is my car safe here?'

That I wasn't sure of, especially with how fancy it was. I caught sight of Ofonime the store owner, she was super nice and I had grown fond of her during my short time here. I waved to get her attention.

'Tiwa, you're here. It's so good to see you. Why are you still outside?' She asked as she cleaned her oily hands on her apron.

'Good evening, ma. Please, can someone watch over his car?' I asked and her eyes wavered to Femi whose arms were folded across his chest like he was watching a business transaction.

'Who's this fine man? Is he your hubby?'

She walked closer to him as if to get a clearer view and gazed at him from his foot to his head like he was up for exhibition.

'No, haba!' I said embarrassingly, eager to go inside, making sure to avoid Femi's eyes.

The cool breeze from outside was beginning to feel chilly. Thankfully, she had no more questions and instead called on one of her men to watch the car. The aroma of the food was even more enticing inside the canteen. There were more than a few people inside. Some were in groups, while others sat alone. I asked Femi where he would like to sit but he insisted I made the choice. So we sat close to the wall, where an antique painting of a mother carrying her child on one arm and another on her back was placed. It had been done by Ofonime's daughter and it was beyond beautiful.

'So, how are you feeling?' Femi asked me, his eyes going around in circles.

'I should be asking you that,' I chuckled, finding this scenery amusing.

'I'm good. I've been to a place like this before with my sister,' his eyes glimmered with pain, raw and sharp as if he remembered something traumatic but he quickly shut it away in an instant and I decided not to press.

'Well, if you say so. Would you like to order now?'
I asked him, as Ofonime walked up to us, her hands on her waist.

'What do you want to eat? Do you want your normal Edikang Ikong?' She asked me and I was so tempted to order that, but I didn't want to embarrass myself, especially because it could be messy sometimes.

'Jollof rice and chicken is fine,' I said, smiling tightly.

We turned to Femi who didn't hesitate in making his order.

'I will have that food,' he said and we both looked at him, confused.

'Jollof rice?'

He shook his head in answer,
'No, Edikang Ikong and just water,' he clarified, drinking from the glass already poured for him while Ofonime gave us puzzled looks before walking away.

I felt more stupid because that was what I was craving but I had asked for something else instead. I thought about changing my order but it would make me appear more stupid.

'I wasn't aware you were into that kind of food,' I said.

'What do you take me for? I eat a lot of swallows. My mum made sure of that while growing up,' he smiled. A half-fond, half-wry quirk of his lips was more like it actually.

'So, I'm guessing you love amala,' I continued, moving away for the waiter to place a jug of water on the table.

'Not really, honestly. I find it bitter. I prefer fufu,' he responded and I laughed, unable to help it.

'Really? I assumed you would hate the smell,' I said and his cheeks flushed.

'That's actually my best. There's just something about it. My mother makes the best fufu.'

He folded his shirt above his wrist as he spoke and I washed my hands on the basin beside the table.

'Aww… that's really surprising,' I said, my heart warm from hearing him talk about his mother this way.

I missed mine. I remembered the grey-haired woman from the first day, and it felt like the perfect setting to ask him about her.

'So how about your former assistant? Do you hear from her?' He grinned widely, dropping his cell at the edge of the table.

'Mama is fine. She's actually my mum's older cousin. She lost her only son to a tumour and she was only working for me temporarily. She insisted she needed to work to keep her occupied. And we couldn't just let her go anywhere, especially with her condition'

I felt my heart ache for the poor woman, remembering how nice she was to me. Now her stronghold on Femi began to make sense. I had my job because of her, actually my trial, I was still not sure if I would get the job yet. But that was a discussion for another day.

'I feel really bad for her. So, where is she now?' I asked him softly.

Our food had come, and the look of his meal made my stomach rumble. The Jollof rice didn't look bad, but who wouldn't care for Edikang Ikong and pounded yam, especially one which looked like this? I was about to start eating when he moved the bowl of soup to me, coupled with the wrapped pounded yam.

'Here, I know you wanted this. Give me the rice'

My mouth was open widely as my gaze flickered between both meals.

'I'm confused, what do you mean?' His lips twitched in what I would have suspected to be a smile as he took the plate of rice from me.

'I lied. I don't like Edikang Ikong. I ate it when I was sick in senior school and it made me throw up. It was obvious you wanted it.'

He gingerly picked up his fork and started eating the rice. He eyed me warily,

'Aren't you going to eat yours? Come on, don't be shy,' he teased and I felt a sudden shyness overwhelm me.

I was embarrassed. But the smell of the food was too enticing for me to miss out on it. I took a fold of pounded yam and bit into it, savouring the pleasant taste.

'There you go,' he said, grinning widely and I smiled warm-heartedly grateful for his display of kindness, especially after my first bad impression of him.

'So, I was right. You don't like swallows,' I countered, and he shook his head in disagreement.

'I do. I didn't lie about loving fufu. I'm just not a fan of this soup', he shrugged.

'So, what did you want to talk about?' I asked.

He was eating his food with so much enthusiasm that I suppressed a smile at the sight of him looking like a kid who had been presented with his favourite food.

'You, I want to get to know you' he said, before gulping down some water. 'Well, what do you want to know?' I bit into the stock fish, careful to not let it spill on my cotton shirt.

'Anything and everything. Why did you decide to move here?'

His question was one I had gotten from a lot of people. I usually just said it was because of the company, but with him, I felt like saying more, and by more, I didn't mean my whole history. Just my desire for a new setting.

'I was tired of the Lagos life. I needed to find myself' That was as far as I could go and I hoped he wouldn't push for more details.

'Oh, I see. Do you have family here?'

He was almost halfway done with his rice and I marvelled at how fast of an eater he was.

'I don't actually. Everyone here is a stranger to me. Well, except the few friends I had made in my short time here’

'Do you still see me as one?' He asked, his brows furrowed, as he watched me curiously.

'Maybe a little. I mean we've hardly had conversations like this. You've been more of a boss to me,' I said truthfully. He nodded as he took in my words.

'I get where you're coming from honestly, and I'm trying to amend my ways. I don't want to be a stranger to you, Tiwa'

I blinked in surprise at the vehemence in his voice.

'Then what do you want? We hardly know each other.'

I was beginning to feel full, but I didn't want to waste my money.

'We can be friends, nothing more. I think about you, yes but I admit that it's still too early to expect more. I don't think I'm ready for something like that yet either. I got out of a relationship not long ago, but feelings can be very surprising.'

My expression relaxed, as I listened. I didn't mind being friends, as much as I was attracted to him. I wasn't ready for something more yet. My feelings were brand new and I needed time to nurture them and be sure that he was even right for me. Sometimes, your mind deceives you into wanting what is dangerous and I was going to be as careful as I could.

'I don't mind being friends, but when we're at work you remain my boss,' I said in a still voice and his smile deepened.

'So, you can't call me Femi always?' He asked with his eyebrows raised.

'Not at work,' I replied and his eyes fluttered close in a pretence at pain.

'You're so dramatic,' I teased with a chuckle.

There's a saying that the bond of all companionship, whether in marriage or friendship, is conversation. I and Femi were testaments of that fact. Ever since our dinner together which he ended up paying for despite my protests, we had a better relationship, but I wouldn't say we were close. It was more or less just more bearable. The arguments were fewer. The greetings were warm, and the conversations were pleasant and very hilarious mostly.

It was three days to the end of my trial. Every time I thought about it that way, it felt like I was caught up in a court case. Zainab had given me much reassurance that I would definitely be given the job but with Femi, I could never be too sure. I could have blatantly just asked him, but I didn't want him to think I was taking advantage of our newfound friendship. I'd rather I got the job because he believed I had it in me than to be considered a charity case.

It was an early Friday morning and my legs were already killing me from standing while waiting for a bike. I waited for seven more minutes till I couldn't bear it anymore. I wasn't a fan of using buses, which were commonly known as *Kabukabu* because they got caught up in traffic a lot, especially this early morning when everyone was in a haste to go to work.
I resorted to using it this time because I had no choice. I sat at the back, with my earphones on. We were not too far from my workplace when I saw a man's calloused hands going around a little girl's bum through the hole at the back of the seat. It was like I couldn't control myself, my hands instinctively went to the man's fingers and pushed them away.

Chapter Nine

Unwanted Feelings

SEEING THE MAN TOUCH HER that way ignited a sudden anger in me that I couldn't control. My hands instinctively went to the man's fingers and pushed them away.

'Who are you?' He shouted, his head turning around to face me. I looked boldly at him and turned my eyes in the direction of the girl who looked like she was not more than eight years old.

'Why were you touching her bum?' I asked him directly and heads turned around to stare at us.

'Shameless man,' the woman beside me said.

'Good for nothing fellow,' a bald lady in the front seat said. '*Oga driver o*, see what is happening in your bus,'

I heard a man's voice say, but the driver didn't bother to turn around, and neither did the conductor whose sole focus was on calling more passengers as the car moved. The woman beside her was busy eating her puff puff as if she had no care in the world. A man beside her patted the paedophile's back.

'*So now na small pikin you dey follow*'

The culprit looked straight ahead like he wasn't just molesting a child.

'Why are you on the bus alone?' I asked her softly and her eyes seemed unbothered as she was not aware of what was really happening.

'My mother sent me to collect yam from her customer,' she pointed at the huge bag on her lap and my heart ached at the thought of her carrying all these alone.

It was horrendous that a man was taking advantage of a little girl, but it wasn't new. Reported cases flashed on my television screen almost every day. It was now beginning to seem very normal which was frightening.

'Do you mind me dropping you off?'

I asked her softly but she shook her head.

'I can't bring anyone to the house, ma'

I was almost at my stop and my eyes went to the man still in the taxi. I felt uneasy leaving her here, and I was almost late for work. In fact, it was when I was supposed to know my fate on if I had my job or not. This man wasn't going to get charged because no one would take it that seriously, anyway. It was depressing being a woman in such a society and as the taxi stopped at my bus stop, I gazed at the girl in front of me.

'At least can I drop you off at your last stop?'

She bit at her fingers as she eyed me warily and I felt my heart boil at what had just happened. Some people would never understand the turmoil sexual assault brought to its victims. She was a mere child, and even if she was currently oblivious about what

was happening, she would grow to hate this moment - when she realises that her body had been tampered with by an imbecile who definitely had more victims.
The bus drove past my stop and as much as I dreaded being late to work today, I couldn't handle the thought of this man touching her anymore. It had taken shorter than I expected to get her home, not home exactly but at least very close by as I didn't want to get her in trouble. Zainab had called me repeatedly thinking I overslept again but I had assured her that it wasn't the case.

I had no idea if my being late would affect my job. I was frightened obviously, but I had no choice. I was weak when it came to protecting myself, but a new strength had obscurely come when I witnessed one personally and I could only assume it came from my late mother. I made sure to send a quick email to Femi to explain that I got held up and I hadn't checked to see if he had replied yet. I already felt panicky and breathless that he would just tell me to not bother to show up at his company again. We were friends but he didn't fail to be stern occasionally.

***

When I finally got back to my desk, I took loud breaths before checking my emails. I had a couple of official ones from Sam, and a few from publishers that requested updates. I saw one from a store where I recently bought some underwear. I smacked my head for giving them my official email address instead of my personal one. I made sure to open the others before finally opening Femi's own.

'Please, meet me in my office when you arrive'

I sat back for a minute, not sure if I was ready to hear my fate. It's now or never, I said to myself as I stood up. When I opened his office door this time, he was standing, staring at the city through the glass windows. He turned around to me but he wasn't smiling. His face was expressionless and if I had any hope left, it fell down the drain. I stood there, unsure of what to expect. His lips were pursed in thought as he gestured for me to sit down.

'You can sit, you know!'

I did, but not fully.

'Did I do anything wrong? Why do you seem so mad at me?' I asked him, unable to help myself.

'I'm usually this way, Tiwa. Why are you surprised?' He asked in a low menacing voice.

'Oh, I'm sorry for assuming. So, I guess you're going to tell me if I have the job or not,' I said through gritted teeth, beginning to feel stupid for presuming our so-called friendship meant he would be the least decent to me.

''Tiwa, really? You know you have the job already.'

He suddenly grinned and for a moment, the sight of a smile stretching across his face and changing his stony but handsome profile caught me completely off guard. I shook my head at him, feeling beyond relieved that I finally got my job.

'You just had to,' I said, my lips curved into a tight smile.

'It was fun while it lasted, and my aunt would probably kill me if I don't give you the job,' he groaned and I couldn't help my laughter.

'I really need to thank her though. She's been so good to me,' I said gratefully.

I had only seen her once, but it seemed like she had made so much impact in my life. Her belief in me was sweet and I understood why they cared for her this way.

'I can always take you to meet her someday,' he offered.

It made me feel uncomfortable because it sounded like I would be meeting his parents even if that wasn't the case. My cheeks instantly burned as my eyes got caught up with his. He stood up, presumably in an attempt to ease the tension and I rose to join him, but he stopped me.

'I wanted to offer you something to drink', he said as he walked to the bar at the end of the office

'You shouldn't bother. You don't have anything I like. I fill up your bar, remember?'
His head went up and down the bar, like one of those bobble head cats on a taxi's dashboard.

'I'm sure I will find something,' he insisted and I laughed.

It was filled with loads of expensive champagne which he usually shared with his business partners or just when he needed to take a break. There was nothing I drank there.

'It's fine, really. I should go back to my work anyway' I said, standing up.

The creaking sound of the chair made me cringe.

'Yeah, I think I need to change that chair,' he said and I laughed, agreeing with him. It looked new but the sound it made felt like a rat's squeak.

'I will make sure of that,' I added softly.

We stood a few metres away from each other. My palms closed, his hands in his pocket as always.

'Thank you,' he said and I smiled softly.

My nerves were building up and as much as I wanted to flee, I felt my heart pulling me to stay.

'Thank you, too, for giving me the job,' I said.
He studied me from the corner of his eye and smiled faintly.
'You deserve more.'

He looked crestfallen as if his words went far beyond the mere meaning. What was on his mind? I couldn't say.

'I think I should go back to my work'

My heartbeat had increased rapidly and my palms were beginning to feel sweaty. It was an enormous space, but it felt like there was no distance between us. He didn't say anything and as I turned to leave he called my name.

'Can we ever be more?'

His words caught me off guard. It was unexpected. He never ceased to amaze me, and I found myself struggling to come up with a response. I wasn't wary of him, which was new to me. I wasn't running away like I usually did. My fright seemed to be decreasing with this man in an unexplainable way. Sometimes, I felt like I could understand myself but that was a lie. I never felt whole, and now that I was growing feelings for a man, for the first time, it made me feel guilty – as if I was betraying my body, especially after promising to protect it no matter what, even if it meant being alone forever.

'I don't know,' I replied.

I didn't turn back to answer. I couldn't bear to look at him, not this way. I felt damaged and I knew that he would see it through my eyes, as enigmatic as it sounded. And I couldn't bear that.
After telling Zainab that I got the job, she insisted we celebrate and I wasn't really in a festive mood. I craved to be in my bed, drowning my sorrows in a bowl of ice cream. My heart felt an ache that I presumed was a heartbreak, it was more depressing because it wasn't like I had love in the first place.

It had been hopeless from the beginning. Why did I feel like I wanted more with him in the first place? I couldn't because my body would never allow it. I felt like a lost puppy that would never be found. My phone rang from my side table and I moved to see who was calling. I sighed as I saw Zainab's name on the caller ID.

'I told you I wanted to be alone,' I said with a groan.

'Yes yes, I'm sorry but Isaac made me do this. He's been begging me to meet you again but I've been postponing, and now he just showed up at my house to ask about you, and I lied that I've told you. I'm in my bathroom now.'

I sat up, trying to understand what was happening. 'Why would he want to know me?' She sighed, clearly exasperated.

'Girl, he obviously liked what he saw. Please, just let me give your number to him. He's my good friend. He means no harm, trust me,' she mumbled.

I wasn't sure I wanted him to have my number. He was still a stranger to me.

'Zainab, I don't think...'

'I'm giving him. He's calling my name. Bye,' she said, before ending the call.

I looked at my phone for a moment, still trying to grasp what just happened. A few months ago, I had no man wanting to do anything with me. Where did all these come from? The next day was a Saturday, and I was going to use it to get rid of any stress I felt right now. At least, that was what I hoped for.

Chapter Ten

A date or Not

FRIDAY NIGHTS WERE USUALLY THE best because I got to sleep soundly without the fear of my alarm interrupting me. My nightmares did most times, but I had become so accustomed to them that it felt unreal if I woke up without one. It was almost noon on Saturday, and the sun was creeping in through the windows. I could hear the voices of my neighbours whose faces I wasn't familiar with. I had met a few and it had been by accident. Not that I avoided them, but I hardly went outside except it was important. And no one had tried to build that neighbourly relationship with me which I was grateful for. The fewer the people in my life, the better.

That was one thing I never wanted to change because it usually caused problems. That explained why the events the day before kept replaying in my head, no matter how much I tried to get rid of the thoughts. Too much had happened - Femi's puzzling question coupled with Isaac's sudden interest in me. I already had enough male predicaments. I wasn't ready for another, and Isaac was definitely still a stranger to me.

He hadn't taken much time to call me. I knew it was him when my phone suddenly rang.

'Hey, it's Isaac,'

His voice didn't sound as familiar as I thought it would from when I saw him at the party. But I had only met him once. It was no surprise that I easily forgot.

'Hi,' I replied.

'You don't sound too surprised to hear from me. I assume Zainab has spoken to you already about me.'

I could hear the television sound in the background. He was probably at home.

'Yeah, she did,' I answered, making a mental note to reprimand her for trying to play matchmaker.

'Well, I'm not going to beat around the bush. I'm interested in you and I'd like to know you more.'

As much as I already expected his intentions to be close to that, it still shocked me. He had only seen me once. He knew nothing about me, so why was he that interested already?

'Umm... You don't know anything about me,' I said, and I could hear the smile in his voice.

'That's why I want to know you more. What do you say about hanging out?'

I could count the number of times I had gone out with men. I was still trying to come to terms with the fact that I allowed Femi to take me out, but with him, I couldn't help it. I certainly didn't want to lead him on, especially when my feelings were already growing for someone else. And even though there was still nothing going on between me and Femi, I wasn't ready to get myself mingled up with someone else. I needed to understand where I was going with one person first. It was my own way of trying to protect myself.

'I'm sorry, I can't,' I said. I heard him let out a sigh.

'It's okay, but just so you know, I don't give up easily'

I had no chance to respond because the call ended immediately. I made sure to call Zainab after that to ask her why she decided to just give Isaac my contact number. She mumbled a couple of he wasn't going to stop asking and it wasn't her fault. The laughter in her voice made it obvious that she gave him on purpose but she wasn't going to admit to that anyway.

Zainab knew I was wary of men, but she didn't know the reason. And I wasn't ready to open up yet which made everything harder. Most times, people found it strenuous to understand where I came from and I couldn't blame them, not everyone had been unlucky like I was. They saw life differently, and they took each day as it came. There was no bad history, no torturous moments that they had to keep fighting away from their thoughts.

I needed to get my mind off everything that was happening recently and the only way I could have done that was to write. I had a novel I was working on, but I hadn't had the time to continue ever since I started work. I usually got home very late and usually felt exhausted. I also needed to set up my writing area, because it sort of gave me motivation.
That was one thing my late mother never failed to provide for me as I grew up. They were used items of furniture, with lots of scratches around them, but because they came from her, they were

beautiful to me. She had also decorated them with lots of sticker notes that gave me my daily motivation. I still had them with me and even if they were not sticky anymore, I would never dispose of them. I just needed to get my groove back. Hopefully, all these mini-dramas would awaken my skills.
I was setting up my movie when I got the text.

'Can we talk?'

It was from Femi, and I instantly dropped my popcorn on the bed nervously.

'Talk about what?' I asked and he was typing immediately. I had less time to process his words.

'What happened back in the office with us?' He asked.

His use of that word caught my breath, there was no us, at least not now. It was more of confusion, me feeling guilty for even feeling this way about him. And I felt like I was caught in the middle of a bridge with no direction to turn to.

'Where do you want to talk?' I asked him.

'Do you mind having dinner together? I can pick you up,' he said.

It sounded too much like a date and I just needed to be sure. As much as it made me feel terrible, the idea of a date didn't disgust me as it usually would. I had feelings for Femi which explained why it was easier to refuse Isaac. As much as it made me feel culpable, they were so hard to get rid of. There was just something about him that drew me close, that made me feel exhilarated at the thought of seeing him on the only day where I got to be alone.

'It's not a date, right?' I asked, dropping my phone on my bed.

I realised that I had no idea what to wear anyway, and I didn't feel like asking Zainab, especially when everything was still uncertain.

My phone beeped,

'It doesn't have to be, but that doesn't mean I'm not paying this time. I will pick you up at seven, and it doesn't have to be at your home exactly. I can wait for you where I dropped you last time.'

A ghost of a smile hovered on my lips as I read his text. He always insisted he paid no matter how much I resisted. The last time when we had to pay for something, his hands had been faster than mine, and he had this manner of making everything seem like a business deal which kind of amused me and it explained why he was so successful in that world.

'See you then, and I'm paying this time.'

I immediately hurried from my bed to my wardrobe, searching for what to wear. I never worried about things like this, I never seemed to understand why female characters in movies stressed themselves over what outfits to wear when they had to meet the male characters. But as I stood in front of my clothes, my sigh loud as I prayed silently that I would find something presentable, I understood them. Sometimes, you couldn't help it.

I made sure to occupy myself with other things and not just look for an outfit before time flew by. I had subtle makeup on, a little more than I usually wore, and I wanted to wear a dress at first but I opted out of it and decided to wear jeans instead. The dress looked too much, and we hadn't said it was a date yet. I didn't want to look eager when I was confused. The black jean was skinny and it encompassed my curves more than the other outfits I wore to work. My purple top was cropped off-shoulder. I usually got lots of compliments from outsiders, but they never did anything to me. If I was having a bad day and someone told me I looked pretty, my day would still be bad. What I yearned for was more than that - just love, to feel cherished again. The only time I had ever felt that way was when I had my mother with me.

After looking at the mirror and deciding to let my hair down, I left my apartment to meet Femi. I tried to ignore the stares I got as I walked. I didn't allow the constant catcalling to bother me. I was a nervous wreck already. My mind was tired because of how occupied it was and it bundled up when I saw Femi's car approach me. He came out of it. He looked handsome in his dark jeans and navy blue sweater. His eyes circled me like a hawk and I held my purse tightly, trying to hide how nervous I was.

'You look breathtaking,' he finally said and I felt flustered.

'Thank you'

I wasn't used to compliments from him, and as much as other people's words never bothered me, his words caught my breath. The way he kept looking at my face and not my body, just my eyes like they were this treasure he had just found, marvelled me. It was why I felt different around him. I never caught him staring at other parts of my body as I did with other men. It made me more comfortable. His uniqueness drew me to him and that was my only explanation for these feelings I had.

'Are we getting in or not?' I asked and he shook his head, a bright smile lightening up his face.

'Oh, sorry'

He walked ahead of me to open the other side of the door and I got in. His car smelt like him, it was heavenly and expensive.

'So, where are we going to?' I asked him and he grinned widely. '

You've not really been around Calabar, have you?' He asked, his eyes focused on the road.

'Well, not really. I've not had the time,' I said honestly.

Zainab had said she would show me around, but we got so busy with work sometimes that we usually just wanted to rest during the weekends.

'Well, consider me your new tour guide. It's a beautiful city,' he smiled softly.

'Hmm, so what's the first place then?' I teased, deciding to play along.

'You will see for yourself', he said. He pulled into traffic, checking over his shoulder.

'That's not exciting,' I lied.

I was beyond elated to spend the day with him. It was in a way that I couldn't control, and I could sense the constant urge to fight that feeling away wanting to eat me up. The drive had been a mixture of silence and funny conversation.

'We're here,' Femi said as he pulled over in front of a fancy building.

We were already at the car park of the Tinapa Lakeside Hotel and it looked beyond beautiful. I knew of the place but had never been here. It was on my list of places to go to, especially because of the lake view.

'You could have just told me' I said.

He laughed as he stopped the car.

'That wouldn't be too fun,' he said as he came out of the car to help me out.

'Do you want to see the lake first? Or you're hungry?' He asked me.

I wasn't hungry but the idea of seeing the lake after felt more pleasant.

'I'd rather eat first.'

He nodded and we walked side by side to the restaurant.

'It's so good to see you sir.'

The receptionist smiled brightly as she saw us. She turned to me, her smile curling into a near sneer as she did a quick appraisal of my appearance. Why wasn't I surprised?

'Good to see you too, my reservation please,' he asked firmly, which made me feel a lot better.

I watched as she typed a few things on the computer in front of her before someone else came over to us.

'Mr Adebanjo, your table is ready,' an elderly man with slightly grey hair said, his eyes turned to me, not hiding his curiosity as to who I was.

Femi was clearly a VIP guest, and with the way they looked at me, I probably looked below the class of women he usually brought there.

'Let's go,' he said softly, driving into my thoughts.

We followed the man in the direction of the table, a good two feet behind him. It was not visible to people and the table was already perfectly set with cutlery, wine glasses, a flower pot by the side, a bottle of wine, and my favourite Fanta drink on top. I laughed at the sight of the Fanta, it looked weird beside the wine.

'I can't believe you actually asked for it,' I remarked.

He grinned, his brown eyes were bright with humour.

'I know you don't really take anything else, so I made sure it was ready before we got here'

The gesture was sweet and I felt grateful. He pointed at the menu, which I picked up, suddenly feeling famished. I didn't realise that we would have been going to a very fancy restaurant, but that was stupid of me, because what else could I have expected from him? The prices of the food made my jaw drop. I still wanted to pay anyway, so I resorted to the cheapest meal I could find.

'What would you like, sir?'

Another waiter stood in front of us, her eyes focused on Femi. He asked for something which sounded like Chinese food, which she wrote down.

'And you, ma?'

I asked for Jollof rice, still marvelled at the price of the meal. Femi's laughter interrupted my thoughts.

'What's funny?' I asked him, opening my bottle of Fanta.

'Just you, what's your own with Jollof rice? Tell me, what did you really want this time?' He asked teasingly.

This man could easily read me in an astonishing way.

'I actually wanted the rice,' I countered.

He raised his eyebrows, obviously not believing me. We spoke as we ate. The food was so good that I didn't feel as bad for spending that much on one meal.

'I'm glad you're enjoying the food' Femi said.

I was on my last piece of chicken which I was struggling with.

'It's not so bad,' I said.

He watched me as his lips curved into a pleasant smile. 'That's why you're fighting with your chicken, right?'

And I couldn't help the laughter that followed.

'I hate you,' I replied.

My smile was evident as I dropped my chicken on my almost empty plate. I felt embarrassed, but not uncomfortable.

'Just finish it,' he continued, his smile brighter.

I felt happy, even if it was just for a moment, and I couldn't imagine being anywhere else. I had already given the waiter my ATM card when I found out that Femi already paid for our meal. He was their usual customer, so it automatically got taken from his account.

'You know I can always pay for myself,' I told him, as we walked to the lake, our hands occasionally brushed at each other and it gave me tingles.

'I know you can, but I'm the one taking you out, so it's my duty to pay,' he said.

I cocked a brow at him.

'I agreed to go with you, so part of the duty falls on me too,' I said.

There was no one around us. Femi said he had his own way of making sure of it when he needed it. I tried to not think that he rented it because that would have been ridiculous. And it would only emphasise the differences in us that I never failed to recall. We were already close to the lake. It was skyline silver, and window clear.

'You never want to give up, do you?' He teased and I laughed.

We were much closer now, our arms brushing each other. I could see our reflection in the water, and I couldn't help feeling like a dwarf beside him. Femi was a tall man. There was so much height difference between us. It was usually easy for me to get caught up in a crowd, with me being just a little over five feet.

'It's really so beautiful,' I said honestly.

'It is,' Femi agreed, but I could see him staring at me.

'I wish I could see more of this. There's this peacefulness they instil,' I said, enjoying the view - the light sounds of birds chirping interrupting the quiet, especially with no one else around.

My instinct made me turn to him. We were so close, no part of our bodies collided, but it felt like I could feel him. I was so badly drawn to him. My heart felt like it was going to burst out of my chest.

'I can show you more places, anywhere you want. I'm your tour guide remember?'

I smiled nervously, unsure why I was still standing so close to him without finding the will to flee. He was obviously joking, but it didn't hurt to play along.

'I've always wanted to go to Iceland. I heard it's peaceful,' I said.

Amusement flickered in his eyes as he took in my words.

'Where else?' He asked.

I put a finger to my jaw as if thinking,

'Rome, Netherlands, Morocco. When I was younger, I dreamt about getting married in a church in Italy. It's ridiculous I know, but I watched this movie where the lead female character got away with wearing sneakers with her wedding dress. I found it so cool, but I'm older now to know that things like that don't happen.' I laughed nervously as I spoke.

'That was when I was still me, way before life had happened and marriage had begun to seem like a horror story. Maybe I could have feelings but marriage was impossible. Could someone ever love me enough to want to marry me? Could I ever get over my fears to want to trust a man so much that I would be willing to get married to him?' I continued.

Femi chuckled, as he shook his head in disbelief.

'You know, it's lovely seeing you this way. There's so much in there and I can't wait to see more. I hope you do get to have what you once wished for,' he said seriously this time.

His beautiful brown eyes were gazing at me. They had so much emotion that I could tell a story just by staring at them.

'Hopefully!' I replied.

My gaze was lowered to his lips which suddenly felt so near. He grabbed my hand and laced it through his. I felt tingles all over me. My body was jittery from so much attraction. I allowed him to rub his thumb over my knuckles, his other hand pushing my chin up softly. My eyes met his and they were lost in them.

'Can I kiss you?' He asked softly.

The moment was hypnotic and I wanted it but as our lips nearly touched, I instantly drew back.

'I can't. I'm sorry,' I said. I was breathing hard and I wanted to let out my anger.

I wanted to be normal. I wanted to be able to kiss a guy I felt so attracted to. Why was it so hard? Why did I feel so guilty when I hadn't done anything wrong? Or maybe I had. I was going against my vows.

'I'm sorry, it's fine. I understand. I didn't mean to,' Femi said, his eyes showing so much guilt that it saddened me to make him feel this way.

'It's not your fault. I do want you. I want to be kissed by you,' I blabbered.

'We are doing this according to your terms, we can take it slow.'

He smiled reassuringly as he spoke, his hands moving to grasp my shoulders softly. And as our eyes met at that moment, I suddenly wanted him as I had never wanted anything else, the longing to touch and feel his lips on mine taking over everything else. If I kept holding on, I wouldn't do it.

'You can,' I said before I could stop myself.

Chapter Eleven

Entangled

I COULDN'T BELIEVE I WAS actually doing this right now. I had just said that out loud. He stared at me, his eyes hazy as he took in my words.

'What do you mean?'

His hands were still on my shoulders as he asked, his lips, slightly parted as he gazed at me.

'I mean you can kiss me. I want it so bad right now that I can't help myself, and if I don't do it now I...'

His hands moved to hold my face tenderly as his face got closer. But just as our lips were supposed to touch, my eyes caught someone lurking in the background for a second. It was at the other end of the lake, quite distant but it definitely looked like someone was watching us or me. I wasn't sure.

'We're the only ones here, right?' I asked, breaking the moment.

Whoever it was had on an all-black outfit, I couldn't say undoubtedly that it was a man. It could have been a female, he or she had a black cap on so there was no sight of any hair, at least. Moreover, I could have seen wrongly because the person was quite far from me to have been accurate in my description. My nerves had gone haywire because whoever that was, the person had a mask on. This one was different from the one I remembered but that didn't do anything to put me at ease. It awoke appalling memories that I had kept locked away for years, and I felt the sudden urge to throw up. I couldn't see anyone anymore when I looked again but I was certain someone had been there.

'Yes, we should be. What's wrong?' Femi asked concernedly.

He looked around us as if to check if anyone was there but no one was anymore. I felt superbly tensed and I wanted to leave.

'Nothing, I think we should leave.'

I suddenly withdrew from him in a way that I was sure stung, but it was too late. I already made my way in the direction of where his car was parked. Maybe this was a sign that I would have made a dreadful mistake if I kissed him.

'Tiwa, what the hell is wrong? Is kissing me such a bad idea? I thought you said I could,' he rasped.

I tried to think of a reasonable response as I turned around, but I couldn't. My words were caught in my mouth as I tried to speak.

'I'm sorry, I...'

'It's fine, I understand. Let's get you home.'

My heart ached with the crystal pain in his eyes. This time, the dull pain slashed me anew, nothing ever seemed to go right when it felt like it was. It was beginning to feel like I was doomed, but he wouldn't understand that this time, it wasn't him. It was my past haunting me, and he didn't deserve to know my horrific tales, no one did. So, it was better for him to think whatever he wanted to.

The drive back home was still and quiet. Femi had made no indication to ask any questions or say anything else. It was the one time I would have appreciated his comic self, but he was definitely hurt. Today's turn of events had probably left him addled.

'We're here.'

I had been so caught up in my thoughts that I didn't realise we had gotten to where Femi usually dropped me. I turned to look at him but his eyes were turned away from mine.

'Thank you for today, I had a nice time,' I said as I unbuckled my seatbelt.

'You don't have to lie to me. I think I scare you, and that's the last thing I want to do.'

His raw confusion ignited the turmoil I already felt inside me. My eyes closed briefly as I waited for my tears to abate. The last thing I needed was to break down in front of him. That would have only made me more miserable than I already was.

'There are so many things you don't understand, things I can't explain,' I said weakly.

His lips were pressed together as he stared at the windshield in front of him, his hands holding the steering wheel in a tight grip.

'Then explain to me, let me know, make it make sense, Tiwa. I'm not even hurt that you didn't kiss me, I'm more worried that I know nothing about you. I feel like I'm trying to get you to feel comfortable but I'm scaring you more. And it's not your fault, maybe I'm being too much. Maybe it's all too fast for you and I don't want to lose you when I don't even have you yet.'

I swallowed with difficulty as I took in his words, my heart pounding repeatedly in my chest at his sincerity.

'I don't know how to explain, and I'm sorry. It's my battle with myself, and I'm still stuck at crossroads. I'm nowhere near finished, talk less of the end, Femi. So, I'm sorry if you think you frighten me, you don't.'

He turned directly to me, his hand moving to tuck a lock of hair behind my ear.

'Then let me in, allow me to fight this battle with you. I have no idea what it is yet but I'm willing. I want to be with you.'

I forced the lump down my throat as I tried to speak.

'Why are you doing all this? Being kind to me? Why me?'

I spoke out my thoughts, and I watched his face soften as he sighed.

'Isn't it obvious? I have feelings for you. I want you. I want to get to know you. There's so much beauty inside of you and I see it. Allow me to get it out of you. Give me a chance, Tiwa.'

His eyes were pleading like he wanted me to believe it too. But that was where he was wrong. There wasn't anything beautiful inside of me. I was damaged.

'You don't know what you're talking about, Femi. You know nothing about me.'

His eyes flinched with what I recognised as pain, as he took in my words, and I began to fidget.

'I know I don't, that's why I'm trying to spend time with you.'

There was something about him that was so vague, he was inscrutable despite how open he appeared to be most times. There was so much more to him than what was visible. I was certain about that because I was the same.

'I'm trying to fight my feelings, Femi. I don't want them.'

I wasn't going to hide that fact. It was better for me, to be honest. He didn't need to know the depths of where my truth came from, this was enough.

'So, you do feel something?'

His lips were pursed together and I noticed a flicker of hope pass through his eyes. I removed his hand from my hair.

'I need to go,' I said, my hand moving to the door handle.

'At least, do you believe me when I say I feel something for you?'

There was so much warmth in his brown eyes as he rambled on, he sounded so genuine. I wanted to believe him, I really did but it was so difficult.

'You can't blame me for not believing everything you've just said. You're my boss, Femi. There are so many women out there. It's hard to believe that you do want me. I'm trying to not get hurt here. I need to protect myself.'

My tears were pricking to flow through my eyelids and I tried my best to hold them still. I wasn't going to cry in front of Femi. He already saw more than he was supposed to.

'I understand that, take your time. I don't like being this way either, and I can't explain why I'm so drawn to you, but I assure you whether you choose to believe me or not, what I feel for you is genuine.'

***

When I got home, I showered and tried to write in a quest to get rid of my hazardous thoughts. Luckily, I was able to at least write two chapters non-stop after so long. I tried to let myself believe that something good came from everything that had happened. We had almost kissed, and my fingers unconsciously went to my lips, as I tried to imagine what it would have felt like. My beeping phone caught my attention and the number looked familiar even if it was not saved.

'Hey, Tiwa. It's Isaac. I hope you don't mind me texting you.'

I sighed loudly, my head resting on the palm of my hands in agitation as if he could see me. Too much had happened in one day, and I was still trying to fight my feeling for my boss, as difficult as it felt. I decided to reply later, right now all I wanted to do was sleep. The next day was another day to solve boy dramas, but my phone vibrated again. This time it was a call. I waited for it to stop ringing before I decided to reply to his text. It was difficult to conjure a reply to Isaac's unexpected text. I minded but Zainab told me to say otherwise, she said I didn't have to be disrespectful. I decided to go in between,

'I'm not sure how I feel.'

It was as nice as I could go. He was typing back a response so quickly that it startled me.

'I would like to know you more'

I shook my head in response as if he could see me. What was everyone's problem with knowing me lately?

'I'm not an interesting person, you really shouldn't bother.'

I decided to drop my phone, not really in the mood for pointless conversations.

***

My first day at work as more than a temporary worker was almost joyful, at least I tried to make it that way for myself. I had this book I was editing that completely blew my mind away. I had chosen it on purpose because the writer, Kenneth Okolie, was one of the most talented writers I knew. He had already published four other books and this was the second book in a series of two. It was about a woman in an abusive marriage and as much as our situations were different, I felt like I could connect with her.

The book was titled *Not Damaged* and I loved it before I even started reading it. No one wanted to feel that way. I was only halfway through, and I was scared I could have missed out on errors from being so invested in the heart-wrenching story.
This was one thing I enjoyed doing. I had access to so many successful books before they became known. I felt like a VIP, as dense as it sounded. It was why I loved my job. I relished reading and being able to edit them which made me feel like a part of the book.

We were supposed to have celebratory drinks because I got out of the trial stage successfully. It was Zainab's idea obviously and she had the backing of most of the other co-workers who looked for every opportunity to throw a party. I gave numerous reasons why this would be a bad idea but they had a counterstatement for every excuse I gave. It was supposed to be after work and I insisted we just take a ride from the office to wherever it would be. At least, I won this round because I made it clear to them that if I went home I wouldn't come back. We were supposed to be going to a club which was Sam's idea but we were all dressed in work clothes thankfully, so we decided to go to Zainab's small apartment as she called it.

But it was much bigger than mine. It had a living room and two medium-sized bedrooms. She said her dad had given it to her. He gave them things to compensate for his absence. She usually tried to convince me that she wasn't bothered but I knew she was. Her consistent need for a man in her life was a way of filling up the absence of the one that mattered the most while growing up. I never insisted though, it was arduous to open up about things that haunted us because we loathed being seen as victims. I hated pity, I couldn't handle it. It made me feel more horrible than I already felt.

The mini party started an hour after work. It took about thirty minutes to get to her place because of traffic. When we got there, a few others were already waiting for us.

'The celebrant is here,' Dami said.

She was the receptionist and the first person I ever met in the company. I laughed as I took in other faces.

'It's not my birthday, guys. You're being extra,' I said, moving to hug Sandra, another friend I had made.

'Wait till you see the cake,' Sam said as he bent to pick something up from his car.

'Really guys? You shouldn't have.'

I ran my hands through my hair, as I stared at the people in front of me. There were about seven others, including Kanayo who was able to come because he had a substitute.

'*Abeg jor*, just say thank you,' Zainab said as she walked ahead of us towards her door.

I laughed loudly as I held unto her shoulders.

'Thank you so much, ma,' I said jokily, loving the light chuckles around me.

I felt like I had a new family as I watched everyone in the living room. More people had come, and everyone was busy eating something or having a drink. Some people were talking about work, while others were conversing about what I couldn't figure out.

Onome, another editor that had also written a book, was talking to Sam and Dayo about how she went about it. That was something I would definitely be interested in. But as I walked to join them by the sofa, I heard my name.

'It's good to see you again, Tiwa'

I looked to my side to find Isaac who stood by a very guilty-looking Zainab.

'I'm sorry,' she whispered before moving to walk past us like she didn't just put me in an uncomfortable position.

'Hi,' I said casually.

He looked good in his khaki shorts and T-shirt, and he smiled at me from where he stood.

'Zainab told me about this, so I decided to show up,' he said, and I nodded, unsure of what to do.

'Oh, well thanks for coming,' I said, as I rubbed my palms together.

'You look beautiful,' he said as his eyes ran through me.

'Thank you,' I responded.

I was beginning to feel worried that people would see us and assume it was something else.

'Do you want to talk? That's actually why I'm here.'

He was a smooth talker. That was obvious from the way he spoke. I couldn't help but compare him to Femi, they had so many similarities, but differences at the same time.

'Umm… What do you want to talk about?' I asked.
He narrowed his eyes, his hands were in his pockets, another thing Femi did.

'I want to get to know you, Tiwa. I find you intriguing.'

His lips were pursed as he spoke. There was no sign of nervousness. How the hell did they do it?

'I've told you you're mistaken. Nothing is intriguing about me,' I said but he raised his eyebrows in disbelief.

'There's nothing you can say to change my mind,' he insisted.

I really wasn't one to engage in small talk. I was beyond tempted to just turn around and go my way. But he was Zainab's good friend and it would seem disrespectful.

'Well, if you insist, we can talk here,' I said dryly.

He shook his head and pointed towards the door.

'Hope you don't mind going outside,' he asked.

I looked around me, and everyone seemed to be having fun. 'We can just go to the dining, no one is sitting there.'

He walked ahead of me, clearly familiar with Zainab's house.

'So Zainab says you guys work together,' he said.
He was sitting across me at the table. It was quite small, so we weren't really far apart.

'Yes we do, that's where we met,' I replied, recalling that day and how much had changed.

'I bet she frustrates you every time.'

He sat back in his seat as he spoke, and I laughed, agreeing with him.

'I also wanted to apologise about Inuobong. I'm still unsure of how he was able to enter my house,' he said softly.

I winced.

'It's okay, it wasn't your fault.'

I was not in the mood to start talking about it. I needed to enjoy myself at least, and getting in a foul mood wouldn't be helpful.

'I just wanted to apologise anyway.'

His face was solemn and I appreciated his compassion honestly but that wasn't why we were here.

'It's fine, Isaac. We can stop talking about it.'

He nodded in response, a wide grin sitting on his face.

'Yeah, let's talk about why I'm here. I asked Zainab already but I'd like to ask you personally, so I know I'm not overstepping my boundaries.'

I narrowed my eyes, unsure of what he was talking about.

'What's that?' I asked.

He looked nervously this time, but he only took a minute.

'Are you single?'

My breath cut as the words left his mouth. I was single but no one outrightly asked me this, so I had been caught unaware.

'I am'

I watched his grin grow wider in obvious hope and I wasn't sure how it made me feel.

'Well, that's good news for me,' he said.

I laughed at the excitement on his face.

'I'm not looking for a boyfriend,' I said blatantly.

'But boyfriends are looking for you.'

I was confused at his use of boyfriends. Did he know about Femi? Because that was the only other guy that wanted something more with me.

'I'm not interested,' I said, already moving to stand up.

'I know you aren't, please just don't shut me out. I'm enjoying our conversation,' he replied and I sighed, sitting back down.

'I'm only doing this because of Zainab,' I said and he chuckled.

'It's fine, as long as…'

'Isaac?'

Our heads turned to see Femi standing just a few metres away from us. His eyes moved between us both as he walked closer. I hadn't expected him to be here. Isaac stood up immediately and they shook hands. I had forgotten that they knew each other, and this just made everything more awkward.

'What are you doing here?' Isaac asked Femi.

Femi's eyes turned to me immediately in question. It was expected of him to be bewildered at me sitting here with his friend.

'I came for Tiwa, you?'

My eyes fluttered close for a second, this was so uncomfortable.

Chapter Twelve

Just Some Guy

IT FELT LIKE I WAS suddenly in those scenes in movies where the female characters had to figure out how to end the awkwardness. Although, in this case, it was more difficult, my lips were sealed and I couldn't form words.

'Oh, I see. Didn't know you guys were close. I came to see her too,' Femi replied.

I tried to focus on anything else apart from their faces, but I couldn't resist. I was not close to Isaac, this was the only other time I was seeing him apart from the party.

'There are many things you never seem to know.'

My eyebrows drew together in confusion at Isaac's words, what exactly did he mean by that?

'Let's not go there, Isaac. I can always see her later, take your time,' Femi said blatantly.

I didn't miss the hint of disappointment in his eyes. He was already turning to walk away when Isaac stopped him.

'You shouldn't, I have somewhere I need to be. Tiwa, it was good to see you. I hope to see you again.'

He walked away so fast, almost like the way he came in. I gazed at Femi who looked nervous. His muscles were taut, and I felt the need to touch them.

'Should I be worried?' He asked.

I looked around and everyone still appeared to be focused on a movie Zainab had probably put up for them.

'Why should you be?'

I was still trying to grasp what just happened and it was hindering me from thinking correctly.

'You know, it's obvious he's interested in you. And I can't stop him from wanting to have meetings like this with you because you're not mine.'

I sighed as I listened. Isaac may be interested in me but I definitely wasn't. Thoughts about him were not what kept me up at night. Femi had more power over me and he obviously didn't know that because I hadn't been the most expressive about my feelings. It was my way of protecting myself and safeguarding my heart.

'I'm not interested in him, Femi.'

I don't know why I felt the sudden urge to reassure him, but I couldn't bear the disgruntled look on his face.

'You're not but you're not interested in me too, and he's someone I know. Tiwa, he's a good guy, maybe better than me. It wouldn't be difficult for you to fall for him,' he ran his hand through his hair as he spoke.

I wanted to speak up, to let him know there was no need to be worried, but I found it hard to. The words were caught up inside of me and it would have been way easier if he could read minds. His hands moved impulsively to hold my face so tenderly, that if I didn't see them move I wouldn't know they were there. I wanted to push his hand away but I couldn't, my heartbeat rate had increased.

'Did anything happen back in the lake? Something felt wrong from your reaction, Tiwa. Was it me?'

I had no idea how he could easily read into me but it frightened me. I wasn't sure of what I saw and I was scared of what could have been out there. It felt like someone had been watching me but who would easily believe that? I pushed his hand down as gently as I could muster.

'Nothing happened, let's get back to the party,' I said, purposely avoiding his eyes.

I was lucky no one had seen the little drama earlier and I'd rather no one saw this. He gave me an amused smile, as he held up the bag in his other hand. I hadn't noticed it before.

'I got you something.'

He was already bringing out what looked like a flamboyant jewellery box when I gasped,

'No, Femi. I'm not collecting that.'

I shook my head for more emphasis as I drew back. It was bad enough that I had feelings for my boss, I wasn't going to start collecting presents.

'It's just a gift for you getting your job, nothing serious.'

He opened it to reveal a silver necklace with what looked like clear round diamonds as the pendant. It looked alluring with the way it sparkled. This necklace definitely surpassed the price of everything I owned, another reason why I couldn't accept it.

'You mean the job you gave me, right? That's enough gift. I can't. I'm sorry, you should return it.'

He held it up, indicating he wasn't listening to me.

'It can't be returned. I threw the receipt away. Please, it's just a gift, no big deal.'

I scoffed, as my arms went up in exasperation.

'Really, do you think I have loads of diamond necklaces hanging around my home? It's a big deal to me. I'm sure you can find someone else to give it to.'

He sighed loudly before his face began to light up again as if an idea dawned on him.

'I'm going to announce that I have feelings for you if you don't accept it.'

I swallowed hard. He knew I hated this much attention. He was so annoying.

'You wouldn't dare!'

He raised his eyebrows at me, indicating that I was taunting him.

'You already know I have no problem with people knowing about how I feel,' he insisted, his grin getting wider.

He was clearly enjoying this. It was when he turned around that I finally relented.

'I'm returning it to you, it's still yours.'

He laughed softly as he turned me around. I let my hair up as he placed the necklace around my neck.

'It suits you well.'

He turned me around and my hands went to my neck.

''Thank you for this' I said genuinely.

I had never worn anything half as expensive as this, and that's why I needed to return it.

'Only thank me if you keep it,' he teased and I smiled, not surprised by his ability to never give up.

'Your perseverance is really something else,' I murmured.

He looked at me, his brown eyes crinkling at the corners with humour.

'And it never lets me down, hopefully.'

The last word he appended was a way of obviously referring to me. He picked up my hand and kissed it.

'You look beautiful.'

I knew I definitely looked less attractive because I was still wearing my work clothes, and my hair was probably disorganised. But the way he stared at me with so much awe made me feel like that was really what he thought about me.

'Thank you. Um, do you want some cake?' I asked and he laughed loudly, attracting a tiny bit of attention to us.

'No, I didn't come here for cake. I came here for you,' he whispered.

'When did boss arrive?'

I panicked as I heard Sam's voice.

'Let's join the party,' I said, placing the necklace inside my shirt in an attempt to keep it from displaying.

'Okay, I think I would like the cake now,' he replied with an indigent smile, making me chuckle.

'Yes, boss!'

Femi was a friendly employer, so it wasn't too awkward when we left to join the others. Of course, the conversations changed to the company, but that was before Zainab got back and used her sweet ways to try to get everyone back to focus on the movie. I had sat close to Femi all through, and thankfully he had behaved properly by not holding my hands or being too obvious.

He showed no indication that he cared what people thought, but I did. I already had more than enough attention to myself, I didn't need more. More so, we had no idea where this was leading. It was still novel and I didn't want to get my hopes too high.

My evening had been pleasant and I was delighted to have such wonderful people around me. We were in Femi's car and he was taking me home, at least to where he always dropped me. I was certain that he definitely wasn't a kidnapper now, but I wasn't sure if my heart was completely safe with him, or maybe it was my own way of still trying to create a barrier between us, as ridiculous as it seemed. Everything was complicated and what happened at the lake certainly wasn't helping matters.

'I'm happy I made it today. I had a nice time,' Femi said, his deep voice, interrupting the stillness.

'Me too,' I agreed, watching the stars through the closed windshield.

'Happy I made it or that you had a nice time?'

I smiled at his words, not surprised at his weird questions. My eyes turned to him and he was focused on the road.

'Even if I say it's because I had a nice time, you're going to believe what you want to anyway,' I teased.

He turned to wink at me and I suddenly felt shy.

'You can't blame a man for trying,' he shrugged and I moved to smack his arm.

'You know that's the first time you ever touched me willingly,' he said softly.

He held out his hand to hold mine and I let him.

'I smacked you, Femi. It wasn't a sweet touch.'

His expression faltered as he turned around to look at me.
'It doesn't matter, it shows you're getting comfortable around me,' he said.

His thumb drawing lazy circles on my palm in a way that felt soothing.

'Is that really a good thing?' I said, voicing out my fears.

He was right, I was beginning to let down my walls, the ones I had built all through most of my life. It was like I had no choice this time. They chose to pave a way for this man right beside me. And it was terrifying.

'It is if you give me the chance. Just one, Tiwa. That's all I ask for.'

We were already parked at the roadside where he usually dropped me off. The sun had set already, and it was a chilly night. I turned to Femi whose eyes were already focused on me. His hands were still holding mine, and I found myself not wanting to let go.

'It's not as easy as you think it is, Femi. It's complicated.'

He glanced heavenwards and sighed, his other palm had lifted to hold my face.

'I never said it was easy. I'm just telling you to allow yourself to be loved, you deserve it. I only want to care for you.'

He brushed a lock of hair off my face, and I looked down, too weak to be locked in his gaze.

'Look at me, Tiwa, what are you so scared of?'

My heart rate had picked up, no one ever cared enough to ask, but I never allowed myself to be this way with anyone anyway.

'I don't know how to explain, what do you even see in me? There's so much baggage that comes with me. You have enough on your plate already. I don't understand how I feel myself.'

I was being honest, maybe he was indeed one of the good ones, but that didn't make it any much easier. I was still my damaged self, no one could handle the dejection that came with me.

'You not even knowing how special you are amazes me more. Apart from being so beautiful, you've taught me so much in just the short time I've known you. You stand up to me when no one does. You're strong even when you don't think you are. You stood in front of me in my office despite how we met to try to get your job no matter what,' he expressed.

'You knew it was highly impossible for you to get it, but you did anyway. If that's not what you call a strong and determined woman, then I don't know what is.'

I chuckled, my cheeks warming up as he continued.

'When I look at you, I seem to forget everything else, all I can think about is how much I want to be with you. You say you have baggage, Tiwa. I have more than that. I'm not perfect, if anything I'm far from it. When others see me, they think about me as the wealthy Femi, no one is genuine with me, and no one believes I have problems. But you don't care about what I think, you don't seem to anyway. You're real with me. I'm old enough to know I don't want anything less.'

A shiver ran down my spine at his words, no one had ever seen me this way. You never know how much you want to be loved till you see the promises in front of you.

'I'm so scared but at the same time I find myself being drawn to you.'

I gazed into his deep brown eyes and watched his head move closer to mine. But he suddenly drew back.

'I don't want to make you uncomfortable, I guess I was caught up in the moment.'

I couldn't blame him for stopping himself this time. I mean, I had stopped him the last time he tried to kiss me.

'It's fine, I was too.'

He was clearly taken aback by my admission, and the car suddenly felt steamy. I needed to leave.

The next day at work was busy. There were loads of meetings to attend too. And a book that had been published had gone below the ratings we expected, so it kind of warranted a little chaos. Zainab already asked me to have lunch with her and I was really looking forward to it. I was famished and we only had thirty minutes of lunchtime before I had to continue my work. I couldn't contain my loud sigh when I saw her walking up to me in her fitted office skirt.

'I'm so hungry, Tiwa. Please, let's hurry,' she said.

I wasted no time in getting my purse and going along with her. At the cafeteria, Sam and Dayo sat with us. We usually ate together and we used that time to catch up on our lives.

'So, how's your new man, Zainab?' Sam asked.

We turned our heads to her. Zainab always had a new man and Sam never failed to tease her about it.

''There's no new man, I'm still looking.'

She drank her coke from her straw as she rolled her eyes at Sam who had a wide grin on his face.

'Really? So out of all the men around you, none of them are good enough?'

She was clearly getting annoyed with his inquisition because of the rare frown on her face.

'What's your business?' She asked.

He shook his head, before letting out a sigh.

'It's nothing, I was just curious.'

He took a bite of his sandwich which he seemed to be struggling to eat. The food here had its days, sometimes it tasted so good that I felt like packing some home, while other days it was like the cooks were in a quest to punish us with tasteless food.

'Then keep your curiosity to yourself, I've told you to stop asking me questions about my love life.'

'Sam is jealous,' Dayo said nonchalantly.

I watched him and noticed him staring at Zainab discreetly. Oh my God, he probably had feelings for her. But how come no one ever noticed, maybe because I hadn't ever seen them in that way?

'I'm definitely not jealous, stop being annoying,' he scoffed, and Dayo held his hands up in surrender.

'All of you are annoying, but not as much as Corinne. Why the hell is she coming here?'

We looked up to see the girl in a black dress that looked a little less professional with her full face makeup walking up to us. She carried a tray that had nothing but a can of sprite on it.

'My God, I can't deal with this talkative,' Dayo sighed loudly, obviously wanting her to know how much he despised her presence.

'Is she that bad?' I asked and everyone turned to look at me.

'See for yourself,' Zainab said as Corinne withdrew a seat from the long table.

'So why do you guys look like your day is going far worse than mine?' She asked.

No one responded. I decided to be nice.

'Today was just really stressful,' I said.

She looked up as if she was trying to make truth to my words.

'Really? Because it seems like you get special treatment from Mr Adebanjo, you can't be as stressed as we all are.'

I gasped as she spoke, clearly not expecting this. So much for being nice, was that really what everyone thought? This was what I was afraid of. The funny thing was my situation was the opposite, I actually had to prove my worth for a month before I got the job. If anything, I deserved this, especially with my credentials.

'I'm sorry, what do you mean by that?'

I hoped I didn't sound as angry as I felt. I couldn't let her get to me.

'You're only saying that because you wish it was you, you've been struggling all year to get on his good sides, so sad he couldn't even notice you,' Zainab retorted.

I heard Dayo's grin. He was clearly enjoying this.

'You have no idea what you're talking about'.

Her words were in between loud breaths, she was obviously getting agitated. And luckily for us, no one sat beside our table. I wasn't ready to be today's topic of gossip in my workplace, that's if I wasn't already.

'Really? Then next time make sure you think before you talk.' Zainab's voice had gotten higher and I didn't want to be the reason for a fight.

'I know nothing about you, Corinne but from what I've just seen I now understand why they treat you as a plague. Please, go sit somewhere else,' I said in my calm still voice, ignoring Dayo's laughter.

'You know what? I hated you when I first saw you. I hate you more now - All of you!'

She stood up and walked away, leaving her Sprite drink. I was dumbfounded by what had just happened and my attention went to the people around me.

'Why is she like that?' I asked honestly.

Sam shrugged as he said,

'I wish I knew. She's not the only one, though. That's why I stay on my lane. The business world isn't as smooth as it appears to be, more people look for your downfall than those that want you to succeed.'

I gulped my drink before focusing on Zainab whose attention was on her phone as she typed.

'Only smart thing you've said today,' she directed to Sam and I couldn't help my grin.

'Had no idea you were counting,' he retorted.

There was just something about them. We were almost done eating when my phone beeped.

'Can we have dinner tonight? I missed you today.'

It was Femi. I had rarely seen him all day because of how cramped the office had been and I would be lying to myself if I said I didn't miss him.

'Not sure if that's a good idea,' I replied.

His response came almost immediately.

'Doesn't have to be for long. You can pick this time.'

'Fine, but I'm returning your necklace.'

He didn't respond to that, clearly on purpose. I had the necklace on me anyway, so I was going to use this opportunity to give it back to him.

'Who are you talking to?' Zainab asked.

I looked around us and I couldn't say who it was because it would raise questions. I needed to at least know where this was going before I mentioned it. It was too much of a risk.

'Just some guy,' I murmured.

Chapter Thirteen

Not the End of Us

I CONTEMPLATED BETWEEN WEARING THE necklace and giving it to him when I saw him. I wasn't sure what option came out nicer. I ended up wearing it with my dress anyway. I was giving it back and this was my way of saying I wasn't returning it because I didn't like it but only because it was necessary.

It was so funny how a tiny piece of jewellery kept my thoughts busy for almost longer than I dressed up. I felt relieved when I finally wore it. I had asked him what to wear expecting him to say anything I wanted as he usually did, but this time he told me to wear a dress.

I had only very few dresses and I had no time to buy something fancy. After looking at my options, I decided to wear a dark blue off-shoulder dress. It was fitted and as much as I liked to downgrade myself, I was only lying if I said it didn't look good on me.

I had to walk to meet Femi where he usually dropped me, so I wore block heels because there was a high chance of me falling with the number of stones around, coupled with the fact that the streets were not levelled. When I finally saw him, I had tingles from the way he stared at me like I was the only girl in the world.

'You look amazing as always,' he said as he hugged me tightly.

Being so close to him usually made my heart beat faster and I struggled to keep myself in check.

'Thank you. You look good too,' I said.

He chuckled as he held my hands and led me to the other side of his fancy car.

'Did you decide on where you want to go?' he asked and I suddenly recalled that he insisted I choose this time.

'I've not thought about it. You can take me anywhere, honestly.'

It wasn't like I knew many places anyway. I was still trying to adjust to this new environment and I definitely hadn't had the time to explore different places.

'Well, I always have the perfect place to take you to,' he teased and I laughed softly.

'Fine then. As long as the food is good,' I teased back.

The drive to the restaurant wasn't as long as I expected. Where I lived was kind of centred around everything, so it was pretty easy to go anywhere.

'We're here,' he said as he turned off the ignition.

This one even looked fancier than the one by the lake. Femi held my hands through the parking space as we walked. The building was magnificent with the street colourful lights surrounding it. I could already tell that the decor would be even more pleasant before entering it.

I was right. The restaurant was elegant inside with stairs in the middle going all the way up. It looked more like a decoration, but Femi told me they actually led to another section of the restaurant.

'It's so beautiful here' I said, and he chuckled

'The food is even better,' he said.

There were lots of people around, but instead of hearing chattering, they were quieter than ever. Their conversations were like whispers, and I reminded myself that this was how wealthy people lived. I couldn't compare Ifoneme's restaurant where the voices were so loud you couldn't even hear yourself to this. We watched a waitress walk up to us. She smiled brightly as she recognised Femi.

'Good evening, sir. It's so good to have you here. Table for two?'

She turned to me, as she held the book with her tightly.

'Yes definitely,' he said.

We didn't have to wait, because he was obviously a VIP guest here. The restaurant was modern with its pristine table linen and leather chairs. We passed by a beautiful piano which I would have loved to play. I hadn't touched one in a while, and there was an entire water tank filled with fish. The small aquarium was beautiful and I paused to look at it more.

'Do you ever wish you were a fish?' I asked as I ran my hands through the glass and he laughed that wholehearted laughter of his.

'Not a fish but I understand where you're coming from. You have an interesting mind. I would give anything to know more,' he said, and I found myself smiling cheekily.

'Really? What else would you like to be then?' I asked curiously.

The waiter from earlier was still waiting behind us, but she didn't seem to be bothered by it. Maybe it was something she was used to.

'A tiger. I have so many similarities with them,' he teases abs I laugh.

I was tempted to ask why but we were keeping the waiter waiting.

'Let's continue this talk at the table,' I said.

We sat at a small booth where we couldn't really see people, and neither could they. The smell of food was arousing and I felt hungrier than ever before. The table was well set, and low music was playing in the background. It was an Italian restaurant and I knew what I wanted to get without having to look at the menu. I hadn't had it in a restaurant before but I had made it myself after salivating for it from an Italian series I was watching.

'You seem to be familiar with the food here,' Femi said gingerly.

'Not here, but I love to experiment with food. I've tried to make some of their dishes myself before,' I said and I could see the amusement in his eyes. It made me giggly.

'You see, there are so many interesting facts about you. I'd like to taste one of your dishes someday,' he said.

'Well, if you're lucky you will taste all.'

I didn't realise what I had said till he laughed. He drank from his glass of water as he continued.

'So, you do know how to flirt'

I felt embarrassed as our eyes met. I hadn't thought about it before I spoke, but as weirdly as it seemed I didn't regret it.

'I wasn't flirting,' I said but he shook his head playfully.

'I disagree. You're really cute, you know,' he said softly.

I felt myself melting from his heated gaze.

'I'm not cute,' I replied.

We kept going back and forth and I had forgotten that we were at a restaurant till our food was brought over. My lasagne looked so good that I felt my eyes watering from so much joy. Femi had gone for their Florentine Steak which looked delicious too.

'Here!'

He held up a fork to feed me a piece and I had many reasons to refuse but I didn't.

'It tastes really good,' I said, enjoying the pleasant taste.

Dinner was so good, coupled with our funny conversation. This time, Femi paid without any resistance from me because his card was already with them, anyway. And as much as I hated to admit it, I felt sad that the night was coming to an end.

'Do you want to walk around for a while? Or I can just take you home if you want.'

It was like he could read my mind.

'I don't mind the walk,' I replied.

He smiled softly before moving to hold my hand. I wasn't sure where we were walking to, but the amazing streetlights made everywhere look like a movie and I would be lying if I said I wasn't having the time of my life.

'So, you've not had a boyfriend before, right?'

The way he said it was like he would have loved it better if I hadn't.

'Nope. I'm sure you've had loads of women,' I said and he laughed.

'Do I smell jealousy?' he teased.

I scoffed. He never failed to believe whatever he wanted.

'Your nose has always been malfunctioning, Femi' I replied.

He laughed so hard this time that I couldn't help joining him too. We were close to his car. It wasn't so dark so I could see his face brightly. He looked even more handsome when he smiled this way. His dimples were so deep that I felt like dipping my hands in them.

'You made my day today, Tiwa,' he stated, seriously this time.

'I wouldn't say you made mine, but I had a nice time,' I said and he chuckled.

'That's an improvement still.'

Our faces were close, and my heartbeat had picked up a race. He did things that I couldn't understand or control to my body. He made me feel alive and I was trying blatantly to resist. I really was, but so help me God it wasn't easy.

'I guess so' I managed to say.

His large hands were on my waist this time.

'You wore the necklace.'

His eyes went to my neck this time. I had totally forgotten I had them on me.

'I wanted to give it back.'

I moved my hands to unhook it, but he held me back.

'Please don't,' he pleaded.

'It's too much for me, Femi,' I protested, avoiding his fierce gaze.

'Nothing is too much for you, Tiwa. It's my first gift to you, so please just keep it.'

I sighed. It was so difficult to resist him when he looked at me this way and I was sure he knew that.

'Fine,' I said.

He smiled before kissing my forehead. His lips felt so soft on my head that I imagined how softer they would feel on my lips. 'What, I would give to kiss you right now,' he said so quietly that I would have missed it if I wasn't so close to him.

'Do it'

I could see his eyes go dark at the invitation. I had no idea why I said that or how I managed to, but every other thing had disappeared to me right then and all I wanted was to feel his lips on mine.

'Just kiss me already.'

He didn't hesitate. His soft lips cut me short, and his hands moved to hold my face tenderly as I felt his feather-light kisses. He caught my lower lip and slowly sucked and I moved my head in tune with his. I sank deeper into his embrace as his hand moved to tighten around my waist.

I could hear the sound of my heart beating rapidly. Why didn't I prepare myself for this? But how could I? How could I have known that a kiss could affect me this way? His tongue teased at the seam of my lips, they coaxed for entrance and I gave into it without any resistance.

'Your lips, Tiwa…'

His lips were parted from mine as we caught our breaths. I tried to talk but I couldn't. I could feel his heartbeat with how close we were.

'I want to kiss you so much more, in so many ways, at your pace. I'm in no hurry.'
His hands had found their way to the nape of my neck as he spoke.

'I've never been kissed like this before,' I confessed.

My feelings had never been put first, men took what they wanted without asking. They saw me as a pawn for their dirty desires. But with Femi, for once in my life, I was given a choice. We stood there for a while, trying to catch our breaths. His hands were still cupping my face, our eyes lost in each other.

'It's getting late. I should take you home,' Femi said.

I could hear the buzzing sounds of flies around us and he bent his head to kiss me again but the sound of someone clapping pushed me away from him immediately.

'I wasn't wrong. I would recognise you anywhere, Femi.'

My eyes went to her shoes first, till they moved past her flattering expensive-looking dress all the way to her angry face. She was stunning and definitely fuming as she stood metres away from us.

'What are you doing here, Amara?'

I could hear the irritation in Femi's deep voice and I felt uncomfortable in so many ways.

'You left me for her?'
She pointed at me as she walked closer to us. I wanted to leave, and my night was suddenly turning horrible.

'I left you before I met her, Amara. Let's go, Tiwa.'

He opened the car door and I was about to get in when her words stopped me.

'You're a real slut you know? I don't have to think twice to know,' she said angrily.

One thing I was known for was my smart mouth, and I wasn't going to let one stupid woman insult me like this and get away with it.

'Your insecurity is obvious. I have no idea what is going on between you both but let me get this straight. If you're here fuming about your ex being with another woman, then you clearly haven't moved on. Save yourself the shame and go on with your life because this man right here hasn't thought about you since you left.'

I got into the car, ignoring her insults. Femi spoke a few words to her before she walked away angrily. I was disappointed and sad. I had finally kissed him after holding back for so long and I was beginning to regret it.

'I'm so sorry about what just happened, Tiwa,' Femi said apologetically as he got in.

'Just take me home, please,' I requested.

He sighed loudly before starting the car. So many emotions filled me. I loved it, and I wanted more, but I felt guilty. I was breaking my vows. I was starting to go against everything I had promised myself. Maybe that was why the heavens decided to punish me.

'Was that your first kiss?' Femi asked and my breath cut.

I hadn't kissed anyone in years. The last time I got kissed wasn't by choice. My lips were taken over by a hungry animal.

'No, it's not' I said.

I looked towards the window at my side, trying to use the view of the busy highway to prevent my thoughts from getting dark.

'You know it's only you that I think about, right?' He said.

My eyes were glued to the window beside me and it took everything in me not to yell at life's capability to bring storms my way.

'I don't know that' I retorted.

'But you told Amara that I've moved on from her,' he said and I wanted to scream at his ignorance.

'You think I said that because I actually believed it? I only said all I said to protect myself. I couldn't let her insult me further. My integrity is all I have,' I declared.

He pressed the horn and I wasn't sure if it was from agitation or because of the road but the loud sound increased the tension.

'I just wanted everything to go perfectly tonight, and it was going to be, but I don't know why she's hell-bent on interrupting my life. I'm sorry she dragged you into this. So sorry, please. Tiwa, know that the kiss we shared tonight meant everything to me,' he pleaded.

'I know it's probably not your fault that she's still in love with you, but we just kissed for the first time and this happened. What more is going to happen if we continue this? That's what is scaring me right now, Femi,' I said, voicing out my thoughts.

'I'm going to sort her out, I don't want all this to end when we've not even started.'

We were already close to where he usually dropped me,

'Are you sure you don't want me to drop you home this time? It's late,' he asked but I had had enough for one night.

'Not tonight' I refused and he nodded.

It was like he could sense my need for tranquillity because he didn't say anything else or ask more questions. I was caught in my thoughts, guilt was eating at me for going against my vows. When we kissed, it was like a magnetic pull. I had tried to resist. I wanted to, but I couldn't. It was hypnotic and overwhelming. I was so drawn to him in ways I couldn't explain. Men had tried to kiss me before, tried to date me too but it was always so easy to resist them. I never had to think twice, and at one point it felt like men were never going to be a problem anymore, as long as I stayed away from them.

But now Femi felt like a more dangerous dilemma. I was beginning to want him. He made me vulnerable and the more I began to feel, it was evident that I would begin to have high hopes that more could happen. And that was the best way to get disappointed. Tonight's turn of events made me feel more right for being scared. Maybe these were signs that the universe was against us, or I was just being dramatic.

'We're here,' he said and I immediately moved to open the door before he would come across to help me.

'Tiwa, wait. I hope this isn't the end of us,' he demanded softly.

His eyes were sad and many voices in my head were telling me to say it was but I couldn't.

'It isn't, but it isn't the beginning either.'

He nodded softly as he stared at me admiringly.

'Know that I'm ready whenever you are. Amara has nothing on me. It's you I want, only you.'

I smiled sadly as I took in his words.

'Goodnight, Femi,' I said and left.

Chapter Fourteen

African Magic

WHEN I GOT HOME, I showered and lay in bed. My fingers kept feeling my lips as images of my passionate kiss with Femi kept occupying my thoughts. My brain kept telling me that kissing him had been a mistake, especially because of Amara but my heart felt differently.

We hadn't really spoken about her. It was only normal that we decided to not talk about his ex in our conversations but now I was getting curious. It was obvious she wanted him back and I had no idea what lengths she would go to for this to happen. She was also more in his class. She came from a rich family, was quite known, and had an amazing career.

The next day at work came with surprises. I met flowers on my table and a note had been planted at the edge of my desk.

'I'm sorry about last night. Thank you for letting me kiss you. I loved it.'

I couldn't hold the smile that followed, he was really good at things like this. I hated to think about him doing the same to Amara, especially since they were together for years. You couldn't really blame her for being so attached to a man like Femi, I was definitely beginning to fall too and it didn't matter that I was fighting it.

After settling down and keeping the flowers, I remembered that I had a meeting, but this time it was with the other proof readers, and that included Corinne. I hadn't spoken to her since that day at lunch and I had tried my best to avoid her. Especially because of how much she got on my nerves. I certainly didn't have enough energy to always go back and forth with someone like her.

As a child, I was made to believe that bullies were only in school, but as I grew older, it was certain that bullies were everywhere. I grabbed my phone to text Zainab about the meeting, her reply was almost instant.

'Wow, you're meeting with that witch. I feel sorry for you.'

'Let's not be negative, it might not be that bad.'

'You know that's not possible. She's a pest and everyone knows it, but I trust you to not take any rubbish.'

I smiled softly. She was right, I never did.

'Exactly, so it's fine. I can handle her, anyway. I need to go now. I will give you the gist later.'

'Wait, you've not gisted me about your secret guy, I saw the flowers.'

I sighed loudly. I hadn't because I had no idea where this was going. But knowing Zainab, she wasn't going to relent till she got what she wanted.
'Fine, I will tell you everything. Bye for now.'

***

We were just five in the conference room. We were supposed to be six, but someone had called in sick. It was going well so far, thankfully. We were discussing new books and trying to conclude on the authors deserving of awards. It all depended on the ones that were selling out fast and getting the best reviews. We had narrowed it down to two options and everyone was going to vote on who they wanted.

'Tiwa, don't you think Okonta deserves it more? I mean that book got to me,' Ndoku said.

She was another nice lady that I barely got to see because we were at opposite ends of the company.

'I'm honestly conflicted. The Anulopo lady really tried too. When I edited her novel, I almost slipped through some errors because of how captivated I was,' I said genuinely.

'Maybe because the main character's life is similar to yours. I mean she was a sadist too,' Corrine said and everyone turned their eyes to her.

'You don't know anything about me,' I retorted, trying not to sound as agitated as I felt. I wasn't going to satisfy her because it was obvious that was what she wanted.

'I never said I did. I only said what I was thinking,' she said with a devious smile, her hands going to pat her hair like she was applauding herself.

'Who do you think we should go for, Corrine?' Ndoku threw the question at her.

'Well, I'm with Okonta,' she said.

While we kept going back and forth, the conference room opened to reveal Femi. His eyes went around the room like he was looking for something till he saw me. Everyone stood up to greet him, as we watched him walk towards me.

'I'm sorry to interrupt your meeting, but I need my assistant immediately. I hope it's no problem.'

They shook their heads and I didn't miss the puzzled look on their faces. Corrine's own was more of anger, not confusion and I felt uncomfortable. He stared at me as I walked past him trying my best to avoid anyone's eyes. I was going to yell at him for this.

'Why would you do that?' We were at his office already when I finally decided to speak. 'Do what?' He queried, clearly trying to play ignorance.

'You know what I mean. I'm sure you don't need me for anything.'

I was leaning at the door and he was at the other end of his huge office.

'Okay, fine. I overheard Zainab telling Dayo that she felt bad for you because you were at a meeting with Corinne. She said she hoped you wouldn't get insulted like the last time. I wasn't thinking. Immediately I heard it, I kind of just wanted to get you out of there. I'm sorry.'

Dear God, how could I stay mad at him when he got to me this way? My heart melted at the solemn look on his face as he spoke. He was perched on his desk, watching me intently,

'You know you can't jump in to help me every time, especially at work. You're my boss and rumours are going to spread. Besides, we're not even dating yet,' I noted.

I was stressed already from the week's workload and then there was Corinne, only God knew what she was going to think from what just happened.

'You said yet. That means you're considering dating me,' he teased as he stared but I tried my best to keep my serious expression on.

'Fine. I'm sorry. I will try my best to control myself from helping you next time.'

He said it as if he was trying to convince himself, and I almost smiled as I watched him walk closer to me.

"Thank you for the flowers and the note. I loved kissing you too.'

He grinned widely, his hands moving to cup my face when he finally stood in front of me. My skin felt warm where he touched me and I savoured his heavenly scent. He lowered his lips to brush against mine

'Do you love this too?'

I could feel my pulse racing, my legs felt like jelly inside out from the way he stared at me.

'Kind of,' I struggled to say.

His lips went to my forehead.

'This?' He asked again as he went to my cheeks.

'Yes!' I whispered.

I was pressed against the door, and I had no idea where my hands were supposed to be, but he placed them on his shoulders like he could read my thoughts.

'Here?'

His lips were on my neck and although it was new to me, I felt tingles all over.

'Yes!' I managed to say.

It was as if my body was responding against my will. I couldn't help it. That was what he did to me. My eyes automatically drifted close from the sensations I was feeling, but I suddenly felt him withdraw from me, the lustful look in his eyes disappearing.

'Thank you for your time, Tiwa. You can get back to work,' he said in a business tone, a mischievous glint obvious in his eyes.

I raised a brow at him, loads of emotions filling me. He was obviously playing around and that was what got on my nerves.

'Really? You think this is funny?' I asked, feeling embarrassed.

He had really gotten to me and as much as I hated to admit it, my body had been anticipating more kisses.

'I didn't say it was, Tiwa,' he replied. I rolled my eyes at him before moving to open the door.

***

After my encounter with Femi earlier today, I decided to occupy myself with loads of work to suppress my irritation. I was irritated at myself for feeling disappointed when he withdrew. I was beginning to want things that I would normally never think of and it annoyed me.

It was late already when Femi asked me to wait for him outside. He usually dropped me off, and we went home late most of the time. So, there was hardly anyone around, which I kind of preferred, especially because there would have been loads of curiosity as to why we were this way.

My heels were very uncomfortable, so it was annoying to walk. I usually brought ballet flats with me in case my feet hurt but I had forgotten them this time. I had stood downstairs for a few minutes when I noticed someone's eyes on me. It felt like that time at the lake again and as much as I wanted to shrug it off, I couldn't. It looked like a shadow from the corner, and I could trace it outside the already opened gate. It looked so distant but there was this uneasiness that I felt from the stare.

Maybe I was being paranoid. I had read a lot that abused victims tended to have paranoia, sometimes it lasted for many years. Some needed therapy to believe no one was after them. But as much as I wished that was the case, I couldn't say it was. It was dark, but

I could swear that those eyes were pointed at me. I couldn't make out a face because it was too far away. I tried to make out the outfit but the person moved away quickly. I had only seen one other face in a mask and it was my rapist. Was he watching me? But that couldn't have been possible. There was no way he could have known where I was, and maybe I was seeing wrongly because it was quite dark, and my tiredness could have made me see what was not there.

I suddenly wanted to go back inside. Kanayo the security was probably inside his apartment because he wasn't out there. But as I turned to go in, someone called out my name.

'Hey, Tiwa'

I turned around to Isaac's voice, wondering where he must have come from. He came out of a car that I hadn't noticed earlier, and it was the only other car there apart from Femi's own.

'Hey, what are you doing here?'

My attention had been somewhere else. I wondered how long he had been here. I hoped he didn't just watch me look around like a maniac. I'm sure he must have been confused. There was no way he could have known I was here except for Zainab.

'I came to see you,' he said.

I hadn't seen him since the mini-party that was organised for me, and neither had I heard from him.

'Oh, I'm on my way home. Maybe some other time.' I said.

'Can I drop you home? We can talk on the way,' he asked casually.

I suddenly felt like yelling at Zainab for putting me in this predicament. I still felt unsettled at what I thought I had seen earlier, and that was enough worry.

'No, please just go home Isaac. Save yourself the stress.'

I was already turning around when he spoke.

'Is it because of Femi? Are you two together already?'
My breath cut, wondering how he could be so plain-spoken.

'We're not but that's not your concern. Please, I'm exhausted from work. I'm not up for a conversation,' I said but he walked closer to me.

'You're still single. I was worried you wouldn't be. I'm not trying to rush anything here. I just want to be able to talk to you. Do it for Zainab if not me.'

I looked back at the company, Femi was still inside. What would he think about this? Zainab, on the other hand, had been pleading with me to give her friend a chance. I couldn't even let him drop me home when I hadn't even allowed Femi to know exactly where I lived yet.

'Fine, you can take me to Zainab's place. I was supposed to see her today anyway.'

I was clearly not thinking well but I was going to use this opportunity to reprimand her about whatever matchmaking plan she had.

'Thank you so much. I promise to not bore you,' he said cheerfully as he moved to open the car door for me.

I made sure to text Zainab immediately to let her know I was coming.

'Yay, finally a sleepover night, enough time to tell me about everything that has been up with you,' she replied and I laughed. After locking my phone, I drew my attention to the car. I had no idea what brand his car was because I wasn't really familiar with vehicles but it looked clean and expensive. There were papers arranged on the dashboard which he immediately removed when he got in.

'Sorry about that, it's from work,' he said softly.

'It's okay. What do you do anyway?' I asked him.

I knew it had something to do with houses from what Zainab had told me earlier but I wasn't sure.

'I own a real estate agency and I'm a civil engineer,' he said as he started the car.

Kanayo opened the gate and we both waved at him when he drove past him.

'Wow, that's something,' I said.

He chuckled as he looked at the side mirror while he reversed.

'It's not as fancy as it sounds, trust me. It gets boring sometimes but enough about me. Have you always wanted to be a publisher?' he asked.

I have always had one answer to that, especially after answering that question more times than I could count.

'I guess so. I've always had a passion for books, so it's expected.' I said.

He nodded as he listened.

'Have you thought about writing your own book? You look like a writer, the only thing is you have no glasses on,' he teased. I smiled back.

'I see. I don't know if I'm supposed to take that as a compliment,' I said.

'You should. I'm amazed by you guys,' he said.

My phone beeped and I saw Femi's name on the notification. I didn't want to reply him because it would be rude to Isaac, so I locked my phone.

'Anything wrong?' he asked softly, and I shook my head.

'Tell me, what do you do for fun?'

I hated when people asked me this because I did nothing interesting. My definition of fun was comfort, being in bed with my PJS on and an emotional movie on my television screen. I hardly went out. Zainab usually had to drag me out most of the time before we went out.

'Honestly, I prefer to just stay in most times. I already told you that there was nothing interesting about me. I'm capable of boring you to death,' I explained and he laughed in a deep throaty way.

'I don't see myself snoring, you know. The fact that you don't know how amusing you are makes you more amusing.'

I pretended to think before responding.

'That's ridiculous,' I answered.

My phone beeped again and this time it was from Zainab. I chose to ignore it, I was going to see her anyway.

'Sure nothing is wrong?' he asked again and I shook my head.

'I doubt it's Zainab,' I said.

The road was kind of rowdy, and the sounds of horns were rampant around us.

'Oh, maybe we should get her something. There's a store close by,' he said.

I smiled at that, eager to see Zainab's excitement when I gave her whatever we got. She was an unapologetic foodie and she never failed to show it. We spent way longer than I thought we would, looking around for what she would like. The drive from there to her place wasn't long. We spoke about other things and it wasn't as bad as I imagined it to be. He was a nice man but that didn't mean this would go anywhere. I had only accepted the ride because of my friend and I was going to make sure to warn her about this repeating itself next time.

'Let me walk you in so I can say hi to her too.'

He helped me open my side of the door. I pressed the doorbell, and she wasted no time in opening the door. She smiled and winked at me when I saw her 'Someone has been waiting for you,' she said. I hugged her and her eyes went to Isaac who stood behind me.

'Oh my God! I didn't know Isaac was coming,' she whispered.

I was going to ask her what she meant when I saw Femi come up behind her.

'Hey!' he said softly.

He was still in his suit, and his eyes were worried, but I watched his eyes go behind me and from the way they instantly grew dark, I knew he had seen Isaac.

'My house has turned to African magic,' I heard Zainab mutter.

Chapter Fifteen

Shattered Hopes

I COULDN'T EVEN LAUGH AT Zainab's joking remark because of how uncomfortable I felt.

'Do you guys want to come in?' Zainab asked but no one responded.

Femi's lips were pursed as he looked at me expectantly. I didn't have to look at Isaac to know his eyes were boring holes in the back of my head.

'I didn't expect you to be here,' I managed to say, hoping I wasn't doing more harm to the already awkward situation.

'I was worried about you. You didn't reply to any of my texts,' he said truthfully.

I felt the sudden urge to smack my head because this gauche moment would have been blatantly avoided if I had read his texts.

'Well, you didn't have to be. She was with me,' he said firmly.

It was obvious he was trying to get on Femi's nerves for reasons unknown to me.

'That doesn't mean anything. In fact, that makes me more worried,' Femi replied, with his jaw clenched.

I wanted the night to be over when it had just started.

'Really? Or jealous?' Isaac retorted.

Zainab stood with her arms crossed and her eyes wide like she was watching a movie and as much as she looked comical, I envied the fact that she wasn't the one between these two men. I needed to end this uncomfortable situation. I raised my head to heaven hoping there could be a divine intervention to this predicament I was suddenly in.

'You two are talking about me like I'm not here. Please, stop. Isaac, thank you for dropping me. There is no need for you to be here anymore. I'm sure you have more important things to do.'

I hoped I didn't sound as exasperated as I felt. 'I came to check if you were okay. I know you are now. So, there's no reason for me to be here too,' Femi replied, and he didn't say another word as he left for his car which I hadn't noticed was packed in front of us.

As I watched him walk past us, my heart ached from his absence and obvious anger at the situation but I managed to sway myself from fleeing after him. It was until he had driven away that I was able to focus on Isaac who still hadn't flinched.

'You should really go home. We've all had more than enough drama for one night.'

He nodded before turning to leave. It wasn't till Zainab had shut her door that I finally let out a sigh of relief.

'Girl, your life is a soap opera. I can't believe I've been missing such all this while. Tiwa, where have you been all my life?'

Zainab bowed dramatically as she spoke and I bent to pick up a throw pillow on her couch. She groaned loudly as it successfully landed on her face,

'It's very compensating that you find my dramatic life entertaining,' I said sarcastically, trying to hold myself from calling Femi to explain why I allowed Isaac to drop me off, especially when he must have waited for me so he could drop me off as usual.

'You just said the word girl, dramatic' Zainab said, but this time the laughter in her eyes had dropped.

'Honestly, I think Femi really likes you, that's if he isn't head over heels for you already,' Zainab said.

I tried to search her eyes for any trace of teasing but I couldn't.

'What makes you so sure?'

I sat beside her, sighing at the comforting feeling of the soft couch.

'I don't know if you are just blind or in denial, but it's so obvious. This night showed it to me alone. I mean he sat here and kept asking questions about where you could possibly be, especially when he went outside and you were nowhere to be found. I've known him for a couple of years and I have never seen him this way. He wasn't even worried that I worked for him, all he wanted to know was that you were safe and I was the only person he could think of to have the answers.'

Her words didn't make me feel any better, if anything I panicked. All she said gave me fewer excuses to push him away. She was giving me more reasons to open myself to the prospect of being in a relationship for the first time in my life, especially after closing the doors to one for so many years. And as much as I didn't want to admit it, or tried to push my feelings away, they were constantly there.

'What about Isaac? I mean he's your friend but it seems like you are trying to push me towards Femi.'

It was a good point because she had given him my number in the first place. She quirked her lips as she looked at me.

'Honestly, I'm not on anyone's side, except yours. You are the one in between these two men, and from what I can tell you seem to be leaning more towards Femi. Your feelings for him are obvious and that's why I was pleased to realise he felt the same way. You've spent more time with Femi than with Isaac so you hardly know him. Don't think about what I would want, think about what you want.'

I held back a sigh as I took in her words. I knew what I wanted but I wasn't sure if the universe did. It felt like someone was watching me, especially this night, before Isaac had shown up. It made me uneasy but I couldn't even bring myself to mention it yet until I was sure my past was not just tampering with my mental health.

'I don't know if what I want is good for me. I have no idea if I'm falling into the lion's den.' I said, accepting the bowl of ice cream she handed to me from what I had bought for her. It had melted but I didn't care.

'How would you ever know if that is happening if you don't take the chance? You need to get out of your comfort zone girl. You just have to open yourself to love.'

Hours after, Zainab was already asleep and I found my thoughts lingering back to when Femi had walked passed us. Would it still be possible for us to be more? I was not sure if he would even want that after tonight. Maybe he could have realised that I was too much trouble and there was no need to keep wasting my time. But as Zainab said, I would never know except if I tried. I picked up my phone to call him and he answered on the first ring.

'Yes, Tiwa'

I almost let out a sigh of relief at the sound of his voice, ignoring the thrill that went through me at the sound of his deep lazy voice as he said my name. I was certainly delighted that he picked up because if not, I would definitely have been discouraged after two failed attempts.

'Well, I'm just going to go straight to the point. I'm sorry about how tonight went, I know you felt awkward'

'I guess I did, but it wasn't your fault. I need to understand that you can take care of yourself. I mean, you've been doing that way before you met me,' he said with a sigh.

'Yes you should, but I understand what must have gone through your mind when you saw me with Isaac, especially while ignoring your texts.'

There was a moment of silence before his next words.

'I would be lying if I said that didn't catch me off guard, but you are still not to blame. It's not your fault you have men fawning over you. I just have to deal with my incessant jealousy.'

I smiled faintly at the agony in his voice.

'I don't have men fawning over me, and I guess it's only normal for you to have been jealous,' I replied softly, and he chuckled.

'That's an improvement at least, you don't mind me being jealous. It shows that you are not upset that I am.'

I could hear the flicker of hope in his voice, and my legs felt like jelly under my duvet cover. I was falling in deep and I could feel myself beginning to let my guard down.

'But the thing is, I don't have the right to be. You are not mine and it makes me feel like a jerk. I'm frightened it's going to push you away, you know. I don't want to be a villain in your life, Tiwa'.

'Then what do you want to be?'

He took seconds to respond.

'I want to be more than a friend. I want a relationship. I want you but I'm not in a hurry, whenever you are ready.'

My cheeks flamed and I curled my fingers around the edge of the duvet.

'What if I am now?'

The words left my mouth before I could stop them and I swallowed hard.

'You really think you are?' he asked softly.

I heard the sounds of sheets shuffling in the background, and the thought of him laying comfortably in bed like I was gave me unexplainable feelings.

'What if I give you an answer to that tomorrow?' I said softly.

The next morning, I woke up with a banging headache and a rapidly beating heart. I was nervous, and if I wasn't careful I would have arrived late at work today, especially after having to hurry home first to change my outfit and get dressed. Zainab had insisted I just wore one of her slim-fitted shirts that I could fit in with my skirt but I wanted the stress of going back home as a way of clearing my thoughts or preparing me for what was going to happen for the day.

I was supposed to answer him today. I knew what I wanted to say but most times, deciding to do something without an outright plan wasn't the best. It came with a bundle of nerves and uncertainty. Was I making a mistake? Would this end up breaking me? Did we even belong together? But these were questions and they would be left unanswered if I never tried.

I thought about telling him immediately I saw him, or maybe I would slip it in a note and keep it on his table when he left for a meeting. I was behaving like a high school teenager but I couldn't help it. I wanted to ask Zainab for her advice but she was going to tease me and I wasn't ready for that.

I had no idea how to get the words out of my mouth, but with him, I did things unexpectedly. I made sure to dress a little fancier than I usually did. My makeup was in between light and heavy. I intentionally used red lipstick so it could match my red jumpsuit. It was very fitted, and it encompassed my curves. It wasn't exposing in any way, which made it more appropriate for an official setting.

When I got to work, I got lots of compliments on how I looked and that made me feel a bit better, at least Femi would like what he saw.

'So you can be fine like this?' Sam had said teasingly.

'So I was ugly before?' I asked him softly and he laughed.

'Nope, never! What's the occasion? Tell us,' Dayo had asked but I promised to answer them later so they would leave me for the time being.

When I got to my desk, my heart had picked up pace unconsciously. It was like I couldn't control it whenever I was around Femi or knew he was a few meters away from me. He wasn't in the office when I checked and I found that a bit odd, considering how punctual he usually was.

I contemplated asking him about his whereabouts, but I didn't want to sound desperate when we were not even together yet. As excited as I felt, all these made me feel weird like I wasn't myself anymore. But Zainab has explained that it was because I wasn't used to this.

Relationships weren't my forte. It felt foreign and it would probably take more time and more special moments before I would finally get accustomed to it. I decided to not message him anymore after going consistently back and forth. Moreover, it would only increase my nerves.

Usually, at times like this, when Femi was around, he would wink at me in between meetings, or just open his office door just to close it again. Things like that made me miss him and as much as I acted like I didn't want it, I cherished those moments. He was definitely not being discreet but it's like he didn't care to anyway. I was just on my way back from a meeting when I got his text.

'Where are you? Meet me in my office.'

I grinned widely when I read the new text, I hadn't realised how much I had missed him till I saw it.

'On my way,' I texted back.

He responded quickly.

'Hurry, I've missed you.'

I had just gotten to the front of his office when I saw her. She was wearing a figure-showing red dress and matching black shoes, I could smell her perfume from where I stood and her wig looked beyond expensive as it cascaded down her shoulders. She held her purse tighter as she gazed at me.

'You again, why am I not surprised?' She asked sarcastically.

I struggled to keep myself in check, watching the way she eyed me warily like I was a piece of garbage.

'How may I help you?' I asked defiantly.
'I came to see Femi,' she said.

'What are you doing here anyway? It's good to know you can look better than you did last time. Saves me the stress of being embarrassed for Femi,' she said as she adjusted her wig.

Her nail extension was blue and so long that I flinched at the thought of her injuring herself with them. She was taller than me, way taller. She had a model figure, and her legs were endless.

'You know, I don't have the time to go back and forth with you, especially not when I have work to do.'

I noticed the way her eyebrows raised at my words as if she had just figured out a huge puzzle.

'I see, you work here. That explains it. You slept your way through this company, didn't you? I mean, Femi has always had an annoying kindheartedness that I've never understood. Especially for sorry cases like you.'

'You will not talk to her that way.'

I hadn't realized Femi had been watching us till I heard his glowering voice. She turned around to him and it took everything in me not to slap her right then, but I wasn't a violent person.

'What are you doing here, Amara?' He asked her.

I knew her name meant kindness and sometimes I found it odd that someone with such a sweet name had such callous behaviour because she acted very differently from what her name meant. I watched as she walked to hug him but he held his hand out to push her away.

'I came to see you, baby. I've missed you,' she said in a voice that I assumed to be her sweet one.

I wanted to leave this ridiculous scenario and I thanked God again that this area of the company was secluded from the rest. If not, there would have been a hot topic on everyone's discussion today.

'Please, leave. You have no right to show up here, not in my company, especially not in front of my girlfriend.'

I couldn't feign ignorance at his words. He had just referred to me as his girlfriend, but I had no time to react and I didn't want to, especially because of the satisfaction that came over me when she turned around to face me. The look on her face was filled with so much jealousy and bitterness that I wondered how Femi was able to cope with such.

'Wow, you really went all the way in, didn't you? Tell me, how many times did you get him to sleep with you? Does he scream your name while you fuck? Does he grab your hair the way he grabbed mine? Tell me, you idiot, you wretch, you...'

'Get the hell out of my company or I'm going to call security on you,' Femi's voice was thunderous this time.

I hardly saw him this way, but I was already agitated at the whole situation. Today wasn't supposed to go this way, he had an annoying ex-girlfriend that seemed determined to interrupt and spoil any beautiful moments we tried to have.

'You sound desperate and I'm only going to tell you one thing. I haven't slept with him yet. I didn't have to sleep with him to be his girlfriend. But if I eventually do, I'm going to take note of your questions,' I said.

I usually preferred to just keep quiet because I didn't want to stoop to her level but she had gone overboard and I wasn't going to let a random stranger make assumptions about my sexual life. Especially when it was something that was so important to me. She looked at me with horror, and I could swear that she wanted to throw more insults but the look on Femi's face must have shut her up. She cursed softly before moving to walk away. The sound of her heels had become faint when I turned around.

'Wait, please,' Femi beckoned but I didn't listen.

I didn't want to face him, at least not now. I was embarrassed and I wanted to be alone. It's like he knew because he didn't follow me. The only thing was, I wish he did.

Chapter Sixteen

Thunderstorms

I WENT HOME EARLIER THAN I usually did. If anyone had noticed my despondent mood, they were quiet about it, thankfully. I had no words to describe how I felt, if anything, I couldn't even figure out if it was Amara's disparaging that irked me or if it was the fact that Femi had gotten into my skin so bad that I still didn't want to leave despite the predicaments surrounding us.

Maybe this was a sign that being with him was a bad idea. We hadn't even started anything yet and all these were happening. I'd cried so badly that my pillow was beginning to resemble a mural because of my smeared mascara and my pink lipstick. I hated myself because I was responsible for this additional suffering.

But what could a girl like me have done? I was weak, maybe even weaker than I thought I was. He had referred to me as his girlfriend, I wasn't sure if it was in order to get rid of Amara or if he had meant it. But he couldn't have, I mean I hadn't answered him yet.

I wasn't sure of how I would handle the situation, especially when his ex-girlfriend seemed to still be very invested in their relationship. I didn't have many pointers on relationships but I certainly knew that never went well. He claimed he wasn't interested in her, but that didn't seem to bother her. She knew what she wanted and was going for it. I sighed loudly as I looked at the ceiling.

'What exactly do I want?'

If I had turned deaf ears to my mindless feelings and Femi's words, maybe I wouldn't be in this upsetting situation. I found myself unwittingly searching for more information about her. I refused to call it stalking. I was only curious, who wouldn't be? She was a year younger than Femi. I couldn't find anything but praises about how good a doctor she was.

She was an only child and there was not much information about her romantic relationships, except the one with Femi. Maybe because he was the only other public figure she had dated. I saw rumours about her being close to Femi's elder brother, Dapo. I hadn't really paid attention to him when I researched Femi in the past.

But as I stared at the man through my phone, I found it arduous to trace any sort of resemblance between them. He was almost the same height as Femi but he seemed to be more laid back from what I read. He was hardly ever in the country but only came around when a family occasion was happening. I got directed to more updates on their sister. She was a fashion designer in Abuja. They looked so close in the images of them I saw together that it was difficult to believe that they were not that close.

Sometimes, I felt the urge to ask Femi more questions but that would convey that he could do the same and I wasn't ready for that. He did talk about his sister sometimes, he seemed to be fond of her as well but he never mentioned his brother. I could have asked the few workers I spoke to or Zainab even but I wanted to respect his solace.

It felt like my knowing less was safer most times. As much as that was dangerous, I didn't find myself wanting to change it. We respected each other's privacy and it was for the best. Maybe, with time, that could change but it wasn't my sole focus.

I could hear the sounds of lightning and I groaned as I stood up to shut my windows. I had clothes spread outside, so I went out to get them from the line. Thankfully, there weren't people around to see how messy I looked. That was what I thought until I saw a very familiar shadow walking towards me. He was holding his suit jacket, and his face looked distraught. I didn't know I could feel more heartache than I already felt till I saw him.

The rain had gotten to him but he didn't seem to be bothered by it, especially with how leisurely he walked. I had more than one reason to be mad at him. My only guess at him knowing exactly where I stayed was Zainab. I needed to talk to her about giving my details out. I was about to turn around and just shut my door when he called me.

'Tiwa, please don't.'

I cringed but didn't want to turn around, it was almost dark and I hoped the neighbours wouldn't complain about the noise. But they would hardly hear us anyway, with the thunderous noise from the rain.

'Please, just wait.'

I stood still, noticing that his footsteps had gotten closer.

'What do you want?'

He was in front of me now, and I could feel droplets of rain running through my face.

'Can we at least get you inside first? You're going to catch a cold.'

My anger flared at how subtle he sounded, his constant capacity to worry about me no matter what annoyed me because it drew me more to him. I could feel myself shivering but I didn't want him inside my house.

'I'm not cold, we can talk here' I insisted, hearing his loud sigh.

'You're going to get sick. I don't have to go in, I can talk to you from outside your door,' he offered, his brown eyes glinting for a second.

He looked genuinely perturbed and I hated that it got to me.

'I don't know what you want, Femi. I just took loads of insults from your ex-girlfriend. And not for the first time. Is this how I'm going to keep getting insulted when I'm with you? You can't blame me for having second thoughts,' I scoffed, lifting my hands in the air.

His lips moved to speak but I raised my hand, stopping him.
'I know what you're going to say. You're sorry that she reacted that way. You didn't know she was going to come, but what exactly can you do to stop her from coming?'

'I'm trying my best here, Tiwa. I didn't expect her to react that way after our break up. She seems like a whole different person. I'm indeed sorry for how she acted towards you. I hope she leaves now, especially after I referred to you as my girlfriend.'

'Yes, that was surprising,' I replied, deliberately avoiding his eyes.

'Well, you were going to answer me today. I'm here for an answer.'

Droplets of rain were around his face and although they had reduced I found it oddly attractive.

'Do you think you still deserve one today?'

He smiled at my teasing, his hands moving to hold my waist, but I didn't resist.

'I don't but I came to plead my case,' he said softly.

'I see. I guess you already answered it for both of us then.'

He was staring at me aimlessly like he was trying to read through me. It was when he grinned widely that I knew he understood.

'Wait, you mean you are mine now?' He asked softly.

I laughed. This was more fun than I had expected.

'Obnoxious much? But yes, I'm yours'

He didn't say anything to that. Femi spoke to me through his lips as he kissed me fiercely, his hands tighter on my waist. My toes were curled from how passionately he kissed me. From a girl that hadn't been kissed before, I was suddenly getting tons of it. And boy did I react? My hands went to his shoulders, head moving in sync with his.

'I'm right here in the rain promising you this, not worried about getting sick or being recognised by a stranger. I promise to treat you the way you deserve. Thank you for accepting me.'

His head moved to kiss me again and I enjoyed the sensual feeling of his lips on mine. I felt lightheaded, my heart beating so fast that it felt like it would explode.

'I feel nothing for Amara and I'm sorry about how she spoke to you.'

He settled me down on my feet, releasing his hold and I suddenly got lost in his eyes. My mouth was still hanging open from the kiss, it was hard to form words, but I managed to.

'It's fine, it's not your fault anyway. I was embarrassed, that's why I reacted the way I did,' I said genuinely. He nodded as he took in my words, he held my hands and I shuddered at how cold it felt.

'Do you want to come in?' I managed to ask and he nodded, as he kissed my forehead.

As we walked towards my broken door, the last thing on my mind was the clothes I left hanging on the line, all I could think about was the man beside me. I hardly had visitors over, so it was weird to have Femi at my apartment. The door still had a little hole and I suddenly felt self-conscious.

'Isn't this dangerous? It's not safe, Tiwa. Have you tried to get it fixed?'

His statement didn't help matters as I held the door open for him to get in. I knew it wasn't exactly safe. I had complained to my landlord so many times but he kept postponing. At this rate, I was going to just fix it myself.

'I know that. I just haven't had the time to get it fixed,' I said, as I collected his wet jacket from him.

Thankfully, I was on the ground floor so there were no stairs to climb. The entrance to my apartment was through my small living room with a small wooden table at the centre which was crammed with my work laptop and crumpled pieces of paper that I had forgotten to trash. There was a carpet at the centre, and parts of it were already torn. The two-seat sofa was okay at least, and the small TV was on a stool at the other end of the wall, with a DVD player which had disks of Grey's Anatomy and a documentary I was currently watching.

I had frames of just me and my mother by the side of the TV, and I had struggled so much to place them properly but they kept falling. So, I resorted to using the leg of the stool to keep them in place. Across from my living room was my double-sized bed, which was the best part of my apartment. It had been super useful, especially with how comforting it felt. But that was what beds were for, isn't it?

There was no door in-between both but there was a slight demarcation. Only my bathroom had a door, which was necessary.

Thankfully, it was clean as I already cleaned my place earlier in the day.

'It's cosy. I like it.'

I turned around to Femi, who was studying the photo frame on the floor.

'You're just being nice' I said, slightly uncomfortable.

This wasn't his scene, and I wondered if he was beginning to realise that we were very different. He seemed to have noticed my uneasiness because he smiled reassuringly.

'I'm a blunt person and you know that.'

I sighed and turned away from him, bending to pick up the crumpled papers from the table.

'Your mum? I see where you get your beauty from. She's gorgeous.'

I turned around, overwhelmed with emotions.

'Yes, she was. She died years ago.'

I watched his face change from several emotions before he pulled me into a hug which I reluctantly accepted.

'I'm so sorry. I didn't mean...'

'I know, it's fine. Can we have a change of topic please?'

I requested and he released me, his hand lifting my face as he peered at me.

'I hope you're able to open up to me one day, especially now that you're my girlfriend.'

Hearing him call me his girlfriend still shook me, maybe it was because I wasn't used to it yet.

I was feeling a bundle of nerves by being so close to him in a place where no one could easily interrupt us. At the same time, I loved the comfort. It was confusing and I wish I knew what I wanted exactly. His hand grabbed mine softly as he spoke.

'I understand if you're not ready now. It takes time for people to open up, or even trust. I hope one day, you see me as someone you can open up to.'

'I hope so too,' I said. He relaxed a little as he hugged me again. 'You've totally made my day, Tiwa.'

'Don't be so excited, I'm still mad at you,' I replied jokingly.

I held him too, my hands wrapped around his back, as they savoured his manly scent despite the wet clothes he had on.

'You're shivering, you need to change.'

I drew back at his words. I had goose bumps from being in the rain and I felt bad for him because of how drenched he looked. I couldn't offer him anything to wear because I had nothing manly. It was like he knew because he smiled amusedly,

'Don't bother. I will take my leave now. I just needed to clear the air and get my answer,' he winked at me playfully, and I found myself smiling happily.

'Well congratulations, you finally got me to succumb,' I teased, as I watched him go to grab his jacket from the door handle, before turning back to me.

'Goodnight, baby. It was nice to finally know your hiding spot.'

They say being with someone you really care about should feel like the best thing in the world, and nothing else matters. Well, I wasn't sure how I felt the next morning, I woke up sweaty, my old T-Shirt felt like it was glued to my skin and my wrist was wet from the droplets of sweat that had come from my forehead.

I had a banging headache and my nose felt like I had tissue bundled up inside my nostrils. As expected, I had fallen ill and I had myself to blame for that. I couldn't miss work though, because the day was going to be hectic. This was the worst day to fall sick, I definitely wasn't telling Femi because he would insist I stay. And I was sure he wouldn't hold back from showing how much he worried about me especially now that we were together.

After managing to dress up and go to work, I made sure to avoid Femi, at least for the very early hours so he wouldn't pawn over me. I had tried my best to control the number of times I sneezed in the last meeting I had, so I only hoped it hadn't been obvious.

I had just gotten to my desk when I saw a light paper bag. I didn't ask for anything, so I was confused, but I saw a note crippled at the side of the bag which I hadn't noticed before.

'It's my first day with you, and I've never felt so lucky'

I smiled a sweet, cheeky smile as I inhaled the flowers. There were boxes of chocolates and my tongue melted at the sight of them.

'Thank you for the flowers and chocolates, I needed them.'

I pushed the send button and decided to try to focus on my work. The sound of footsteps across me caught my attention. I smiled brightly as he held out his hand to hold mine and held me up.

'Hey, baby'

He bent his head to kiss me but I refused, worried about someone seeing us. He had shown that he wasn't bothered but he was an employer, so it wouldn't look bad on him. I wasn't ready to be seen as one who got special favours because I was with the boss. Especially when people like Corrine already assumed that. I had my own dreams and it was going to be because of my capabilities.

'You can't kiss me here,' I murmured and he nodded.

'Are you ashamed of me?' he asked teasingly, but I shook my head and I shouldn't have done that because the pain that followed caused me to groan.
'Tiwa, what's wrong?' he asked worriedly.

He didn't wait for me to respond before taking me with him to his office.

'I'm fine, Femi.'

I said, as he closed the door. His lips were in a thin line as he watched me. He obviously didn't believe me.

'I just have a bad cold, another reason why you shouldn't kiss me.'

He raised his eyebrows, clearly bewildered as he felt my neck.

'My God, you're burning up. I'm really stupid. I shouldn't have let you stay in the rain.'

I rolled my eyes as I watched him. For a man, he was really dramatic.

'I'm an adult, it's not your fault I stayed in the rain. I was there on my own accord, and you're only going to make me feel worse if you keep blaming yourself.'

That made him stop. He looked at me for a minute as if he was trying to find the truth in my words.

'Fine, but you're leaving for home now. I will take you,' he said softly.

His fingers were running through my hair soothingly, and as much as I knew I needed to rest, I wanted to wait till it was time to go.

'Not yet, I still have work to do,' I protested.

'You wouldn't be able to do any work if you drain yourself. Let me take you home, baby.'

With him talking to me that way, it was expected that I would find it hard to resist.

'Everyone is going to see you take me home,' I said, and he sighed loudly.

'We're together now, that shouldn't matter,' he said but I refused.

'It does to me, at least at the beginning We just started this, so let's not rush to make rash decisions,' I said but he smiled softly.

'I don't see how it means we're taking rash decisions but fine. You have to stay on my couch then, I will get someone to get you medicine.'

He didn't wait for an answer, before moving me to the very comfortable chair in his office.

I watched him pick up his phone to call for drugs for my fever and also for food.

'Why're you looking at me like that?' He asked when he dropped his cell.

'Because I'm happy,' I said.

Chapter Seventeen

Melted Hearts

IT TOOK A WHILE FOR me to become accustomed to dating someone. I wasn't sure I was ready yet, but I had gotten to the next level emotionally if I was going to put it that way. We were discreet at work, at my request. I was grateful he, at least, listened to me. We were just at the beginning and we needed to be sure of where this would be going first before I took the risk of letting my co-workers know.

The comical thing was that a few people probably suspected already, despite us not being that public with our affections. Little things like his dropping me home could have been noticed. We had been together for almost two weeks now and each day felt like just the beginning. I had begun to realise that he was going to keep being extra because that was who he was.

I had a meeting this morning, and I had been extremely nervous about it because I was the one presenting. It was on new ideas for incoming books that we would publish. It had been a lot of work and I only hoped to not embarrass myself. I usually hardly led meetings, I preferred to just write down what was said, but Femi had insisted that I needed to come out of my shells. I walked in to find him very close to the door. He pulled me to hug him as if he hadn't seen me in days.

'I could have hit you with the door,' I said, feeling pleased for the physical comfort.

Hugs definitely did wonders, they were the most underrated thing ever.

'I don't care!'

I could hear the smile in his voice.

'Obviously, I'm the one that's going to get into trouble for hitting my boss,' I said sarcastically.

We were still hugging and as much as I felt the need to breathe, I didn't want to let go.

'I'm your boyfriend, Tiwa.'

He kept pointing it out as if it wasn't plastered at the back of my mind every second.

'And my boss who I directly report to'

I couldn't see his face but he groaned softly.

'Do you want me to step down?' He teased and I laughed.

He was definitely more dramatic than I was.

'No!' I said.

'Do you want to resign?' I shook my head in response.

'No!'

I decided to put him out of his mystery.

'What do you think is going to happen when everyone finds out about us?'

Okay maybe I was doing the opposite but these were crystal clear questions that needed answers to them.

'I can't say, and that's why I'd rather just get over with it now, I don't care.'

He shrugged, and I raised my brows at him, not surprised at his indifference.

'I came here for my dream too, you know. I don't want it to get tarnished because of my love life.'

He sighed, his eyes looking worried and his hands moved to hold my shoulders in that comforting way of his.

'I understand that, you weren't even supposed to be working so close to me anyway. You can go back to your own office. Actually, on second thoughts, maybe not that one. I don't trust Dayo and Sam,' he frowned and I laughed at his jealousy.

I was friends with them, and in such a short while I was getting used to being around men, especially when there were loads of them in the company. I had been able to avoid them in the past, but it was inescapable here because I signed a contract to be professional and I couldn't really take my personal problems to the business world.

'So, I'm not your assistant anymore?' I asked.

'You weren't employed as an assistant. I guess my subconscious already wanted you close to me.'

My heart did a catapult at his words. I always knew this day was going to come, we both had just not been ready to say it. I already worked as a publisher but my office hadn't changed. I loved being so close to him that I had no care for where I stayed.

'Me too,' I said honestly and he bent to plaster a quick kiss on my lips.

'Tell me, what else do you want to do?'

He held my hand and pulled me with him to the couch.

'I have a meeting soon, Femi.'

He just rolled his eyes and sighed.

'That's why we're getting you to talk. You need to let go of your nerves. Now sit.'

I pouted but sat and I couldn't help the smile that followed from seeing the satisfaction on his face.
'Now to my question, what else do you want to do?'

He persisted, as he sat next to me.

'I want to start with being an author,' I said and he smiled like a satisfied father listening to his child say they got a first class.

'Wow, have you started any books?'

He pulled me closer to him, and I could feel my nerves lessen.

'I have actually. I've not really been able to continue lately because of work. I also need to get my reading table and just do some setting up, but I've been occupied you know. And I don't want to let you or the company down.'

He kissed my forehead, as he raised my chin so I could meet his eyes.

'You can't let me down, baby. Believe in yourself! You know you work yourself hard these days, you've been getting home later than you're supposed to. Take time for yourself to write. I don't mind assisting you with setting up.'

My heart melted as I listened to him. He was making me fall more for him in ways I couldn't control. As much as it frightened me, it reposed me. I never knew that I had it in me to feel this way. My mother would be happy if she could see me right now.

'You don't have to,' I said, my eyes lost in his very brown ones.

'With you, I have to.'

He bent to kiss me again, this time it was longer and I loved every second of it.

'Why are you so good to me?' I asked him softly.

He studied me with a bemused expression on his face like he didn't understand why I would ask such a question.

'If you think this is me being good, then I wonder how your exes treated you.'

I had never told him about my past, at least relating to men. He never insisted, which I appreciated.

'I don't have any exes,' I responded blatantly, and I could see the amazement on his face.

'You mean, I'm your first boyfriend?'

I rolled my eyes, already beginning to feel embarrassed.

'Yes, Femi' he grinned widely as he removed a lock of hair from my face.

'Wow, then it's a privilege to be with you, Tiwa. I assure you, I'm going to take care of you so well, till you begin to know that you deserve it and so much more.'

It suddenly dawned on me that he had never written a book before. It was weird because he was working in a publishing company.

'Why do you own a publishing company?' I asked him, his eyebrows rose in surprise at my question.

'No one has ever asked me that before,' he said in surprise.

'Well, I'm asking now. You do not even write, all you do is manage the company,' I continued.

He sighed softly as he ran his hands through my hair.

'Well, technically my father started the company. I just took it over,' he explained.

'So, it's not something you really wanted for yourself then? Why couldn't any of your siblings have taken over?' I asked, suddenly feeling too curious.

'Well, my siblings found a way to escape and it would have broken my father's heart if none of us took over. I don't particularly hate it. I'm doing very well for myself so it's not so bad. I grew up with lots of books around me. My dad loved to write but that has never been my passion,' he further clarified. 'Then what do you love?'

I asked him. For someone who had never written his own book, he handled this company really well.

'Well, I love arts. I paint and draw but it's like a hobby right now. I make a living out of running companies,' he said, but I could tell that he was not entirely happy with that fact.

'Why can't you make a living out of it? You already have the name, and your father is famous so you would be easily recognised'

I said suddenly feeling curious to see one of his artworks.

'Well, I haven't been able to paint in years,' he said.

The pain in his eyes was visible despite his smile.

'Why is that? Only tell me if you are comfortable,' I said and he kissed me softly.

‘It’s a long story but I promise to eventually. Right now, let’s focus on you, not me,’ he said before pulling me in for a hug that I did not know I needed.

Femi was clearly an expert in calming nerves because I certainly felt better after our talk. My meeting had gone better than well, at least. I was on my way back to my desk when Zainab pulled me.

'Girl, you would never guess what happened'

She had a disgusted look on and I tried to think of what could have happened as I waited for her to talk. 'Sam got a girlfriend' I raised my brows in surprise, but I was more puzzled about her reaction to this news. Not the news per se.

'Really, I'm happy for him now. Why do you look so angry?' I asked her.

She attempted to smile widely, but I knew her well enough to know it was fake.

'I'm not, please. I'm just wondering who she is,' she said. I sighed suspiciously.

It was obvious she wasn't happy about this information and the only reasonable explanation for this would be that she had feelings for Sam.

'How did you find out?' I asked her.

She walked towards my direction and I followed her.

'I overheard Dayo congratulating him. I'm waiting for him to come and tell me. I'm usually the first person he tells when anything happens, but he decided to keep it a secret this time.'

'How are you sure it didn't just happen yesterday? He couldn't have had the chance to tell you. And honestly, you guys have been having unnecessary arguments lately. What do you expect?' She hissed in response, and I had to try my best not to laugh out loud.

'Well, that's his business. He's been very annoying too. Always judging me about my lifestyle, but that's not my problem now. How's your new boo?' She asked a little bit too loud.

I, instinctively, moved to cover her mouth with my palm, before someone would overhear this conversation.

'Shhh… no one knows yet, Zainab. Your voice is too loud.'

She eyed me warily as she pulled my hand from her face.

'You're too humble. If it was me, everyone in this Calabar would know. Then, I would be having weekly interviews with Punch newspaper to talk about my relationship progress so that the whole of Nigeria would know. Me, I don't care what people say o. It's jealousy that makes them talk. You're just too slow for my liking.'

I shook my head in laughter as she spoke. This was the difference between us. I was more laid back, while she had this energy that I couldn't explain. Sometimes, I wished I didn't lack in that department because it would definitely lessen most of my worries.

'I trust you, but we're fine. He's been so romantic, honestly. We are supposed to go on a date this evening. I'm not sure where but I'm super excited and nervous. I have no idea what to wear.'

'Well, that's why you have me. I'm going to dress you up. It's going to be so much fun. I'm coming to your place after work, okay?'

***

Life definitely threw surprises at you. That was what explained the novel changes in my life. I had a date to go for, our first date as a couple, and it made me nervous and excited at the same time. It was an irony because this was Femi's way of trying to get me to be more comfortable with him.

Honestly, I felt like I was. I allowed him to hold me more than I had ever allowed any other guy. I was happier, everything was going positively for the first time in a while. And my look tonight didn't leave room for any doubts about that.

'He doesn't have any idea what's going to hit him,' Zainab said as she adjusted my dress from behind.

When I told her what had transpired between me and Femi, her facial expressions had altered into different ones in only a few minutes. From her hearing about his ex to our incoming date, it had been understandably hard to take in. She had given me tips on how to handle that Jezebel as she called her and I hoped I would never see her again so they wouldn't come in handy.

'Are you sure I don't look too much?' I asked her.

She insisted I wore the dress on me. It was a black velvet dress. It had a slit at the front which went all the way to the lower part of my thighs. The neck was v-shaped, so a little cleavage was showing which I wasn't really comfortable with.

'It's a date, you're supposed to look too much' She eyed me warily

'And whose manual is that?' I asked her, trying to raise the dress a little.

'The universe, Tiwa. You have no idea where this man is going to take you. You can't afford to just go out looking basic.'

My hair was in a high ponytail which emphasised my natural contour.

'You think everyone is like you, *abi*? You can dress up for Africa.' She laughed in response.

'Well, that's your friend for you. Never to be caught not fresh,' she said and I laughed.

I didn't have time to respond because my phone beeped.

'He's here,' Zainab said as she read my text.

I suddenly felt wrapped in a bundle of nerves. My thoughts were haywire as I stared at Zainab for help.

'You will be fine. I'm on your emergency dial, so just call me if anything happens.'

She hugged me before shoving me out of the door. Femi already knew where I lived, so he insisted he picks me up directly from here. He was standing in front of his car when I saw him. A few of my neighbours were outside and I could hear their murmuring sounds as I walked towards the man in front of me. I was suddenly glad that I wore this dress because of how dapper he looked.

He was in a three-piece black suit, which kind of complimented my dress. He looked way taller despite my 4-inch heels which I was struggling with. He had his jaw open as he stared at me with so many emotions. He bent to kiss my forehead softly, patiently not caring about the people around.

'You look stunning, baby' he said, and the smell of his expensive cologne drew me in.

'Thank you,' I said nervously.

'I'm trying so hard not to kiss you right now. Let's leave.'

He held my hand as he moved to open the door for me. I felt myself getting excited even if I had no idea where we were headed to.

'Where this time?'

I watched him buckle his seatbelt as he smiled mischievously.

'You will see.'

We laughed a lot during the ride there. It was like nothing had happened before. But it was our own way of trying to just let go for once according to his own words. I didn't know what Femi meant by spoiling me silly till I found myself in front of a yacht.

'What is going on?'

He was still smiling in that suspicious way of his as he motioned for a man with a very full beard to come to us.

'Is it ready?'

The man smiled as he pointed to the dock where the massive white luxury yacht sat.

'Everything is set, sir,' he said.

Lots of people were around us, families taking photos of each other by the beach side, a few people pointing at us. Couples held each other as they stared at the water waves.

'Shall we?'

Femi led me to the dock as I gazed in astonishment at the yacht in front of us.

'I didn't expect this,' I said and he smiled gingerly.

''That's the point.'

He helped me up the dock, as I used my other hand to hold unto the side of my dress. Another man arrived in front of us and Femi shook his hands.

'Tiwa, this is Udeme.'

He gave me a pleasant smile as I shook his hand.

'Nice to meet you,' he said and I smiled in return.

I marvelled at the vessels of the yacht, it was my first time being on board in one.

'So first things first, let's have dinner.'

We were at the cockpit and lights were bouncing around as reflections of the harbour. It was early evening, but the colourful lights made it seem like it was midnight. The table was already set and Femi was holding flowers which I hadn't noticed before.

'I hope you like them,' he teased.

I laughed as I took them from him and inhaled.

'They're beautiful.'

Music had started playing in the background and I could tell what he wanted to say before he did.

'You're beautiful, dance with me,' he murmured in my ear, as he wrapped his arms around my waist.

'I don't know how to dance,' I said truthfully, but we were already moving to Rihanna's *Stay with Me*.

'You're not doing so bad.'

His hands held my waist tighter and I could feel the yacht beginning to move.

'That's you being nice.'

My hands were on his shoulders and my head was laid on his chest.

'Not with you, baby. I'm never nice. I'm honest,' he said.

It wasn't a chilly night, yet I shuddered, emotions were rolling. I was engrossed in this moment.

'I hope so,' I said honestly and he raised his eyebrows in a very quirky way that I was beginning to get used to.

'So are we really dating now?'

I laughed at his question which was clearly him trying to reassure himself.

'Yes, we are' I said, holding onto his shoulder tightly.

'You're an angel,' he said, and his head bent to kiss me slowly.

I engrossed myself in the kiss, our heads moving in sync.

'You make me so happy,' he said softly.

His hand was holding my waist tightly, and as I laid my face on his chest. I couldn't think of any other place I'd rather be.

'So do you.'

I suppressed a smile as the song changed to another favourite song of mine. Ben King's *Stand by Me.*

'Who would have thought that Tiwa would be saying I make her happy?' he teased and I suddenly felt shy.

He grinned widely as my hand moved to cover my face in embarrassment. He removed it immediately.

'You're making me want to change my mind' I said and his laughter doubled.

'You're the cutest,' he whispered.

He bent to kiss me, and I met his lips as I stood on my tiptoes. It was a slow sensual kiss, and I felt fireworks in my belly. I wasn't single anymore. I was taken by the most amazing man.

Chapter Eighteen

Tears and Twisted Hearts

TO LIVE IS THE RAREST thing of all. It's that way because life finds it easy to throw so many predicaments at you that you forget about living. And that's why Femi and I made sure to go on loads of dates over the past few weeks. It was our way of trying to get past Isaac's never-ending proposals and Amara's incessant demands from Femi. Too many things had happened that we were failing to grow our relationship. It was like we were being torn apart at just the beginning. I had no idea if that was a good or bad thing.

We went for dinners, and I was better at eating exactly what I wanted. I was becoming more comfortable with him and I loved it. We had more talking moments and it was fun to know about him. He had studied for his university in America but had decided he wanted to come back to start his own company. Obviously, he had the means and it hadn't been that difficult for him, especially with the full support of his parents.
He never really mentioned his brother in our conversations, but whenever he spoke about his sister, his eyes lit up and he smiled that rare cheeky smile of his. It was obvious he was very fond of her, but he said that he hadn't seen her since the year before. She was also in the country but she stayed in Lagos instead.

I assumed she would be living with their parents but he said she had moved out a few years ago. She wasn't married but she had her own fashion business which occupied her. The irony was that whenever he opened up to me about his family, I couldn't say much back because there was really nothing to know. He knew about my mother and me already. I wouldn't say my life had been boring. If anything, it was phenomenal in its own way. Before anything had happened, I had been so accustomed to my simple life with my mother that it seemed normal. We were happy despite the struggles. There was genuine love, and I was too much of a bookworm to worry about other things anyway.

Our date today was at Femi's house. I was nervous and elated at the same time. As astounding as it was, I had come up with the idea this time, not him. We had been thinking of where else to go and it dawned on me that I had never visited him. He had asked a couple of times before, but I never felt ready.

Obviously, we were together now and it was only proper that I would know where he stayed, and besides, I was curious. I had come up with loads of images in my head of what his place would look like that I needed to know for sure. We were supposed to watch a movie together and eat whatever he prepared. That also fuelled my curiosity. He kept insisting that he was a good cook, but that was Femi. He claimed to be able to do everything.

I was waiting for him at my place as usual. I was dressed in a simple sweater and jeans this time. It was quite chilly and I was glad we would be indoors, at least. When I saw his name on my caller ID, I went outside without answering the call.
His grin was wide as he stood in front of his black Porsche in front of my house. The car looked so out of place in the rural area and it usually caused a lot of attention from people around. I walked into his open arms, his hands moving to hold me tightly.

'I missed you,' he said softly.

I smiled into his sweatshirt, inhaling the familiar scent I had come to love.

'I missed you too,' I replied.

He kissed my forehead before helping me get into his car.

'So, are you excited?' He asked.

He was reversing, so his eyes were directed towards his back.

'A little,' I said truthfully.

He waited for him to be back on the right track before moving his hands to join mine on my thigh.

'Make it very. I'm cooking, remember?' He said and I laughed. He was clearly proud of his kitchen skills.

'What exactly are you making?'

I decided to play along. His eyes left the road to face me as he answered.

'It's a surprise,' he said.

I rolled my eyes, already expecting that. Everything with him was a surprise. It was definitely his best word.

'Of course, you and surprises,' I teased.

He smiled widely as he pressed the horn.

'You never get disappointed. You look beautiful today.'

His compliments always managed to get to me no matter how subtle they were. Maybe it was the way he said them, or how unexpectedly they usually came.

'Thank you. You stay alone, right?'

He already told me he did but I needed to make sure.

'Yes. It's just Kanayo the gatekeeper who stays around, and the housekeeper comes to clean daily. She doesn't stay at my house. I actually told her not to come today so she wouldn't interrupt my time with you.'

My heartbeat rose as he spoke. We would be alone and it definitely wasn't the first time but this was different. It was his territory and as much as I trusted him, I wasn't sure if I trusted myself.
Lately, my body chose to betray me with urges I wish weren't there. We were both attracted to each other, but we tried our best to not go overboard. He was still being a gentleman and it kind of made me want him more.

'We're almost there,' his voice broke through the silence.

I noticed the GRA as he drove. It was placid as expected and I caught a glimpse of so many fancy houses, with some looking to have more floors than others. A few people were jogging on the streets. And it was when he drove into a magnificent black gate that my mouth opened widely. The building was huge, maybe bigger than I expected. The kind that you saw in the movies, the ones that seemed too unreal. He waved at Kanayo who opened the garage which was already filled with cars I hadn't seen before.

There were at least six more cars there, but I had only ever seen two. He only drove one of them to work and the other maybe when we went for outings. It was like he shuffled between the two when there were many others. There was a marble fountain with clear water, dropping in fast drops in a way that resonated with the surrounding silence.

It was a three-storey building, painted white and it looked uniquely neat in a way that drew you in. I wondered how he lived in such a place all by himself, but he was probably hardly ever home to notice anyway.

'Don't you ever get lonely?' I decided to ask.

He held my hands tightly as he walked me through the front door which could definitely accommodate a family of giraffes.

'Not really, I'm used to staying alone,' he said.

When the doors opened, my eyes went to the polished wooden floors and the beautiful high windows. There were velvet drapes that framed the curtains and they matched the burgundy couches which were mixed with the black expensive looking divan at the sides of the parlour. There were flower vases at almost every corner and the centre was a glass table that looked so clear in a way that you could mistakenly walk over it.

'You have a nice house,' I said honestly.

It was my first time being in a place like this, and it was definite that there was still so much more to be seen.

'Thank you, baby. I would love to show you around, but you can start doing that yourself while I get dinner ready.'

He kissed me soundly on my lips before walking away to where I would assume was the kitchen. My eyes went to the huge plasma TV on the wall, and I noticed photo frames hung above it and from what I remember, they were photos of his family. There was one with his brother but that was a full family one. His sister has no smile on as if she had been forced to take a picture. There was also one of him with the elderly lady that I met on the first day of work. She was hugging him tightly and I felt my heart warm at the sight. I smiled as I saw a photo of Femi with a graduation cap on. He looked almost the same only that his dimples looked deeper in person and his smile wasn't as wide anymore.

There was a long corridor to my left and I decided to look around since he already permitted me to. There was a library, as expected when I opened one of the doors along the corridor. It had huge bookshelves with books that had been arranged neatly. I wanted to feel them, and go through all of them if I was given the chance. A single light burned, creating a cosy environment which kind of made reading more interesting.

I was just about to close the door when I saw a photo frame resting on a table by a bookshelf. I walked closer and as I picked it up, my heartbeat raced faster uncontrollably. I was dumbfounded because it was beside his reading glasses or his work laptop, meaning he looked at it often. I was shocked because the girl in the picture was me. Do you know that moment when it feels like your life is crashing down before your face? That moment where you are too numb to move because your fears become a reality. Femi was a liar. What was my picture doing in his place? It wasn't a recent photo of me. It was a picture of me in my graduation gown from the university and I couldn't remember ever taking this picture. Was he my stalker? Had he known me all this while?

I suddenly couldn't breathe. All I could think of was that I needed to leave. I suddenly turned around but Femi was standing in front of me.

'Have you been watching me?' I asked him immediately.

I moved to pick up the picture and threw it at him not missing the shock on his face as he caught it easily.

'What? I don't understand, what do…'

'Have you been watching me?' I asked him again.

I was already thinking of an escape route because of how scared I was.

'I have not. Why do you look so scared of me, Tiwa? What's happening?' He asked as he began to walk closer, but I moved back.

'Don't come any closer to me. Explain why you have my graduation picture. Oh my God! Femi, I let you in. I was beginning to trust you,' I exclaimed in between pants.

I was struggling to breathe and I knew that the more I stayed here, the higher the chance I would have a panic attack. I watched him look at the picture in shock.

'I'm just seeing this for the first time. The first time I met you was the day I almost hit you on the road,' he explained, but I shook my head as I walked back more.

'How am I supposed to believe that? Someone has been watching me. That day we almost kissed, someone was watching, someone…'

'What? Why didn't you tell me? Tiwa, how could I be watching you if it was me you almost kissed? Someone must have put this picture here. I have cameras. I can have them checked. Tiwa, you have to trust me.' he said softly, but my head was all over the place.

It was true. He was with me when I felt someone watching me, but how did the person know I was going to be there? This frightened me more. How could I possibly hide from someone that knew my every move? Femi was on his phone already, whispering instructions to security. It wasn't long before I saw two men barge inside.

'Watch the cameras. How can I be paying you so much for you to let someone easily break into my home?' he said as he dropped the picture on the chair.

It was turned upside down and that was when I saw the small writing in the corner. I hadn't noticed it before. I picked it up to read what was written.

'You are not allowed to forget me that easily.'

I didn't know I was crying till it dropped on the picture.

'What's there?' Femi asked me and I gave the picture to him, noticing that the two men had left.

'Son of a bitch,' he said before pulling me in for a hug but I drew back.

'I'm scared, Femi. I want to trust you but I don't know if I can. Even if it's not you, how am I supposed to feel safe with any man after what has happened to me?'

'Do you really not trust me? Do you really think I could hurt you in any way? Why would I leave your picture hanging around if I knew you were coming? Tiwa, tell me you don't feel safe with me right now and I will take you home because I would never want you to feel unsafe.'

How could he expect me to tell him this when he was looking at me like this? I had no idea why, but I believed him. There was nothing familiar about him. The voice was different. I could never forget that voice. He was taller as well.

'I believe you,' I said, not missing the relief from his voice.

'Do you want to tell me what happened to you? Why would someone have put that picture here? Do you have any idea who has been watching you?' He asked as he ran his fingers through my hair.

I sat down feeling breathless but I was ready. I was ready to say the words out loud after so long.

'I was raped.'

It's no secret that most victims fear that moment when you let it out. When you finally say the words out loud, your words are rusty, maybe feeble, almost in whispers because you're still trying to convince yourself you can speak out. That's not all, for a second you think that you can let it out, but thoughts seem to come like thunderbolts, so you change your mind.

Eventually, it's like you finally find someone to whom you can pour out your soul. I mean that's how I felt with Femi. And as he's holding me right now, I wonder if I would have told my mother if she were alive, but honestly, I don't think I would want her to experience that pain. The heartbreak of knowing that someone you cherish the most has been damaged, what do you do in such a situation? Knowing her, she would have blamed herself, and held the guilt for so long.

I couldn't do that to her. I have no idea why I just told Femi, but I did. When my tears finally stopped flowing in big drops, I tried to withdraw myself from his grasp.

'Who did that to you? Please tell me he's in jail right now,' his voice was low, but I could hear the anger in them.

'I don't know who he is.' I met his eyes as I spoke.

'What? How?'

If a man's body and soul were to be thoroughly tortured, he would look like Femi did now. If he really was the one stalking me, then how could he look this way? Why wasn't I feeling the urge to run even if my mind was telling me otherwise? The heart really can be weak. I was seeing that for myself right now.

'I don't really want to go into details right now. I've said enough.'

He held my face softly, his fingers brushing away the bits of tears on my cheeks.

'Thank you for telling me. I know how difficult that must have been for you. And I have no idea what's on your mind right now, but I want you to know that I would never do anything to hurt you and I never have. I have never stalked you or thought of it. The day you met me by the road was also the day I met you, Tiwa. So please, don't push me away,' he rasped, his brown eyes shining with tears.

'I believe you' I said.

Just three words but they meant so much more to me. They were my way of saying I was thankful that I had been heard - my pain had been heard and they weren't shoved aside.

'Thank you so much, baby. Thank you.'

He closed the small distance between us and held me tightly again, this time I didn't hesitate. I held him back, reliving this moment again and again.

'We should get back to dinner,' I said.

He nodded but then reached for the home telephone on his table. He spoke to whoever was on the call with him about a security breach before ending the call.

'Someone brought that picture here and I'm definitely sure they wanted you to see it. We need to be careful, Tiwa. I can get you bodyguards, I have this set of…'

'No, Femi. Please don't.'

I shook my head, stepping back. I didn't need more attention than I already had. If I got one, the stalker would be aware that I knew what was going on. And who knew what other lengths he could go to?

'Please, it's only for your safety,' he insisted.

'You once said all these would be according to my terms, remember?' I retorted. He nodded.

'This is different,' he said but I refused.

'It isn't, so. Just listen to me this time. No bodyguards, no anything. We just have to be careful.'

I said but his eyes showed he clearly disagreed.

'At least we can inform the police.'

He held my shoulders firmly, showing how serious he was.

'We can't, I don't think he wants to kill me or something. I'm not even sure if it's linked to my rape, and I have no idea who my rapist even is. It's been years, Femi. Who's going to believe that he was wearing a mask? This is real life, not a movie. I would need to be sure or at least have more evidence before I let this secret out. Please, don't make me regret opening up to you.'

I knew I was probably hurting his feelings right now but he needed to know.

'You seem to forget that I have the means to make this different. You can use me to your advantage, and I'm not attempting to be arrogant. All I'm trying to do is help because of how worried I am about you.'

My heart twisted, I wanted to hold him and kiss him. I felt like comforting him even if I was the one that had been hurt.

'Thank you for worrying about me, but I'm not going to use you. There are so many others like me who don't have you. I'm going to find a way to do this on my own so they know they can too. I don't mind you being at my side as I do, Femi. I only need your support.'

He sighed as he bent to kiss my lips softly. It was sweet and slow, undemanding and I felt the impact everywhere in my soul. I leant unto him, wanting to be as close as I could. My arms encircled his neck and I suddenly forgot everything else. I forgot that I was scared inside too. I forgot the battle I was fighting, all I could think about was this man who seemed to be saving me in ways I can't muster.

'All I want to do is support you, to be by your side, Tiwa. You don't have to ask, I'm here to stay.'

I'm not sure which was having a great impact on me, his words or the sizzling kisses, but I didn't want the night to end.
I ran my hands through his face all the way to his stubble, enjoying the look on his eyelids.

'So am I. Let's go eat,' I said.

He held my hands as he led me to the dining. As we ate together, with light-hearted conversations in between – for once in my life – I began to think that my mama's words could be true. Maybe I could find love after all.

I woke up with mixed feelings the next day. It was a mixture of my emotional conversation with Femi and my fear of my tyrant. We both had no idea how the picture had gotten into the house.

Femi insisted we reported to the police, but I wasn't ready for that. Talking to the police came with more questions and I wasn't ready to tell any other person my secret. My body was sacred to me and the fact that it had been devoured in such a horrible manner made me feel so shameful, even though it wasn't my fault.

Or maybe it was, maybe I had wronged the universe unconsciously. Or maybe I was just born unlucky. I was one of those people that were born to face trials every day of their life. Either way, I just wasn't ready to come out. I needed time, and I hoped to God Femi wouldn't go behind my back to do anything stupid because that would be him breaking my trust, something I didn't give out that easily.

The sound of my phone ringing drew me from my thoughts. I yawned loudly as I got up. I smiled when I saw Femi's name.

'Hey' I managed to say in my very sleepy voice.

'Hey, baby. Did I wake you up? I'm sorry,' he pleaded.

His voice had an edge to it, more serious than it usually was.
'No, it's fine. Are you okay?' I asked him, as I adjusted my pillow.

'I should be asking you that. I'm worried about you,' he said softly this time.

'Don't be. I'm fine, Femi. It happened years ago you know. It doesn't hurt as much as before.' I assured, trying to encourage both him and myself.

As much as time went by, thinking about it never ceased. It was that kind of pain that stayed with you. Your only choice was to learn to live with it.

'You don't have to hide your pain from me. I know it hurts, especially if I'm feeling this terrible and scared, Tiwa. I'm worried whoever hurt you isn't done yet. We still need to know how that picture got to my home.'

We looked at the cameras, and security saw a man with a mask on climb through the fence. Thinking about the video gave me shivers but it gave me more assurance that it was not Femi.

'You're right, but I'm not ready to tell the police. Do you think I didn't want to years ago? I had no idea who he was. I didn't even see his face. The odds were not in my favour. As disappointing as sounds, my case is hopeless, Femi,' I said honestly.

I wasn't going to lie to myself. It felt relieving to be able to have someone to talk about it with, someone I could share my fears with.

'I have the resources. I have my ways. I will make sure they find that bastard, Tiwa. You just have to give me the go-ahead.'

His voice was louder this time and I wondered where he was because I could hear the sound of traffic.

'Where are you off to?' I asked him.

'Oh, I have this emergency to handle,' he replied.

I heard the sound of a loud horn and I cringed at the disturbing noise.

'I hope everything is fine,' I asked worriedly.

'Yes, baby. I couldn't stop looking at your picture last night. I don't know what his motive was for bringing it here. Maybe he wanted to come in between us, but how did he know you were going to be here? Everything is so confusing,' he uttered frustratingly.

'I have no idea too, but I don't want you to keep dwelling on that. It might even be just a random person trying to play with our minds. Can we please talk about something else? You're supposed to be at work in two hours,' I said light-heartedly, hoping he would take the hints and change the topic.

'Good attempt at changing our discussion, but I will indulge you. I wish work was in a few minutes so I can see you sooner,' he said softly and I swallowed nervously.

Hearing him say such sweet things to me did things to my soul.

'Why do you want to see me sooner?' I asked, taunting him. He chuckled.

'Well, I've not kissed you in about ten hours, and I'm dying to. I miss your smell. I miss gazing at your beautiful face. I want to see the smile you have on your face right now. I want to hold you to remind myself that you're mine and I'm not dreaming. I want to comfort you and reassure you that I've never felt this happy to be with someone. Should I continue?' He asked teasingly and I inhaled as I took in his words.

'Wow, all I want to do is get dressed right now so I can see you,' I said truthfully.

'Why don't you? I'm waiting for you outside.'

I looked at my window instinctively completely stunned. 'Oh my God! Really?'

I could hear his laughter as I hurried to get the door open. He stood handsome, fully dressed in his usual work outfit, a black three-piece suit and he looked more pleasing than ever.

'So, I was the emergency' I said.

He laughed at my stunned expression and he pulled me close to him tightly.

'You sure were,' he said.

I held onto his shoulders fiercely, not wanting to let him go.

'I missed you,' I said.

'I missed you more, baby. You haven't showered, right?'

He sniffed my neck jokingly and I withdrew from him embarrassingly.

'You snob. I had no idea you were coming,' I said and he laughed softly.

'I love seeing you this way. Let's go in so you can get ready. We're going to work together' he said.

I nodded and held onto his hand as we walked inside my slightly messy apartment. But that wasn't what made me hold my breath nervously when we got inside, it was the fact that I was going to have to shower and get dressed with him in my home.

Femi's eyes moved through my apartment like this was his first time here

'Seeing where you live is so heart-warming,' he said.

His eyes went to the pile of newly washed clothes on my couch. I had been postponing folding them up and now I wish I had. I had a few dishes that I hadn't done, an empty bowl of ice cream by my bed from last night, and a very unmade bed. Hopefully, he didn't think I was always this disorganised. Last night's drama had me too overwhelmed and exhausted that I couldn't tidy up.

'I'm sorry you have to see my room this way. I didn't think you would come,' I said nervously.

'You don't have to feel embarrassed. In fact, I like seeing this side of you. It feels intimate.'

He moved to kiss me and everything suddenly span around me. That's how much his kisses got to me.

'I really need to shower,' I managed to say and he nodded in response.

'Sure! You should go,' he said slowly.

I wanted to get my underwear but he stood in front of the locker where my underwear was and I had no idea how to get them without him noticing.

'Excuse me' I managed to say.

His eyes followed me and I wasn't sure if I wanted to get my underwear anymore.

'What's wrong?' He asked again.

He moved his hand towards the drawer.

'Do you need any help?' He asked.

I stopped him immediately. My heart rate had gotten faster and I had no idea why my nerves were this way. Or maybe I did.

'I wanted to get my underwear,' I said.

The smile that appeared on his face seconds after annoyed me and made me want him at the same time.

'I see! Go ahead then,' he said teasingly.

'Not with you watching me,' I replied.

He laughed at my response before raising his hands up in surrender.

'Fine, I'm going to go sit down.'

I watched him walk towards my bed and there was just something about him sitting down on the unmade bed that did wonders in me. I had never felt this way before. Men disgusted me but not Femi. His coming into my life awoke significant sensations in me that I never knew existed. I picked up my underwear before moving to the bathroom. Femi was on his phone and I was curious to know if he could feel the same sensation I was feeling and I hoped I didn't harbour these feelings alone.

My shower was shorter than it usually was. My nerves were all over the place and all I could think about was the fact that a man was in the room. But not in the way that frightened me, I felt elated and I knew these feelings had to do with the fact that I was aroused. It felt embarrassing to admit it but I was, and I couldn't help it. When I came out, Femi was standing by my door.

'I'm getting this fixed today. I couldn't sleep well knowing that your door was faulty. We can't afford to take risks like this, Tiwa,' he said as he turned around to face me.

'Oh, wow!'

Femi gazed at me in awe as I stood in my towel, but all I could think about was the fact that he said we.

'We?' I asked him.

'Yes, we! It's you and me now, Tiwa. Whatever affects you, affects me too. So, please I need you to take care of yourself and if you can't, I will take care of you for the both of us.'

He bent to kiss me slowly before suddenly pulling away.

'I should wait for you outside.'

He didn't wait for an answer before walking away so fast that if I didn't know how he felt for me, I would think I was a plague. I wondered why he left like that but I didn't bother to stop him. After dressing up as quickly as I could, I told Femi he could come back in.

'I'm ready,' I said softly.

His eyes ran through me. They were usually hard to read but this time I knew what he was thinking, especially when they focused on my lips.

'You look beautiful as always.'

He stood up and walked towards me.

'Thank you,' I responded.

His head bent to kiss my glossed lips and I kissed him back wholeheartedly. My hands moved to his shoulders for support, while his ran through my back. When his lips moved to kiss my neck, I was weakened. Femi had me in the palm of his hands and I wasn't sure if that was good or not.

'I've never wanted anyone the way I want you, Tiwa' he said hoarsely.

'We should stop,' he muttered.

But his lips said otherwise as they moved from my neck to my lips. I couldn't speak, couldn't move. I was lost in his embrace, his manly scent drawing me to him more. He withdrew from me suddenly, and I felt disappointed but thankful at the same time.

'We're going to be late for work. We should really go before we get ahead of ourselves, babe. I don't want you to do what you're not ready for,' he said sincerely.

I could see something else in his eyes. It felt like he was scared but I had no idea why. I insisted he drops me a few minutes away from work but he refused. He didn't mind people seeing us together but I did. I hated the unnecessary attention that came with it and I already had more than enough.

'No, no, no! Not here!'

I shook my head as I refused to kiss him in the car. He was packed in front of the building but that wouldn't stop preying eyes from watching us.

'I'm going to my office, Femi. I'm almost late and my boss wouldn't be happy about that. You should do the same,' I said in an attempt to be stern and he sighed frustratingly before releasing my hand.

'I really hate your boss right now', Femi said and I laughed.

'Well, good to know you hate yourself,' I retorted before walking away quickly.

Femi must have waited for a few more minutes inside his car because he wasn't behind me. I smiled to myself at the memories of this morning. We had just been together for a short while but it felt like years. He made me laugh like no other. I suddenly remembered him telling me to go shower when he hugged me earlier this morning and I laughed loudly.

'Is something funny?'

I turned to the well-dressed man in front of Femi's office door and my heart stopped.

Chapter Nineteen

Sibling Feud

I HAD NEVER MET HIM before, but he looked oddly familiar.

'I'm sorry, do you have an appointment here today?' I asked him noticing how closely he was watching me as if he found me intriguing and was trying to figure me out.

'I don't need to,' he said with a light smirk.

He wasn't dressed formally, if anything he looked really casual in just an expensive-looking polo shirt and pants.

'Why wouldn't you need one?' I asked already beginning to feel uncomfortable at my weird conversation with this mysterious man.

'Dapo, what are you doing here?'

I turned around to Femi's firm voice behind me and it was then that it dawned on me. Femi's brother's name was Dapo, which was why he seemed so familiar, and it wasn't from him having so much resemblance with Femi, it was from when I had researched Femi and saw images of his brother.
From what I found, they had a bad sibling relationship.

'I came to see my brother. Is that a crime?' Dapo said sarcastically.

I suddenly felt like I didn't belong in the conversation, so I turned around to leave.

'Wait, don't go' Dapo said.

It wasn't just me that was confused by his words. Femi certainly was too with the puzzled look he had on.

'I just wanted to say it was nice to meet you,' he said.

I smiled back in return before walking away as fast as I could. When I got downstairs, I searched for Zainab so she could tell me more about Femi and Dapo. I found her by the dispenser, and it seemed like everyone was already talking about Dapo's visit to the company because I could hear lots of murmuring around me.

'Hey, what's happening?' I asked Zainab who was taking big gulps from her cup of water.

'The boss's brother came visiting and everyone is waiting for a drama to occur,' she said and that awoke more nervousness in me.

'What do you mean? Have they fought here before?' I asked her and she held my hand before taking me to the bathroom with her.

'They have. It happened the last time he was here, and it was really brutal. It's like they hate each other sometimes. There's so much feud,' she said and I knew she wasn't exaggerating from the genuine expression on her face.

‘I’m sure they don’t. They’re siblings. It’s normal to have fights and disagreements but I don’t think they can hate each other.’ I said, but she shook her head at my words.

‘Trust me, Tiwa. Something must have happened between them because there is a lot of hatred. One of them has been rushed to the hospital before because of a fight they had,’ she further explained.

‘Yes, I remember reading that. It was Femi. How horrible! I know they have another sibling, but I wonder how their parents must feel. No parent wants to have their children hate each other’ I remarked and she nodded in approval.

‘Definitely not, and I’m sure they’ve tried to stop what’s happening. I really don’t know much about their sister. she’s really private about her life. I only know much about her fashion business and she’s such an inspiration, and so hardworking. Femi adores her from what I’ve heard, they’re really close,’ Zainab said.

I made a note to try to research more on their family when I got home. Femi was my boyfriend and I could easily ask him but I felt uncomfortable asking such intimate questions. By the way, he never disturbed me about my past. He knew what he knew because it was time for him to find out about it, I guess.

‘I just hope no fight occurs today. I can’t help but worry about Femi,’ I said with a loud sigh.

The sound of the bathroom door opening caught our attention and at the sight of one of the office’s main gossip, Corrine, we both left. I watched Dapo leave Femi’s office a few minutes after I got back to my desk. He smiled at me and thankfully didn’t utter a word as he walked away. I sighed in relief because he was coming out the same way he went in which meant there had been no fight. I was genuinely worried about Femi and all I wanted was to be with him. So I moved to knock on his office door, he didn't respond but I opened it anyway.

He was standing by his large windows, his tall frame barricading the sun that shined brightly. I walked closer to him and hugged him from the back. His hands instinctively moved to encompass mine at the front of his waist.

'I'm sorry you had to witness that,' he said defeatedly.

'I didn't really witness anything. It was all just awkward I guess,' I said and he nodded.

'I know it was. I didn't expect his visit.'

He said it so softly that if I wasn't closely listening, coupled with the room being very silent, I wouldn't have heard him.

'Is that why you're this sad?' I asked him worriedly. He sighed before turning around to face me.

'No, he said he's moving into town. He wants to expand his business here.'

I knew why Femi wouldn't want this. It would increase the chances of them running into each other, and Femi probably hated seeing his brother.

'You shouldn't feel so bad about it. Maybe you guys can take this chance to rekindle your relationship. He's your brother, Femi,' I said softly but he shook his head.

'He stopped being my brother a long time ago. I can't let him move here, I just can't. Both of us can't be in the same city at once. I have to stop him,' he said before pulling me into a tight hug that screamed of anger, hopelessness, and hatred.

What could have happened to them? I wanted to ask but I held myself. He would tell me when he was ready to.

'Don't you think that's being too extreme?' I asked but he shook his head in refusal.

'Never, please let's not talk about him anymore. Just hold me,' he said as he kissed my forehead.

And I did. I stayed for a while with Femi in his office. We ate together and made sure to talk about other things. He tried to act like everything was fine with him like he usually did but as much as I wanted to tell him that it was fine for him to be vulnerable with me, I didn't. Femi hated pity and I didn't want to make him feel more horrible than he already felt.

'You know, I've been with you in just a short while but it feels like you've seen me at my worst more than anyone ever has,' he said softly.

His thumb ran through my fingers and my eyes kept lingering at his face in an attempt to read through his feelings.

'I feel the same way, and that's why I want you to know that being here with you right now soothes me. I can't say you've seen me at my worst but you do know my deepest secret, Femi. That alone draws me closer to you. I hate seeing you this way.'

I watched his eyes grow more vulnerable at my words, and it took everything in me not to kiss him right then.

'I feel very deeply about you, Tiwa. So deeply that I can't put it into words yet. You're beautiful inside and out and you've just given me a reason to fight. I don't care if my brother wants to stay here. Maybe I do, but I'm going to try to not let him ruin this beautiful moment I'm having with you right now. He's not worth it.'

He moved to kiss me and I kissed him back in my most passionate way yet. There was a time in my life when I always felt jealous of my friends whenever they spoke about their annoying siblings. The tales were always so funny that I usually ended up imagining me having at least one little sister or brother. I made sure to never mention that to my mother because she already felt sorry for things that weren't even her fault. Knowing her, she would have beat herself up about not giving me a sibling.
But who was I to ask for anything? She had picked me up from the streets not because she had to, but just out of the kindness of her heart and that alone made me feel an overwhelming of love for her that it encompassed any sort of jealousy or longing that I felt for a complete family.

Seeing Femi and his brother's fractured relationship broke my heart. Why was there so much hatred between them that he couldn't even stand being in the same city with him? The sound of Zainab's incoming footsteps drew me from my thoughts.

'Girl, you've not dressed up still, what are you still doing there?'

Her loud voice led to me covering my ears with my hands.

'I'm dressed up now. Isn't this enough?'

She eyed me warily like I was a masquerade and I sighed in exasperation. We were going for a small get-together at Dayo's place. There was no reason for the party. It was just them wanting to have an excuse to drink and I wasn't much of a drinker, so it wasn't really my thing.

'Your outfit is not it, Tiwa. This is something you wear at home. Please change that skirt,' she commanded as she wore her earrings.

She was exaggerating just because she wanted me to really dress up and I was lazy for that. Femi had just dropped me home and he was all I could think about. I was wearing a black midi skirt and a white body suit. It wasn't party like but it looked acceptable or reasonable. Zainab was a pest and I didn't hesitate in making it clear to her again.

'Why do you like tormenting me? There's absolutely nothing wrong with this outfit. I'm not in the mood to wear something short. Me I'm ready, *sha*. So, it's you we're waiting for,' I said with a smile, and she sighed frustratingly like she wasn't the troublesome one.

'I will leave you just this time. Let's go,' she said.

It took us over thirty minutes to get to Dayo's place because of the light traffic. There were just a few cars parked outside. It was relieving because I wasn't really a fan of being around too many people. I didn't tell Femi about it because it had been impromptu.

'My girls are here finally. Come in,' Dayo said as he opened the door.

I didn't miss the look of longing he gave to Zainab. Of course, she ignored him because her eyes were focused somewhere else.

'Thank you. I'm sorry I don't look *partyish*. Manage me like this,' I said and he laughed loudly.

'Please don't listen to that girl. All she knows how to do is embarrass me,' Zainab said.

She then walked away to meet God knows who. There were about ten people inside already and everyone seemed to know each other.

'You look good no matter what you wear, Tiwa. You should sit down. You've not told me anything about your mystery guy yet.'

We moved to sit on an empty couch by the flat-screened TV. It was surprisingly easy to hear him over the loud noise which I felt grateful for because I didn't have to yell.

'Hmm, what mystery guy? I'm sure Zainab must have told you,' I teased but he sighed softly.

'As if she bothers to tell me anything lately.'

I followed the direction of his eyes which were focused on Zainab and a guy I didn't know. They were conversing in a very familiar way and she was laughing continuously that I wasn't sure if it was fake or real.

'Why don't you tell her?' I asked.

He drew his eyebrows together as if he had no idea what I meant.

'Tell her what?'

He tried to play ignorant but this was so obvious to everyone, not me alone.

'How you feel about her. Dayo, you're head over heels for Zainab. It's so obvious that sometimes I think she's blind to not have noticed already,' I pointed out.

He opened his mouth to refuse but he kept quiet like he decided there was no use in him denying it.

'She's never going to be interested in me. She has her type and unfortunately, I'm not,' he lamented and I patted him on his shoulder

'How do you know her type? You and I both know Zainab doesn't really know what she wants. She flirts with so many guys that she doesn't know which one she wants exactly. You will never know if you're her type or not if you never tell her, Dayo.'

I was shocked at myself as I spoke. I wasn't one for a love story till a short while ago. Now I was even giving advice. How things have changed.

'Who would have thought Tiwa could be such a good relationship counsellor?' Dayo teased.

'Well, you never…'

'Is that you, Tiwa?'

I got drawn from my thoughts by the sound of a very familiar voice.

'I was right. It's you.'

I turned around to see Isaac staring at me with a wide smile on his face. But it wasn't the sight of him that increased my nerves by a thousand folds. It was the person at his side, Femi's brother - Dapo. How the hell was I supposed to handle the two of them?

Chapter Twenty

Coming to Steal You

IN THE PAST FEW DAYS, I had been in lots of awkward scenarios that it was beginning to feel like the new normal. I hadn't seen Isaac in ages, especially after our dramatic last encounter. Maybe I could have handled him alone but there was no way I could handle him and my boyfriend's sibling at the same time.

'Tiwa, right?'

Dapo said and I nodded, remembering our encounter back in the company.

'I had no idea you guys had already met,' Isaac said with his eyebrows raised.

He was holding a glass of wine, while Dapo had his hands in his pocket. There was really no resemblance between him and Femi except for their tall height. If anything, they could pass as just friends, especially now that there was a huge rift between them both.

'You must find me interesting to be watching me that way,' his voice drove me out of my thoughts and I suddenly felt embarrassed.

'I'm sorry. I'm surprised to find you both here. I had no idea you were friends with Mr Adebanjo,' I said to Dayo, who clearly looked confused as well.

'We aren't. Isaac asked me to come along. I hope you don't mind,' Dapo said amusedly and Dayo shook his head.

'Not at all. It's an honour to have you here,' he said as they both shook hands.

'How about you, Tiwa?'

The music had gone down so there was a little bit more attention on us which made me feel uneasy.

'Of course, I don't, Mr Adebanjo. It's not my party, anyway,' I said softly.

I attempted to stand up but he stopped me.

'Please call me Dapo. You don't work for me,' he cautioned.

He was staring at me like he was trying to read me. I tried to avoid his eyes but I ended up locking gazes with Isaac.

'I have not gotten a chance to say hi yet. Do you want to talk?' He asked.

I shook my head even before my words came out.

'No, I'm beginning to feel tired. I should go home soon,' I said, trying to stand up again.

Thankfully, no one stopped me this time.

'How's Femi?'

I turned around to Isaac's voice behind me. It suddenly felt like I was in a battle between three men and I had no idea why.

'He's fine,' I managed to say.

Dapo kept gazing at me intriguingly. There was just something about the way he looked at me that made me feel uncomfortable. I guessed it was because of his bad relationship with Femi. When you care about something, whoever annoyed them usually began to get on your nerves. I wasn't really sure if that was the case but it was a possibility.

After managing to leave them I searched for Zainab and later found her talking to a guy that looked too drunk to have a proper conversation with.

'Hey, baby! Are you having fun?'

She hugged me tight immediately after she saw me. I sighed loudly when I realised she was also drunk.

'We need to go home. I really shouldn't have come to this party,' I protested, as I struggled to get her to walk with me.

I searched for her car keys in her bag, knowing I would need to drive and probably spend the night with her. Making it a sleepover, but with a drunk friend.

'Is she okay? Let me drop her home,' Dayo offered worriedly.

Zainab was beginning to fall asleep and as much as I felt like I could handle her, she was too big for me to carry alone.

'She's gone, but I don't know if I want to leave her alone with you. I just need help with getting her to the car,' I requested.

I knew Dayo wouldn't do anything to hurt her, especially with how much he cared about her, but there were some things you just must not do. Never leave your drunk friend with a boy unless he's her boyfriend, at least.

'How are you going to get home, then?' A voice came from behind.

I turned around to Dapo's voice and I couldn't hold my sigh.

'I will stay with her,' I said.

'I can drop you guys off,' Dayo insisted but Dapo held his shoulder.

'Don't leave your own party. I can just drop them off,' he offered but I wasn't sure I wanted that.

'Never mind. She came with her car, anyway. We will be fine. Just help me get her to the car, please.'

I wasn't going to let a stranger drive us home. He was Femi's brother but still a stranger to me.

'Thanks a lot,' I said to them both when they turned to help me get her to the car.

My phone rang and I smiled when I saw Femi's name. I really needed him after such a long night but I wasn't sure I wanted to tell him about what happened today. Knowing him, he would get so mad and want to go with me to every party I went to.

'Hey baby!'

His deep voice sent chills down my spine and I suddenly wished I was in between his arms.

'Hey love, I can't believe how much I've missed you,' I said as I started the car.

'I've missed you more, but where are you right now?' He asked, his voice already having hints of his protectiveness.

'Nowhere really. We went grocery shopping. We're on our way home' I said.

'Okay then, but it sounds like you're the one driving'

I nodded as if he could see me.

'I am' I said, thanking God that Zainab's place wasn't so far away.

'That's dangerous driving, Tiwa. Call me when you get home,' he said before hanging up.

I hadn't driven in a long time but I still had it in me. I learnt how to drive before finishing from the university. I had thought it was essential for me to know how to even if I had no car. It had really been a struggle, especially with a man teaching me.

As I got close to Zainab's house, my phone rang again. It was Femi still.

'For someone who cares about me, you're definitely luring me into dangerous driving by distracting me with your phone calls,' I said and he chuckled.

'I just called to let you know I'm on my way to see you, I'm missing you as well' he said.

My heart skipped excitedly at the thought of me seeing him.
'I'm not home, remember?' I said.

'I'm coming to Zainab's place, tell her I'm coming to steal you.'

He ended the call and I smiled as I got to Zainab's gate. She was asleep but she wasn't going to mind anyway. Sometimes in life, you are keener to go for events that you regret than the ones that you actually enjoy. At least, that's what my experience has taught me so far. It didn't take Femi long to get to Zainab's place. I always saw myself as someone who loved the artsy kind of attention, so I appreciated efforts like this. We both knew he was busy, yet he was willing to spend as much time with me as possible.

I kind of wished he had come earlier because it was a real struggle to get Zainab to wake up. I definitely couldn't have carried her because I wasn't Wonder Woman, so I had forcefully woken her up.

'So are you going to tell me where you really were?' Femi asked as I got into his car.

I couldn't just let Femi stay with me overnight in Zainab's place, she obviously wouldn't have minded but I did. Thankfully, the door to her apartment could lock without the need for a key. I only just had to leave a note to tell her Femi came to get me.

'Are you purposely ignoring my question?' He asked again as he turned the music on in the car. It was soft so I could hear him clearly.

'What makes you think I didn't just go to get groceries?' I asked him teasingly.

The brief look he gave me made it clear he wasn't really in the mood for my teasing.

'Zainab is drunk and very dressed up. Isn't that enough answer?' He said as he shook his head.

'Fine, we went to a party' I said with a sigh. There was no need to keep going back and forth.

'Something significant must have happened there for you to be keeping it from me,' his lips twitched slightly, and I rested my head on the car door.

'Isaac was at the party,' I said.

To my surprise, he let out a sigh of relief as if he expected something worse.

'Well, he's fond of appearing where he's not wanted,' he said as he pressed his horn and overtook a *keke* beside us.

It was a chilly night, so the loud noise added to my goose bumps.

'I guess so, but your brother was also there,' I said softly.

After several seconds he responded,

'I see! Did he say anything to you?' He asked.

I noticed his knuckles harden as he held unto the steering wheel tightly.

'See, I knew you would get worked up,' I protested.

He was trying to act as if the information didn't do anything to him but it was obvious it did and that was why I hesitated in speaking at first.

'He offered to drop me and Zainab but I refused obviously' I continued, this time with my eyes fixated on him.

'Well, thanks for letting me know,' he responded.

We were already close to my apartment and I could see kids running around the street playfully in their underwear. Their parents watched them from the stools they sat on and I imagined the millions of mosquitoes they would be battling with especially at this time of the day.

'Are you ever going to tell me what the problem between you and your brother is?' I asked, and his face hardened.

'I don't really want to go into that now. I planned to have a good night with you today and I'm not going to let anything get in the way.'

His hand moved to touch my thighs and I held onto them totally understanding where he was coming from.

'Good night? What are you planning, Femi?' I teased and he laughed softly.

'Well, my plan is only going to work out if you want the same thing.'

My face suddenly turned red at his words, and I felt hot all over.

'I'm not sure if it's safe to park my car here overnight.' he said.

He looked around my rural neighbourhood and I couldn't agree with him more. A few boys were playing football and I wondered how they managed to especially when it was so dark, but I guessed it was something they were already used to.

'I agree with you. We can go to your place instead.'

The words left my mouth before I could think twice about them and I watched him blink rapidly like he was trying to absorb my words.

'Are you sure?' He asked and I chuckled.

'I didn't say I was going to do anything, you bad boy. I only said we could go to yours,' I replied as I gestured for him to drive us to his house.

'If I didn't know you, I wouldn't be surprised by this. You have no idea how happy I feel right now,' he said as he grinned widely.

'I already called the carpenter and he is coming to fix your door tomorrow. Since you will be at my place, I will ask Kanayo to come and watch him while he works just to be safe,' he continued and my heart softened.

How could someone care about me this much?

'Thank you, Femi' I said and he held my hand tighter.

'I just want you to be safe,' he said.

Femi's home still looked magnificent as ever that it was easy to forget that I had been there before. My heart was beating rapidly, but not at the fact that I was shivering from this cold night, it was from the way my insides were feeling. I was going to spend the night with Femi, my boyfriend. Of course, we weren't going to have sex because I certainly wasn't ready yet. But this was a major stepping stone in our relationship and my life. I was trying to come out of my comfort zone, and I trusted Femi to believe I was in safe hands.

'So, are you sure you want to spend the night in my home? Is that really okay with you? I mean I can stay in one of the guest rooms, you only have to pick any bedroom you like. I can show you all your options, I have one bedroom that's…'

'Can you breathe, Femi? You're sounding even more nervous than I am. Someone who doesn't know us would assume you've never had anyone here before.'

I tried to sound reassuring but my words seemed to put him in a sombre mood. 'Well, I haven't had anyone sleep over, not in my home,' he said.

I couldn't hide my surprise. He had dated his ex long enough for anyone to assume this was normal for him, so hearing this was a shock to me.

'Really? How come?' I asked genuinely.

We were on his couch and they were so comforting that I felt like I wouldn't mind sleeping off in them.

'It's a long story, but I'm not scared of being in the same bed with you, not that I'm saying I want you to, but I'm just saying I wouldn't mind that,' he said.

He bent to kiss me softly. I kissed him back fully, wholeheartedly. He nipped a trail of kisses down my neck, sending ripples of desire through my belly and I grabbed his arm to steady myself. I felt his hands move to grab my waist, as he carried me to his hard thighs, and my heart skipped when I felt his hardness.

I could feel myself getting surprisingly excited and I shifted my body, needing more contact and instinctively he pulled me closer to him. He captured my mouth with his back again and I whimpered. His tongue slipped in possessively and skilfully into my mouth, and I began to feel so much buzz in my lady parts. My brain was going haywire, and I was just about to feel how hard he was when he withdrew. My mouth felt empty and cold as I struggled to calm my breathing. Femi's breaths were equally ragged as he panted in rhythm with me. As my brain returned steadily from the blissful haze, I realised that I could still feel his hardness under me so I was certain he didn't stop because he wasn't interested anymore.

'I promised to not overstep my boundaries, not till you say you're ready. I want you to know that you can tell me if you don't want me to touch you. You've been through so much and I know how much trauma you must have. Please, Tiwa, do only what you are comfortable with. You are beyond precious and I want you to know that your needs come first,' he explained as he kissed my forehead.

His eyes were so intense, they resembled glowing coals. I was so tempted to say that I was ready, to throw all my fears to the wind and admit that maybe, just maybe I could erase my sexual fear with the loving memory of his, but I was a coward.

'We should go to bed,' I said instead.

This was going to be a long night.

Chapter Twenty-one

Past Horrors

HE HAD SHOWN ME AROUND the first time I came here, but the house was so huge that I had easily forgotten the directions of where anything was. He took me to a room on the topmost floor of his home. It was a three-storey building and the floor of the bedroom was made of coloured marbles and arranged in perfect patterns. I could site a big Jacuzzi from where I stood at the door, it seemed so far away which made it unreal that this was just one room. The walls were covered with blue silk cotton but I could still make out that they were glass walls. I wondered how beautiful the city view would look from there. The ceiling had silk banners that hung from them. The bed was king-sized with about four pillows. There was a huge flat-screened TV on the wall, and I couldn't see any wardrobe but only a locker that definitely couldn't fit so many clothes.

'The closet is over there.'

I had been so engrossed in the magnificence of the bedroom that I totally forgot he was here. The closet was even more attractive. It was huge with so many sections. Some were high, some low. There was something that looked like a shoe rack but it was so massive that my shoes would only fit one section.

'You like it? I know women love their closets' he asked from behind me and I chuckled.

We definitely did but I would need to shop for ten years before my clothes will fill this closet, especially because I rarely shopped.

'You're sounding like the room is mine,' I said and he grinned.

'It's yours whenever you want it.'

I didn't know how to answer that so I decided to change the topic.

'It's unreal that your room is bigger than this. I know I've asked this before but don't you ever get lonely?' I asked him softly.

He stood with his arms crossed as he leaned on the door.

'I'm too busy sometimes to feel lonely, but I do admit that it feels good to have you here.'

Our eyes met and I smiled at him softly.

'I think I'm done with sightseeing for now. I should go to bed so I'm not late to work tomorrow. I have a very demanding boss.' I said and he laughed.

'I'm sure he wouldn't mind,' he responded as he opened the door for me.

We were staring at each other as we looked at the bed before he spoke up.

'I should leave you to sleep right now. My room is next door, so feel free to call me if you need anything.'

I nodded and he bent to kiss me softly before walking away.

I didn't expect the disappointment I felt at his absence. I puzzled myself sometimes with how I reacted whenever I was around him. I hadn't come with any nightwear. I also hadn't come with clothes for work tomorrow. I was going to have to wake up very early so I could go home and get them. I went to the bathroom to pee and I noticed a silk night dress hanging by the edge of the bathroom. I hadn't noticed it before. I moved to get it and the soft feeling of the outfit was so comfortable that I imagined what wearing it would feel like.

I picked up my phone to call him. He answered on the first ring. 'Is the nightgown for me?' I asked and his response was immediate.

'Yes, I hope you like it. I kept them in case you ever decided to sleep over. Didn't think that time would come anytime soon, but I'm glad it did. Zainab told me your size, by the way.'

My heart melted at his words. It felt like he had so many plans for our future and that alarmed me because anything could happen. What if this ended and everything right now became just a memory? Would I survive it? Especially because I was already so attached.

I shook my head in an attempt to get a grip on my thoughts. I wore the dress and it fitted like a glove. He deserved to know what it looked like. His room was next door so it wasn't that hard to find.

I knocked softly on his door. The short seconds I waited for felt like years because of how nervous I was feeling.

'Come in,' he said and I opened the door.

'Wow!' he whispered.

He looked at me like I was this goddess that he had always wanted to see. My eyes went to his shirtless chest and I couldn't look away. This man made me feel like a real woman and not only was I grateful for that, but I was also frightened. Without the slightest warning, he stalked towards me and my breath got stuck in my throat. I definitely had no self-control around him which explained why my hands moved to touch his chest.

'Come here,' he said as he grabbed me into his room while his lips met mine fiercely.

My eyes closed in pleasure as we kissed passionately. Kissing him always felt like we were in another universe. I could feel his hard chest and I sighed when his head moved to kiss my neck softly. I almost melted at the sensual feeling. He moved to grab my lips again, this time we were moving towards the bed. I felt his hands move to touch my boobs but I could sense his hesitation.

I wanted to move his hand towards it further but I couldn't because I suddenly saw him through my closed eyes. And by him, I meant my villain. I felt the force. I felt the shudder and before I knew it, tears filled my eyes.

'Tiwa, what's wrong?' He asked as he held me tightly.

'My God, did I hurt you? I'm so sorry. I shouldn't have. I'm sorry, Tiwa.'

I shook my head as I leaned on his shoulder.

'No, you didn't. I'm sorry. I don't know what's wrong with me, I...'

'It's fine, I understand. I'm so sorry you are going through this. I wish I could take the pain away,' he said softly and I tried to get a grasp of my breath.

'No one deserves to feel this pain I'm feeling, Femi. You're everything I've always wanted ever since I was a little girl and I'm so worried I'm going to mess it up because of my past horrors.'

My eyes met his and he was gazing at me, his brown eyes intense with worry.

'The last thing you should be frightened about is you losing me. I'm here to stay, baby and I'm going nowhere. If all I have to do is hold your hand while you heal, then so be it. I'm always going to be at your corner protecting you from any more terror. You're my girlfriend and I protect what's mine.'

He nuzzled my teary face with kisses and I chuckled at how nice it felt. How beautiful this moment was. I wished time could stop. I knew I loved him. I could feel it. My heart pumped in excitement as I admitted that to myself. He hadn't told me he did yet, but his actions didn't show anything otherwise. My fingers moved to touch his face softly.

'Thank you for finding me,' I said and his eyes closed briefly as he held me tightly.

'No, thank you for finding me,' he replied.

I understood why people said the best bridge between despair and hope was a good night's sleep. That only emphasised the fact that sleeping was one of the best things in life. Femi had offered to walk me back to my room even if it was just next door, but I had refused. I was too frightened to be on my own and the amount of love I was feeling at that moment was so massive that I needed to feel his presence.

'I could stay like this all day,' he whispered as he nuzzled my face with his knuckles.

My head was on his chest and our legs were wrapped around each other. He was so warm, all I could think about was the fact that it would be more difficult to sleep alone after this night.

When I woke up the next morning, the bed was empty. I yawned as I picked up my phone to check for my alarm but I still had over three hours to go. I saw a note on the table and I read it out loud.

'In case you wake up before I'm back, there's breakfast for you downstairs. Help yourself to whatever you want and I permit you to tour my room or wherever you like if you're bored and can't help your curiosity. Don't miss me too much,' I chuckled as I folded the note.

Where could he have gone this early in the morning? And why was I awake at this time? It was a few minutes to five and I usually found it easier to go back to sleep when this happened but I couldn't. I wasn't in my domain and despite Femi's bed being the most comfortable bed I had ever slept in, my curiosity kicked in. I looked around Femi's room through my hazel eyes, it was the biggest room in the house as expected. The floor was similar to the one I was supposed to sleep in.

The room was a big square, with big windows along the left side. I found a remote control by the side stool and pressed the first big button I saw. At least I wasn't so behind in technology. It opened up but it was still quite dark outside. Dawn hadn't arrived yet. There was a massive TV at the other end of the wall. It was almost like the same one in the living room. They could both be used in a cinema room and no one would complain. I stood up and walked a bit further, there was a drinks cabinet in the corner. There was a small door linked to the bathroom, then another door that led to his magnificent closet. The difference between his and the other room was that it was occupied with different colours of suits, and a transparent drawer that had so many ties, more than I could ever count. The shoes were in different forms. I was beginning to feel like I was prying but I wanted to know how he lived.
There were no pictures except that of his sister. From what I knew, they were really close and I was curious to know more about her. After looking around, I kept trying to wonder where Femi was. There were no workers in the house, except the gateman from what I knew. How could he live alone in such a massive place? I kept looking around till I found myself in the library. My thoughts went back to the first time I was here and I was immediately frightened. My picture had been here and we still had no idea who kept it there till now. The picture wasn't here anymore. I wondered where Femi must have kept it.

I saw another picture of him and his family. He looked so young here, with a smile so bright that it could light up the world. He looked like his mum, they had similar smiles and his sister looked more like her father. I couldn't really make out who Dapo looked like but he was a cute child too. He and Femi sat close together and I imagined they were closer then.

'Those were the good old days.'

I almost lost grip of the picture in shock.

'Geez! Don't sneak up on me like that,' I said and he smiled as he walked closer to me. He was in grey sweatpants and a sweatshirt and I could smell his arousing manly scent as he got closer.

He kissed me and I thanked God I had brushed my teeth before coming downstairs.

'I'm sorry, didn't expect you to be up so early though. Were you missing me too much?' He teased and I rolled my eyes playfully.

'Don't flatter yourself. I used one of your extra toothbrushes if you don't mind, and I kind of stalked your room,' I said as I jabbed a finger on his hard chest.

'You can use whatever you want and I permitted you so it's not stalking. Did you like what you saw?' He teased and

I pouted like I was trying to think.

'Well, it wasn't bad,' I said and he moved to tickle me so hard that my eyes began to feel teary.

'Please Femi, please…,'

I begged as he carried me to the couch without stopping.

'Then say the correct thing.'

I shook my head and he continued, this time all over the sides of my waist.

'Okay, I loved it. The best thing I've ever seen in my life. It's epic, trust me, I doubt there's any other room like yours. It's better than that of President Obama.'

He suddenly started laughing as I spoke and I used that time to wriggle from under him.

'Obama isn't even the president anymore. I don't think I've laughed this hard in a long while. Where have you been all my life?' He asked.

I was about to give some smart remark when I noticed that his hands were ready for another attack.

'No, please. I was always here, you just needed to find me.'

He smacked my lips with his.

'Good girl'

His car keys fell from his pocket and I recalled that he went out.

'Where were you?' I asked.

He kissed my forehead before holding my hand and taking me with him to the living room. He pointed at the two filled bags on the centre table.

'They're yours. I went to your place to get you something you could wear to the office because I noticed you didn't bring any. I also wanted to show the carpenter what he needed to work on. Kanayo is with him right now as well. I found your house keys in your bag, I hope you don't mind. I could have bought you something new but no stores were open and I didn't want you to have to go back and forth.'

It was possible to feel butterflies in my stomach. It was also possible to feel an outburst of emotion that words couldn't just be enough to justify or express them. Those were what I was feeling now. How could someone be so thoughtful? It was something little maybe, but I cherished this. If I wasn't sure that he loved me before, I was now.

'Are you mad at me? I'm sorry…'

I moved to kiss him, and he accepted my lips as expected.

'If I had known this was the thank you I would receive, I should have done this sooner,' he teased.

'You could only have done it now. It's my first time in your house, remember?' I said and he suddenly looked sad.

'I'm going to miss you when you go,' he said.

'You're so dramatic! I've only been here for a night,' I replied as I tapped his shoulder subtly.

'We should go back to bed, at least before it gets bright.'

He bent to carry me across his shoulder as he took me up the stairs into the bedroom and though I was elevated in the air, I felt close to his heart.

Chapter Twenty-two

The Box

THANKFULLY, I DIDN'T GET TO work late. Despite Femi's effort to get me my clothes from the office to prevent me from going late, he was still bent on cuddling in bed. I had to threaten to leave on my own before he finally came back to his senses.

'Girl, you need to give me full gist not that half gist I'm hearing,' Zainab protested.

She kept insisting that something worse would have happened because I slept at Femi's house but I was trying to assure her that nothing did. At least, nothing out of the ordinary.

'Trust me now. We only just cuddled. You know how I am. I'm sure he would have been willing to go further,' I explained, and she raised her eyebrows as if contemplating.

'Hmm… True, *sha*. You can be a grandma sometimes. Anyway, that was the first time, next time better have more,' she said jokily.

'I need to go back to my work now, but I've heard you.'

I kissed her cheek before pressing the button on the elevator. I wish I had taken the stairs instead because I saw Corine inside.

'Good morning' I said, not really expecting an answer.

She rolled her eyes when she saw me and I chose to ignore her.

'I don't think my morning will be so good now that I've seen you,' she hissed and I tried to compose myself.

'Nothing about you can be good, so that's no surprise,' I said.

Her mouth opened wide to give a comeback but the elevator opened and I walked out as quickly as I could.

'Saved by the elevator,' I murmured to myself.

My table was almost cleared up, unlike when I had had piles of manuscripts on it. I had finished most of the books I was supposed to cover much earlier than expected and it benefitted me a whole lot because I was left with time to write mine.

It was a story about a girl that was exactly my opposite but similar at the same time. She had been in lots of relationships, but none of them ever lasted because of how self-sabotaging she was. Her pain from a bad relationship with her father defined most of her relationships and until she met someone who would show her that she deserved a love that was almost perfect, she would keep having horrible relationships with men.

I had written three more chapters when I noticed that a paper had been stuck at the edge of my table. I smiled because I assumed it was Femi, but it disappeared when I read what was written.

'I'm watching you very closely. You can't be happy unless I permit you to be. Stop that charade you have going on or you would not be the only one to get hurt.'

I suddenly gripped my table so tightly that my wrist began to hurt. I had only a few people on my list that could be hurt. The closest one to me at the moment was Femi and the thought of him getting hurt sucked the air out of my lungs. My heart wasn't just beating, it was galloping and my bladder suddenly felt full. I stood up and tried to push myself down the elevator. I needed to know who dropped this here, it must have been this morning.

'Did anyone ask for me this morning?' I asked Damilola the receptionist.

She shook her head before she spoke.

'None that I know of, why?'

'Are you sure? Or maybe he didn't ask for me. Did you see anyone that doesn't work here or have you seen anything suspicious this morning?'

I knew I was sounding uncanny but I couldn't help it. I was paranoid and I had good reason to be.

'Tiwa, what's going on? Did anything happen?'

She was beginning to look worried and that was the last thing I wanted. I mustered a smile that I hoped was believable.

'Nothing really, someone is supposed to have come visit by now and I'm just worried.'

She sighed as she nodded.

'Oh, I understand. I'm sure he or she is still on their way. It must be a family member for you to be so worried, you can ask security,' she said.

I thanked her before stepping outside.

'Are you sure you really didn't see anyone?' I asked Kolade.

He was the one on duty today and this was my first time ever speaking to him.

'At all. I've been here every second, no one that I don't know has passed me, Aunty,' he assured.

When it dawned on me that nothing would be said, I nodded and left.

'Why is your face that way? What's wrong?'

I didn't realise Zainab had noticed me from her office.

'Nothing, we will talk later,' I replied.

Femi still hadn't come out of his office all day and it was lunchtime already. I was frightened to face him, especially after the threat I got today. I couldn't tell him, I couldn't tell anyone. Not when their lives could be in danger. I heard the sound of his door open and I smiled at him, hoping my nervousness was not obvious.

'Hey, babe. I've been so busy, are you hungry?' He asked as he tried to kiss me but I resisted.

'We're in public, Femi. Comport yourself,' I warned.

He looked around as if to confirm.

'There's no one here, so we're not in public.'

He moved to kiss me again.

'Stop, we can't afford to be too careless. Let's go and eat,' I requested.

I was beginning to feel like I was being watched, because how else would he know where I work? Femi sighed softly and I could feel his eyes watching me closely.

'What's going on? Is everything okay?' He asked worriedly.

'Yes sure, why wouldn't it be?'

The disbelieving look on his face indicated he found no truth to my words.

'I know when you're keeping something from me, Tiwa,' he insisted.

'I've been trying to write my novel but I think I have writer's block. I keep getting stuck on the same page,' I explained.

It was partially honest because ever since I had read the note this morning, I hadn't been able to write anything.

'I'm sorry, baby. I can try to help you. I don't mind reading through it.'

I was so relieved that he believed me that I kissed him. He grinned in satisfaction.

'Now, that's my girlfriend,' he said.

Lunch went by fast. I kept hoping Femi didn't notice that something was bothering me. It wouldn't do us good if he found out. He would be extreme about it and that could even put him more in danger. Femi asked if we could go for dinner and I really wanted to say no but that would only give him more reasons to suspect that something was wrong.

'I will pick you up by seven-thirty,' he said and I nodded in response.

'Sure'

He kissed me and I waved as I watched him drive away. I turned around and sighed loudly as I opened my door. The landlord still hadn't gotten back to any of the tenants about changing the door locks. It looked like something that could definitely be easily broken into and with everything happening now I wasn't sure I could keep risking this. I would have done it myself but he was against self-repair because it was his property. I made a note to myself to remind him again.

I went into my bedroom and had just removed my coat when I saw a box. I moved back in fear, my eyes going around the four corners of my home. Who could have dropped this here? I wanted to just leave and run but I moved towards the table where the box was kept. I carried it and the weight of it was intriguing, even if I had ordered something they usually called before they delivered.

I struggled with unsealing it because of the tapes used. I found a blade I had just opened by my bedside which I used to open it. Foil paper was used to wrap what was inside the box and I felt my heart beating even before I saw what it was. I removed the last bit of foil paper and after a horrified glance, I ran to the sink and threw up. The snake wasn't just dead, it had been mutilated. It was wrapped in plastic probably to keep the horrible smell from alerting anyone before opening the box. There was a piece of paper under the plastic

'You're not escaping me this time, princess. Your new man better back off,' I read out loud.

My eyes were blurry from my uncontrollable tears. This was the second fright in a day and I didn't think I could handle this myself. I unconsciously picked up my phone and was about to call Femi when I hesitated. I couldn't. His life was in danger. This was even more of a warning. I couldn't drag him into this, he deserved so much more. What if this was a warning about what could happen to him and not even me? This fellow knew I had a boyfriend, he knew about Femi. We needed to be more careful. My hands shook as I called Zainab. She picked up on the first ring.

'Zainab, Zain…' I stammered as I went silent.

What could I have said? How was I supposed to explain all this? Did she deserve this too? But could I handle all these alone?

'Tiwa?'

My terror must have been obvious in my voice because Zainab sounded worried.

'What's wrong? Are you okay?'

I could tell she was in a very busy place because of the noise and I tried to make myself sound clearer, but my voice still came in a whisper.

'There's a dead snake. Ummm… A snake is here, a note too. I met it here. I um…'

'A snake? Wow, I understand your fear. Isn't Femi with you? You can call one of your neighbours to get rid of it.'

I could hear the teasing in her voice. I shook my head but realised she couldn't see me.

'No no. It's dead. I need help. It's dead, Zainab. It's been mutilated. The blood is in the box. It's a threat. I'm scared, Zainab.'

'What? Did you find a dead snake in your room or you killed it? You know what, I'm coming there. I don't understand anything.'

She cut the call immediately. She got to me in twenty minutes. I waited for her outside by the door because I couldn't bear to be inside on my own. I was sweating profusely and that was what she noticed first.

'My God! You're such a scaredy-cat! See how you're sweating. Where's the snake? Isn't it dead already?' She asked and I nodded.

'Yes,' I responded and nodded towards the door.

She pouted before walking inside.

'Jesus Christ of Nazareth!'

I heard her loud scream from inside and I hurried to meet her. She was panting as she held her chest.

'Who sent you this? I don't think I will be able to sleep for days. Tiwa, what's happening?'

I looked around unsure of what to say but I couldn't stand seeing that box anymore.

'I will explain everything to you but we need to get rid of that box first. It can't stay here,' she looked towards it and nodded.

'We need to take it to the police. It's evidence, and why isn't Femi here?' She asked and I shook my head.

'No, no! He can't find out. The person is also out for him, it's in the letter,' I said and she raised her eyebrows like she hadn't noticed it.

'Tiwa, we need to call the police. I feel like I'm in a horror movie. I can't believe I'm witnessing all these.'

She walked towards the fridge and grabbed a bottle of water.

'We can't call the police l. I don't know what to say. This goes way back, Zainab. He knows me.'
She drank a large gulp of the water before dashing the empty bottle into the bin.

'I don't understand, who is he? Did you get in trouble without letting me know or why else would someone send you this?' She asked me. And I sighed.

'I can't fathom it either, but I will tell you everything that has happened so far.'

Her eyes were filled with tears as I finished telling her about everything including the note at the office and the fact that I felt like I was constantly being watched.

'I'm so sorry you went through all that. How could you suffer all these alone? How?'

She asked and I shook my head because I couldn't understand how myself.

'I don't know. I guess I just kept living. There was no one to turn to. I went to the police but they told me I wanted it and that was why I invited him to my home. That's why I have no faith in them now. They laughed at me. They mocked me. They called me a prostitute and said I didn't even know the face of the person that raped me. But how could I have? He wasn't even invited, he found his way in. The memory, it's…'

'I'm here now, my love. I'm here, you must have felt so alone. I never knew. Now I feel horrible for throwing you on Isaac and even Femi. Speaking about him, I hope he's being good to you.'

She rested my head on her shoulder as she spoke.

'He's perfect, that's why he doesn't deserve this. He's only shown me so much happiness and now his life is being threatened. I'm a curse, I really am. Anyone who sees me should run away.'

'No, you're not. He deserves to know, don't you think? But you don't have to tell him now. If he's been good to you, he deserves to know. You can't handle all this alone, you have us now. I love you, sis. Let's go to my place. We need to still go to the police either way, at least let's try. Maybe this time we will be lucky. We can't just throw this snake ourselves,' she insisted and I nodded.

'Fine!'

Zainab had just called the police who said they would be on their way when my phone rang. It was Femi. We were supposed to go for dinner together. He was supposed to pick me up in an hour and it had totally slipped my mind because of everything that had happened.

'Are you going to answer?' Zainab asked but I shook my head.

'No, I will just tell him an emergency came up with you. We both know our police are very unreliable when it comes to being on time. So, we need to wait,' I said and she nodded.

My phone rang again and I chose to ignore it but then we heard a banging on the door. We both looked at each other in fear when we heard his voice.

'Tiwa, I'm dying under this sun, open up.' My breath cut at the sound of Femi's loud voice. Everything was here, and the police were on their way. What the hell were we supposed to do?'

Chapter Twenty-three

Uncertainties

WE BOTH STOOD THERE NONPLUSSED as we stared at each other. Zainab was definitely dumbfounded because she hadn't said a word, and Femi was still banging on the door. At the same time, my phone was ringing.

'You shouldn't leave him out for that long. I'm sure he's getting worried,' she finally said.

I was too frightened to hold the box, so Zainab and I moved to open the door and immediately he pulled me into a tight embrace.

'I was so worried. I thought you had collapsed or something. Why didn't you answer your calls? Were you asleep? But you don't look like you just woke up,' he said.

I was still too shocked to talk, so I just shook my head.

'You don't look good. What's wrong? Let's go inside.'

He held my hands as we both went inside and I felt my heartbeat skyrocketing.

'Hi, Femi,' Zainab said to him, his face hiding no indication of his perplexity.

'You're here. Now I understand why you weren't so eager to open the door. I only called earlier because I needed to tell you that I just got a call from the police about the picture we found in my library.'

'What do you mean? I thought I told you not to go to the police,' I said but his eyes weren't focused on me. He was staring at the box.

'What's that?' He asked and I swallowed.

I watched him go closer to it and I closed my eyes even before he spoke.

'What the fuck is this?' He yelled.

He picked up the note from the bed and read it out loud.

'Tiwa, what in the hell is going on?' He asked as he faced me.

I wasn't sure how to answer so I looked at Zainab hoping she would say the cops had arrived but she shook her head. I shouldn't be disappointed because that was the typical Nigerian police system anyway - unreliable.

'Tiwa? Why didn't you call me immediately after you saw this?' He asked.

There was so much fury in his eyes, in a way that I hadn't seen before. 'I didn't want to trouble you,' I said.

Zainab left the room quietly to go outside. I felt terrible that she had to witness this.

'Trouble me? Why then are we together? Your life is in danger and you think you can go through this yourself? Don't you trust me?'

My eyes were beginning to water. He must have noticed because he sat me down and knelt down as he held my hands.

'How many times am I going to tell you that you never trouble me? Isn't it obvious how much I care about you?'

His hand moved to hold my face.

'I know, I'm sorry, I…'

'I need to make a call, hold on' He stood up rapidly and reached for his phone from inside his pocket. 'Who are you calling? I asked but he held up his hand.

'I already called the police,' I said.

'They aren't here yet, are they?' I shook my head in response.

'Commissioner Orji please,' he stared at me, his expression daring me to protest

'Commissioner Orji, this is Femi. Please I need you in Krinose street, number 34. Yes, the one beside the hospital. It's an emergency, it's my girlfriend's place. She just got a threat, yes a life-threatening one. Okay, please do. Thank you.'

He hung up and sighed as he turned around.

'You can continue with your story,' he said.

'You didn't have to do that, we already called the police.'

I said and he shook his head in annoyance. 'I needed them to come quicker.'

'They're here,' Zainab said from behind us.

'You see,' I said as I hurried to open the door.

I was baffled at the sight of the very tall man that stood in front of me. Behind him were five other men with big potbellies which was a common thing among the policemen in this country.

'Commissioner Orji,' he called and I sighed as Femi came over from behind me.

'I told you I could handle it,' Femi whispered to me before focusing on the police.

'Thank you for coming, sir. There's something you need to see.'

They both walked inside and Zainab hugged me tight as we followed them into my bedroom.

'Chineke! This looks horrible. How long has this been here' he asked, his heavily bearded face tightening with disgust as he looked at the carcass. He had a thick Igbo accent which wasn't surprising from his name. 'I saw it here when I got back from work,' I explained.

He shook his head as he called one of his men to carry it away.

'I've seen so many horrible things in my job but nothing this disgusting in a long time,' he said as he bent to pick up the note from the floor.

'How many times have you gotten notes like this?'

He asked me. Femi looked at me expectantly as if waiting for the answer too.

I knew he would be mad when he heard it.

'I saw another one earlier today,' I said.

'When today?'

Femi scowled and I avoided his eyes as I answered.

'At the office' I replied.
He ran his hand through his face in frustration.
'And you went for lunch with me without seeing the need to let me know?'

'You also reported the picture to the police without my consent,' I retorted. If he was thinking I was going to ignore that part, he was wrong. 'I'm supposed to be the one asking questions here. You can sort out your issues later. Did you keep the note with you?'

The commissioner asked and I nodded. I picked it up from my bag and handed it over to him.

'This person is really after you. Did you have a fight with anyone? Do you have any idea of anyone that would do this to you?'

I wasn't ready to start telling him about my rape. Femi must have noticed because he asked the commissioner to go outside with him. They came back a few minutes later.

'I'm not going to trouble you with many questions, but who else knows about this? Is it just both of you?'

He asked and I nodded.

'Yes'

I wondered what Femi must have told him but I couldn't ask now.

'Let's keep it that way. I will try my best, Mr Adebanjo. I expect a significant reward for my hard work.'

He turned towards Femi who nodded at him in response. I shouldn't be surprised because this was the norm in Nigeria. Most times, you couldn't achieve anything without having to pay someone off. People with no means to do this were usually left unprotected. It was despicable, but the sad reality.

'I will be going now. Inform me if there is any update'

'What did the police tell you about the picture?' I asked.

His facial expression showed it wasn't anything helpful.

'They said it's not enough evidence for them to look for the culprit. They believe a picture is not harmful.'

'And you expect them to be able to find him now?'

The police never failed to be disappointing, so I prevented more heartache by having less hope in them.

'I believe so. This was threatening and Commissioner Orji is an old family friend but anyway you should come home with me,' Femi said from where he stood and I looked at Zainab who nodded.

'Why do I feel like you wouldn't allow me if I said no, anyway?' I murmured and he chuckled.

'Good that you know. I'm not leaving you alone, especially not now,' He replied, and despite so many uncertainties in my life right then, I knew those words were true.

'You must have been really frightened' Femi asked gently, hunkering down in front of me and taking one of my hands. His hands were warm as opposed to mine which were always cold. 'I was,' I said through stiff lips. 'I'm worried about you. I'm thinking of getting bodyguards because…'

'No, please' I cut him short.

'Why must you be so stubborn? You are being threatened, Tiwa,' he said as he moved my face downwards so my eyes could meet his.

'You're being threatened too and expect me to keep going to work with bodyguards? You know I can't afford it. I want a normal life. I can't have huge men following me everywhere I go, Femi' I said.

I was adept at reading his face so it was easy to sense his frustration.

'I can take care of myself. You already know I'm willing to pay for that and more, you just have to let me.'

I shook my head before I spoke,

'I can take care of myself too. You also know I can't accept that, so please let's change the topic. I need to sleep. I have work tomorrow.'

I stood up, held his hands, and took him with me to the bedroom. We were going back and forth and we obviously weren't going to come to an agreement.

'You've been through a lot, I think you need time off work,' he said but I ignored him.

Work was a distraction I needed right now. The next morning was evenly warm, the sun hadn't shone brightly and I chose to take that as a sign that today would be a good day. I had slept off immediately after I laid in bed, and Femi had said that he did the same as well. Despite Femi's insistence that I don't go to work, I had gone. I needed to be strong. We had no idea who it was and we couldn't keep hiding because he would know he was succeeding.

At least, I didn't feel so alone anymore. I had Femi and Zainab to rely on. I hoped today would be less dramatic but it wasn't. Femi kept fawning over me. He would come out of his office every five minutes to check if I was okay. I had only gone downstairs to say hi to Zainab when he called my name from behind.

'Thank God you're okay. I was worried,' he said as he hugged me.

A few people were watching us, including Corinne the company gossip.

'What the hell are you doing? People are watching,' I said but he didn't relent.

'I don't care, let's go.'

He pulled my hand and Zainab was smiling so brightly as she waved at me. I tried to ignore the many eyes on us as walked away.

'Femi, what's wrong? Don't you care about people finding out anymore? You're even more paranoid than me,' I noted when we got to his office.

He shook his head as he rested on his mahogany desk.

'I never cared. It's you that has always cared,' he replied.

'I want to keep you safe. I can't even stand the idea of you going back to your place without me being able to watch you. What if something worse happens?'

I knew he was going to bring this up. The landlord had called me this morning to tell me the door had been fixed. He also apologised for what happened to me. It had to take something so scary to happen before he did what he was supposed to do. Femi obviously wasn't keen on it, he would put me in a cage with thousands of men barricading the door if he could. But I wasn't used to this, I needed to protect myself.

'You know you can't change my mind. The police are handling it already and I'm choosing to believe in them for the first time in a while, so just stop being so paranoid, okay!' He sighed as he kissed me.

I felt his tongue instantly and I moved mine in sync with his. We kept going at it till his phone rang. He ignored the first ring but it rang again.

'You should really get it' I murmured but he shook his head

'I don't want to.'

He lowered his head as he kissed me back, but it rang for the third time.

'What if it's the police?' I continued. That caught his attention immediately because he walked to answer without confirming if it was actually them.

'Hi, mother. I'm sorry, I've been busy. Of course, I haven't forgotten you. In town? Today? You should have given me a warning or something.'

I went to the bathroom to adjust my hair and my blouse. I definitely had to go back to my place today because his mother was coming. At least, he couldn't stop me now.

'Kanayo will come to get you from the airport. Don't bring him to my house. You can see him at his place instead.'

From the edginess in his voice, I could tell he was talking about Dapo. I wondered how their mother felt knowing her sons couldn't even stand each other.

'You look beautiful' Femi's hand slid through my waist from behind as we both looked at the mirror.

'I guess I'm sleeping at home tonight then. You need to attend to your mother' I said and he groaned

'Why don't you stay with Zainab?'

'Her family is coming over too. They're planning her sister's wedding and I don't want to be a burden,' I replied.

It suddenly felt like a family weekend with everyone's family coming over. He turned me around to face him. I could tell what he was about to say was serious from the way his brows arched.

'I don't mind you meeting my mother, I'm sure she wouldn't…'

'No, Femi! I'm not ready, just focus on her okay? I will be fine. The door has been fixed already.'

I tiptoed to kiss him before walking away. My heart was still beating so fast from the thought of meeting his mother. He hadn't told me he loved me yet. I knew I did, and he did too. But hearing it was different. Maybe I would say it to him first. I didn't have to wait for him. I didn't tell him that I was frightened to sleep in my

place, or that I couldn't bear knowing that my rapist knew where I lived. I was finding somewhere else to live. I would make sure I found one in a week. I only just had to budget more for my rent and cut down on other costs.
My phone beeped.

'Do you want to come stay with me tonight? You can meet my family for the first time. Dayo will be here too,' Zainab said and I smiled softly.

'You invited him? To meet your family? I don't know why that makes me so happy,' I said sarcastically.

'I only did because he knows my siblings already, and my mother, she insisted.'

I knew that was only part of the truth. She felt something for him but wasn't ready to admit it.

'Femi would be busy with his mother anyway and I don't want to stay at home alone for that long. Sure!' I replied.

Chapter Twenty-four

Family Weekend

THE DOOR TO MY APARTMENT had been fixed but that didn't erase the fear I felt at going inside. There were so many people in my neighbourhood, yet it felt so lonely. I had always been a misanthrope so it was no surprise. I took in a deep breath as I closed my door behind me.

After a quick shower and a change of clothes, I called Zainab to tell her that I was ready. I wanted to call Femi but I wasn't sure if I should, especially because he would be with his mother by now. I sat up when my phone beeped.

'Hey girl, I'm going to be extra late because my sister's flight has been delayed. I'm still waiting at the airport for her.'

It was from Zainab.

'It's fine, I can come over instead. I'm too scared to keep staying here.'

'Okay love, you know where my extra key is. Be safe,' she replied instantly.

I sighed loudly as I stood up and picked up my bag. I was just about to go outside when my phone rang.

'Hey baby'

I didn't know I had missed him so much till I heard his deep voice.

'Hey, have you picked up your mum?' I asked.

I could hear the strain in his voice. He was exhausted.

'Yes yes, it's good to see her but she has started her trouble again,' he replied.

'What do you mean?' I asked as I went back to sit waiting for him to respond.

'She keeps talking about you know who,' he said suggestively. I tried to think of who he could be talking about but I couldn't.

'I don't understand' I said honestly.

He sighed like he hated having to say it.

'She wants me to get married,' he said softly.

He didn't have to keep talking. I understood him totally.

'Amara! Does she think you guys are still together?' I asked; a new worrisome feeling had begun to overtake me.

One I had always feared but always kept at the back of my mind. I had no family that Femi had to be concerned about but he, on the other hand, had this huge wealthy family and I wasn't sure if

I would be accepted. We'd been dating for months now but it felt like years.

So much had happened, so many memories had been made and I felt more connected to him than ever.

'She knows we're not. I told her I'm with someone else but…'

'She doesn't want you to be,' I said painfully.

His silence spoke volumes.

'But I'm going to change her mind. I want you to come for dinner. Join us. Let her get to know you.'

I shook my head in response, forgetting he couldn't see me.

'Please no, not now. I'm not ready.' I pleaded.

'Fine, I guess you have a lot to worry about. I don't know how long she will be here for but I hope you do meet her before she leaves,' he said and I imagined his hand running through his face as he spoke.

'How are you doing? I've been worried about you, aren't you frightened?' He asked worriedly.

I looked around my room like there was an answer there.

'I'm scared but I'm going to be with Zainab. I won't be alone so you don't have to worry,' I assured.

'I'm always going to worry about you. Call me if you need anything, okay,' he said.

I assured him that I would before ending the call. The journey to Zainab's place was short, there was no traffic. I had been seated in Zainab's living room for only a few minutes when there was a knock on the door. I checked my phone to see if Zainab had told me that she was on her way already but she hadn't even responded to my last text.

I was usually a paranoid person but my paranoia increased rapidly after the incident in my room.

'Who's there?' I asked loudly.

'It's me, baby'

I was so shocked at the sound of his voice that I couldn't speak.

'What are you doing here? Aren't you supposed to be with your mother?' I asked, but Femi kissed me soundly as his hands moved to my waist.

'Yes, I told her I needed to run a quick errand. I just needed to see that you were okay. I'm glad you are.'

My heart melted instantly and I tiptoed to kiss him back softly.

'I am, babe. I'm so lucky to have you, Femi. I can't imagine being with anyone else,' I said wholeheartedly. His deep brown eyes brightened as his hand moved to my face.

'Baby, I …'

A knock on the door diverted our attention.

'I think Zainab is here,' I said.

He moved to open the door and I was shocked to find who was at the other side of the door.

'What are you doing here?' Femi asked Dapo in an aggressive tone.

'I believe you have no right to ask me that. It's not your house. Is that Tiwa? Good to see you,' he replied and Femi kept me behind him protectively like Dapo was going to do anything to me.

'Don't talk to her,' he responded and I rolled my eyes as I wriggled away from him.

'It's good to see you too. I'm sorry I don't think Zainab has ever mentioned having any friendship with you. Why are you here?' I asked him, ignoring Femi's angry look.

'Yes, I don't know her personally. Her elder sister, Aisha, told me to wait for her here. We have a business together,' he explained and I nodded, still confused because Zainab had never mentioned anything like that.

'You can have a sit' I said, letting him in.

'Well, you can stay if you want. I'm taking Tiwa with me,' Femi said as he held my hand but I withdrew it from his grasp.

'What's wrong with you? You can't keep putting me in between your fight with your brother', I whispered to him.

'I'm fine. I'm supposed to wait for Zainab I can't just leave. I'm sure he isn't so bad, maybe I can get him to mend things between you two,' I continued but he shook his head, clearly not ready for that.

'Please don't do anything like that. I have to go now,' he said.

I nodded, aware that Dapo was watching us. But who wouldn't? Femi was acting like a child.

'Don't worry about me okay,' I said and he nodded before kissing me hard.

'I will be leaving now,' he said with a frown.

'Mum invited me for dinner tomorrow, and I don't intend to refuse,' Dapo said.

Femi turned around to face him and my eyes went between both brothers. Their stance was similar, and their body builds almost the same, but they looked nothing alike.

'I don't want you anywhere near my home,' Femi said and I sighed.

I would be embarrassed if Zainab and her siblings were here to witness this.

'Have you told mum about her? You should invite her for dinner with us. By the way, have you heard from kikelomo?' Dapo replied.

The mention of their sister seemed to fuel Femi's rage more because his knuckles folded immediately. I was bewildered at how serious this blood feud was. I hadn't done anything for Femi yet but maybe I could stop this, maybe if I tried to talk to Dapo I could find the root of the problem and help them mend their wounds.

'Don't you dare mention her,' Femi said.

I was confused. Kike was their sister, and her personal life was very private. I only knew about her very successful fashion business.

'What the hell is wrong with you? You can't stop me from worrying about my own sister, you can't go that far,' Dapo retorted as he walked forward.

I was about to pull Femi out myself when his phone rang. He turned towards me,

'It's my mother, I guess I have to go. I'm sorry you had to witness this, I will try to not let my brother get the best of me next time,' he remarked ruefully.

'I wish I could help,' I said. 'I don't want you to.'

He kissed my forehead before leaving instantly. Now I was left all alone with the other angry brother. God help me. I turned around and I saw Dapo watching me closely.

'I'm sorry you had to witness that. I don't know when our situation got so terrible,' he said mournfully.

I sighed as I motioned for him to sit down. He did and I sat at the chair opposite him, it wasn't so far away because of the way Zainab's home was set up.

'How long has it been this bad?' I asked softly.

'It's been years. I felt the same anger towards him at first but now I don't. If anything, I'd rather things were better,' he said.

This intrigued me. It was exactly what I was looking for.

'So you don't mind mending things with your brother?' I asked and he nodded.
'I don't but it's not that easy. Femi is the most stubborn person I know.'

I agreed with him because it was true.

'Do you mind telling me how it started?' I asked, hoping I wasn't going too far.

'Well it started with…'

We both turned our heads to the sound of the door opening.

'I hope we're not too late' Zainab's loud voice filled the air.

'I'm sorry it's my fault,' a beautiful petite lady in a blue sundress said as she held unto her suitcase.

'Everything is always your fault,' a guy who looked too much like Zainab said as he came towards my direction.

'Wow I didn't know you were this beautiful,' he said as he hugged me tightly.

'She has a boyfriend, Mustapha' Zainab said and I laughed.

'It's nice to meet you, Mustapha' I said.

'He was right about you being beautiful, Tiwa. It's nice to meet you,' Zainab's sister Fareedah said.
'Thank you.'

I smiled as I hugged her back.

'Dapo, you made it. I didn't think you would,' she said as she hugged him. So, they really did know each other.

'I didn't know you knew him all this while,' Zainab said to her sister who kept talking to Dapo.

'You don't have to know all my friends, sis. Those were your words, not mine,' she said and Zainab rolled her eyes.

'I'm working for his brother. That's enough reason for me to know,' Zainab said clearly getting annoyed.

'No please, not today. We just got back, you guys shouldn't bring your problems today. I don't mind being the referee for tomorrow,' Mustapha said as he went to shake Dapo's hands.

I laughed loudly already getting entertained.

'You're always so dramatic, Mustapha. Anyway, sorry if I didn't tell you about my friend, Zainab. I met him just a year ago when I travelled to England with mummy. He helped me find my way when I got lost. He's also coming to my wedding, I invited him,' Fareeda said chirpily.

I gasped. I had totally forgotten she was the one getting married.

'Yes, your wedding. Congratulations! Zainab told me about it,' I said hoping I didn't sound as nervous as I felt.

I was around people I had never met before, I didn't want to sound so much like the misanthrope that I was.

'Thank you, beautiful. So you will help us with the planning then. I'm psyched. It's in two months but it feels so close. I would marry him today if I had a choice,' she said dramatically.

Zainab said her sister's fiancée was a good man. She had even joked about him being too perfect for her annoying sister. Some people were indeed really lucky with love.

'You've said that a million times already,' Zainab teased. 'He's a very lucky man,' Dapo said with a smile.

'I should leave now. You guys have things to plan and I have work to do. It was nice to meet you Mustapha. I already knew Zainab and Tiwa,' Dapo said.

I watched Fareeda hug him tightly thinking of how to get to him without it being awkward. I was determined to do this for Femi and that was all I could think about.

'Tiwa?'

He made it easier by calling my name when he got to the door.

'We were discussing my brother,' he said softly and I nodded.

He seemed interested in making amends with his brother which was going to make everything easier for me.

'Yes, I'd really like to help with mending things between you both, but I need to know more. I'm sure Femi loves you, he just needs to be reminded,' I opined hoping I wasn't taking things too far.

'Thank you for wanting to help. We can have lunch at a time of your choice, just tell me when you want to, but you know Femi can't know about this, right? It's going to push our relationship ten times backwards,' he said ruefully.

'I do. He won't know, but he's already meddling in my own affairs because he wants to help. He shouldn't be so angry if I want to do something for him too,' I said trying to encourage myself with that too.

His eyebrows rose inquisitively at my words but he didn't ask about it thankfully.

'Hmm... I see. Well, thank you. See you when you're ready,' he said before walking away.

I sighed loudly hoping I wasn't making a huge mistake by trying to end the blood feud.

'What were you guys talking about?' Zainab asked from behind me.

'Femi,' I said frustratingly.

'Well... What's up with Femi?' She asked and I laughed.

'I will let you know but let's go join your siblings for now' I requested.

She nodded as we both walked to the living room.

'So Tiwa, have I told you that you're gorgeous?' Mustapha said from the couch.

I laughed nervously unsure of how to respond.

'You really need to stop flirting. She's not single' Fareeda said and Mustapha shrugged.

'I'm only giving a compliment, are you sleeping over?' He asked and everyone laughed.

'Yes, she will be in my room with me, while you're sleeping on the couch. If you don't stop, I'm going to report you to Femi myself,' Zainab said scornfully.

'I'm only trying to entertain her. I don't want to be rude to your guest,' he said.

'You're the guest here,' Zainab retorted.

I caught Fareeda's gaze who shrugged like it was something she was used to.

'We're here to plan my wedding, remember? Can we start that now?' Fareeda asked.

'But after I shower and eat, I'm famished' she continued and my stomach suddenly grumbled.

'So am I' I said and everyone laughed.

'Okay, I'm going to make dinner,' Zainab said as she walked to her kitchen.

I decided to join her, but my phone rang. My heart sank when I saw that it wasn't Femi. I had missed him. It was Dayo.

'True, he was supposed to be here' I said out loud.

'Who?' Zainab asked.

'Dayo' I said as I answered his call.

'He's outside,' I said.

Zainab rolled her eyes, but I didn't miss the glint of excitement on her face. As much as she wanted to deny it, she liked him and she could only hide it for so long.

Chapter Twenty-five

Matchmaking

DAYO LOOKED AS NERVOUS AS he sounded over the phone. 'Hey, Tiwa' he said as he pulled me in for a hug.

'Hey, I can see that you're excited to see Zainab,' I said teasingly, and he groaned frustratingly.

'Is it that obvious?'

He smiled but there were hints of sadness in his eyes.

'What's wrong?' I asked him even though the answer was quite obvious.

'I don't think she feels the same way. I was excited when she asked me to come but then she said she wanted her sister to meet me and that Mustapha asked for me. I thought maybe she would have begun to see me as something other than a friend by now, but I guess not,' he shrugged and my hand moved to hold his arm.

'Don't be so negative. She cares about you deeply. I see it but she's not ready to admit it to herself, you know. You just need to be patient. Now let's go inside before she comes out here.'

Zainab was still in the kitchen when we got inside. Mustapha was in the living room watching football and he stood up at the sight of Dayo.

'Hey, man. It's good to see you,' Mustapha said as he shook Dayo's hand.

'Wait, *na match you dey watch*? Thank God. I thought I was going to miss it,' Dayo grinned as he joined Mustapha on the couch

'You *no fit miss this one o, e be like say Chelsea go soon get red card sef*,' he responded.

I rolled my eyes, knowing fully well that I couldn't contribute to the conversation. I wondered what the obsession with boys and football was. It was like nothing else mattered whenever they were watching a match. Their eyes were continuously glued to the TV like it was going to flee from them.

'Dayo is in your parlour,' I said to Zainab.

She kept stirring the pot of jollof rice in an attempt to hide her excitement.

'That's good then. Tell them food will soon be ready,' she said.

'Aren't you going to go say hi? I can check the food for you,' I offered.

She shook her head rapidly as if I had asked her to do something unimaginable.

'I will see him when I drop the food. We've not had a proper conversation in a while. I only invited him because of Mustapha. I wasn't happy to see him,' she expressed and I nodded.

'Yes, but he's also here for you,' I responded.

Now I understood why she kept trying to play matchmaker with me, it was definitely fun.

'You need to stop you know? Not everyone can be like you and Femi. Besides, Dayo is not my type, and you know that. I have my eyes on millionaires or their children at least. Dayo works in the same place as me. We earn almost the same salary. Yes, he has a car and a nice house, but that's not enough, Tiwa. I can't stoop low or start managing. I don't even feel anything for him, so there's no need for all this stress,' she surmised before breathing loudly as if she had thought about it for a while.

'He's just at the beginning of his career, Zainab. We both know how hardworking he is. You can't just judge his life and financial stability at the beginning. If that's the only thing keeping you from being happy with him, then I don't think it's a valid enough reason,' I countered hoping our voices weren't loud enough for them to hear us from the living room.

'You can't understand where I'm coming from because you have a wealthy boyfriend,' she retorted and I felt suddenly disappointed.

'Really?

'So you think I'm that shallow? Do you know what background I came from? Of course, you do because I've told you. Do you think I'm comfortable with being with someone so wealthy that sometimes I wonder if I will ever be accepted by his family? Do you think it's easy just because he's wealthy? Do you think…'

'I'm sorry. I don't think any of those. I'm sorry, Tiwa. My words came out wrongly. I just… I'm scared of how I feel. He's just so different from my typical kind of guy. Everything about him is different, well except for the fact that he's so attractive but everything else.'

I waited for her to finish washing her hands before I went to hold them.

'I'm not trying to rush you into anything. I'm only trying to help you see what's right in front of you. But don't push it for now, okay? I'm sorry if I tried too hard. Thank you for inviting me to meet your siblings today, it means a lot to me.' I explained, and she pulled me in for a tight hug.

'I'm coming to join that hug.'

I heard Fareeda's voice before I felt her arms come around us.

'I can smell something burning,' Mustapha's loud voice came from the parlour.

We quickly retreated, laughing loudly as Zainab hurriedly turned off the gas. When we got to the parlour, Dayo hugged Zainab.

'It's good to see you, I was beginning to think you were hiding in the kitchen,' he teased and Zainab laughed. 'Why would I hide? Would you like to eat now?'

'Yes please' Mustapha said and I laughed.

'Not you, ode. Go and serve your food yourself,' she said.

‘Sure, thank you’ Dayo said.

Zainab nodded before walking back to the kitchen. Dayo caught me staring at him and he chuckled as he shook his head. We spent the next few hours talking about the wedding and choosing an adequate venue. This was so new to me but I welcomed the feeling wholeheartedly. So, this was what having siblings felt like.

‘Have you ever been a bridesmaid?’ Fareeda asked me cheekily.

‘Never!’ I responded without hesitation.

I had never been close enough to anyone to go to their wedding talk less of being a bridesmaid. I was too much of a loner and it still felt strange that I had made new friends in such a short while.

‘Do you mind being one of mine? I can reserve an extra spot for you,’ she said and I felt my eyes beginning to tear up.

‘Wow, really? Are you sure?’ I asked and she nodded.

‘More than sure, consider us your siblings too.’

‘Not me, please. We can’t be siblings,’ Mustapha said and everyone laughed loudly.

‘You never give up, do you?’ Zainab exclaimed.

She definitely found humour in this from the way she was smiling. My phone rang and I couldn’t contain my joy when I saw who it was. I stood up and went to Zainab's bedroom but not without hearing Zainab tell them it was probably Femi that called.

'Hey, babe! I'm so sorry I've not called you,' he pleaded.

'It's fine, babe! I've just missed you, that's all' I replied.

'Handling my mother is not easy but guess what?' He asked excitedly.

'What?' I asked.

'I told her I'm with someone else and she said she wants to meet you.'

My heart leapt rapidly at his words. Not because I was joyful but because I was suddenly so nervous.

'Really when?' I managed to speak up.

'Tomorrow,' he said.

'Just calm down. I'm sure it wouldn't be so bad,'

Zainab said from behind me as she zipped up my dress. I was a nervous wreck. I had no idea how today would go with Femi's mother. So many things were happening at once. We still had scary matters to solve but the police still hadn't gotten back to me. I was sure Femi would have told me of any new updates but that didn't stop my paranoia.

'Tiwa, are you there?'

I didn't realise I had zoned out till I saw Zainab who was now in front of me.

'I'm sorry. I'm trying to calm down. It's so difficult, I honestly don't know what I'm doing. So many things are happening at once. I still have a stalker case hanging and as much as I tried to ignore it for a day, it's still always at the back of my head. I'm not sure if I can handle Femi's mother, especially' I said, feeling a tiny sense of relief that I had let it out.

'You already agreed to meet her. It's just your nerves talking. You've got this, okay? He's going to be here soon and I'm sure this dress will get you into his mother's favour,' she beamed and I rolled my eyes.

'As stupid as you just sounded, I'm really hoping that happens,' I retorted as I stared at the mirror.

It was a burgundy dress. The top part fitted but the downside was pleated. It looked pretty but very decent. Zainab had borrowed me because I hadn't packed for a dinner. I was really lucky it fitted. She said she had got it when she was slimmer and had kept it to remind her of the good old days. Sometimes, she spoke as if she was in her sixties. I didn't even see this coming.

'I assure you it will, when is he…'

The sound of my phone ringing cut her short. 'He's probably here,' I said as I picked up my phone.

'Hey, baby. Ready?' He asked.

I shook my head knowing fully well that he couldn't see me.

'Sure, I will be out now' I said as I ended the call.

'Thanks for letting me spend the night. Tell Fareeda bye for me when she gets back from the store. Mustapha too, when you find out where he went to.'

'Don't mind him. He doesn't ever stay in one place, but yes I will. Have fun, okay? Call me if you need anything.'

She hugged me tightly and I turned to go but I needed to say something else.

'Please talk to Dayo, okay?'

I didn't wait for a response before leaving. The ride to Femi's apartment was a little bit slow because of the heavy traffic. I was glad because that gave me more time to compose myself. I knew he could tell that I was nervous from the way his hand occasionally moved to hold my thigh comfortingly.

'It will go well, Tiwa. Apart from the fact that you look amazing, she will realise how smart and loving you are. It's pretty hard to miss,' he reassured me softly.

'I hope so. I don't have any parents for you to meet, I have just yours. I'm really hoping it goes well you know' I replied and he nodded.

'I understand. We're here now.'

Hearing that increased my heartbeat rate. He held my hands as we walked from the car park to the house. I was grateful for that because I needed comfort.

'I had some of my housekeepers come over because she's around. You know I don't have time for all this mass cooking' I smiled nervously.

'Yes, I figured you would have them over' I responded.

When we got to the door of the living room, he kissed me softly.

'You will be fine okay,' he said and I nodded.

She sat by the fireplace. She held a punch newspaper which she dropped immediately after she sighted us.

'You're back' she said as she stood up.

It was then that I noticed how much Femi looked like her, although she was quite short. Femi must have gotten his height from his father. She was wearing a black long dress and her nails were done in a bright red colour.

'Mum, this is Tiwa,' Femi said as his hands went around me.

'Good day ma, it's nice to meet you.'

I bent my knees as I greeted her hoping I wouldn't fall because of my high heels.

'Good day to you too. You are beautiful indeed,' she said.

But she looked so intimidating that I wasn't sure if that was a good sign. She wasn't smiling either, her face was hard to read. The way she looked at me made me feel like I was under scrutiny.

'Thank you ma. You're beautiful as well,' I said hoping my voice didn't sound as shaky as I felt.

'You're welcome. Paulina should be done with the food by now, shall we go to the dining?' She asked and I nodded.

'Paulina!'

An elderly-looking woman in an apron came from the kitchen immediately.

'Yes ma! Good afternoon Mr Femi, you too ma,' she said courteously and I smiled not really used to being referred to as ma.

'Our guest is here. Please have the table served' Femi's mum said before walking towards the table.

'Just breathe, baby. I'm with you,' Femi whispered to me.

I smiled at him, grateful for the constant reassurance.

'So Tiwa, Femi tells me you work for him,' she mentioned.

'Yes ma,' I replied.

She nodded as she drank from her apple juice.

'So how long have you guys been together for?' She asked.
I tried my best to chew my chicken quickly so I could answer.
'Almost six months now,' I answered.

She nodded as if a thought suddenly occurred to her.

'That's not really long. I guess you and Amara were still in love not that long ago.'

'Mother, please' Femi warned as his hand held my knee from under the table.

'I'm only saying. You don't have to be so defensive, son' She turned her attention to me.

'So Tiwa, what does your father do?'

I expected that question but now that it was out there, it was difficult to answer a question I didn't know the answer to.

'Well, I don't know who my dad is, I…'

'What do you mean you don't know?' She insisted.

'I've never met him, I'm adopted,' I said.

I was not sure how true that was. My mother never went through legal adoption. She had me as a baby, so everyone easily assumed she was my mother.

'I'm sorry to hear that. What about your adoptive parents then?'

'Mum, can you stop with these questions? It's beginning to sound like you're investigating, not trying to know her' Femi said defensively.

'Well, how do you expect me to get to know her without asking about her family?' She responded.

I held Femi's hand trying to assure him that it was fine.

'I only had a mother. She died years ago' I replied.

'You poor thing, so there's no one that the family will meet if your relationship with Femi goes further? Uncles, Aunties?' She probed.

'No, I don't have anyone.'

I was on the brink of tears and I kept praying silently that they wouldn't drop.

'I'm sorry about that, it definitely complicates things further. Femi has such a big family, his ex-girlfriend did too. I hope you can handle it since you probably have no idea what a family is.'

I heard Femi's chair scrape the floor as he stood up. 'She's not going to tell you she's uncomfortable with the questions out of respect for you and me. But I'm not going to just sit here and watch you talk to her this way, mum.'

His voice was a little loud, and I suddenly felt worse. She would probably hate me more for this.

'Femi please sit down,' I pleaded but his eyes were on his mother.

'My God! Son, I'm doing this for you. I didn't say anything wrong did I? Do you really think this will last? What do you know about her? Do you even love her?'

'I love her and that's why I'm not going to watch you talk to her this way,' he responded and my heart stopped.

He just said he loved me. I had been waiting to hear that so much but obviously not in this way. What if he only said it to stop his mum from being rude to me?

'I remember you telling Amara how much you loved her repeatedly the last time I was with you both. You've not said it once in this dinner,' his mum replied as she wiped the edges of her mouth with a serviette.

'Because I did love her then. You weren't throwing questions at her like you are now with Tiwa and that dinner was two years ago, mum. I don't love her anymore. I love Tiwa now and it's either you accept that or…'

'Or what, Femi,' she asked.

At this point, my tears had dropped. I couldn't hold them anymore. Her phone rang and Femi pulled me to walk away with him.

'I'm so sorry, baby! I'm sorry!' he whispered to me.

'Wait, dinner isn't done yet. Your brother is here,' his mum said.

I felt Femi's anger increase a thousandfolds from the way his hands held me tightly.

'I'm sorry. What? Did you tell Dapo to come here? We need to leave, Tiwa'.

'You're going nowhere. I'm your mother! Do you want to keep disrespecting me Femi? In front of this girl? You both are my sons and I choose to have dinner with you,' she blurted out as she stood up too.

I felt so uncomfortable being in this situation, I wanted to leave but I didn't want her to resent me more.

'Let's stay please, for me?' I begged him silently.

He stood at a spot for a while before sighing loudly and going back to sit down.

'Thank you. He's here,' she said at the sound of incoming footsteps.

She walked towards Dapo who Femi refused to turn around to see. This was going to be a long day.

Chapter Twenty-six

I felt like I belonged

'I hope I'm not too late' Dapo asked as I watched him hug his mother.

'Not really. In fact, you came at the right time,' she replied him chirpily as if she and her other son didn't just have an argument.

'Come to the table. Your food will be served soon' She turned her direction towards the kitchen.

'Paulina!' She called the woman's name so loud that you would think she was millions of miles away.

'Mum, I'm not hungry. I only came to see you,' Dapo remarked as he came over to the large dining.

'What do you mean you're not hungry? You have to eat.'

Paulina had already come with a large tray of food and I watched Dapo sit across from Femi who was still fuming. He was struggling to control his anger and I was beginning to regret making him stay. Maybe I should have left with him.

'Hey, Tiwa! I hope I'm not intruding,' Dapo smiled at me.

I struggled to see a resemblance between him and his mother as I did with Femi.

'Of course not! It's your brother's home' I said casually.

'Well, that doesn't mean I'm wanted' he riposted.

But the response was obviously for Femi who was still quiet. I patted his thigh lightly hoping to help him calm down.

'So Dapo, you've met Tiwa before,' their mother said.

'I've seen her a few times. So it's a yes,' he responded. 'And what do you think about her?' She probed.

I was beginning to feel like I was in my own world and not in front of them because they were talking about me like I wasn't here.

'I think she's beautiful and amazing, mother. At least I can support my brother's decision on this one which is very rare,' he remarked.

I was in between expressing my gratitude and yelling at him to stop trying to get on Femi's nerves.

'I can't stand you being here,' Femi said sternly.

'I'm here for mum not you,' Dapo responded.
'I'm not going to watch you both go back and forth. What do you think your father would do if he were here?' She yelled.

'You shouldn't have invited him,' Femi replied coldly.

'Why are you like this to your brother? What did he do to you?' She sighed loudly and I suddenly wanted to leave.

'Yes, bro! What did I do?' Dapo asked.

This wasn't something I should witness.

'I think I should go,' I managed to say and all eyes turned on me.

'It's good that you know your place. Only family should witness such havoc,' she responded and my gut clenched with pain.

'I really can't handle this. I'm leaving too.'

Femi stood up from his chair, our hands still locked together.

'You're going nowhere,' his mother warned but Femi was adamant.

'I love you mum but I need to go.'

'You don't have….'

'Shhh! You are coming with me,' he cut me short.

He walked away so fast that if he wasn't holding me firmly, I would have fallen.

'This is your home, where do you want to go to?' I asked him when we got outside.

Now I was certain that his mother loathed me. Not only was I without a family, but I also made her son walk out from her. I knew today could go bad but this was way worse than I had anticipated.

'We would have gone to yours but it's not safe. So let's go to my apartment' he said casually.

'Just how many buildings do you have Femi? I asked and he laughed.

'Not many' he said.

The building was huge but not as big as his other place. The living room was bigger than my whole house.

'I stayed here when I first moved to Calabar. Many of my new business ideas came right here,' he explained.

The couch was black, similar to the one in his house. The floor was tiled and there was a big flat-screened TV on the wall.

'How long did you stay here for?' I asked him as I walked towards the small dining. It was a table of four and the chair looked so comfortable that I couldn't help but sit on it.

'A few months. I think four actually,' he replied and I nodded as I enjoyed the comfort of the chair.

I stood up and walked to the kitchen. It was the most empty kitchen I had ever seen. It only had empty pans and plates which looked like they hadn't been touched in years. But that was expected.

'It looks really clean though,' I said as I kept looking around. Nothing was in the cupboards except a lighter and a cereal that I was certain had expired.

'Yeah, someone occasionally cleans it.'

'True, I should have thought of that,' I teased.

His lips were curved in a smile as he pulled me in for a tight hug.

'I love being here with you.'

Hearing the word love suddenly reminded me of what had happened earlier today. He had said he loved me and I wasn't sure if it was true or just a ruse. But thinking about it made me feel so close to him than I ever had.

'What's on your mind?' He asked.
'Oh, nothing. Just thinking about how much your mother must hate me now,' I said. It wasn't entirely a lie because I was thinking about that too.

'I'm sure she doesn't, but I understand your feeling that way. She gets on my nerves sometimes. She's a handful. I'm sorry she acted that way towards you, baby. I didn't think it would be so bad.'

I could tell he was beating himself up about it even if it wasn't his fault.

'Thank you for standing up for me. It's not your fault. I guess she's just being a protective mother,' I said.

'This discussion is making us gloomy, let's change it. Are you hungry?' He asked and I shook my head.

'I'm not, I just ate, remember?'

'Yes true, you want to go to bed then? It's a three bedroom so you can pick a room,' he said.

'Actually, I don't mind sleeping with you' I replied.

His eyebrows rose at my words and I realised how my words came out.

'I mean in the same room, not in that way.'

'I know what you meant, come let's go to bed.'
He held my hand as we both walked to his bedroom. It wasn't as huge as the one in his house, but it was beautiful. The king-sized bed looked so comforting that I wouldn't have minded sleeping in it for days. There was a mahogany desk at the other end of his room and I imagined him sitting on the chair while thinking of all his business ideas.

'Here, you can sleep with this.'

He handed me a shirt from his closet. It smelt like him and I smiled as I took it and went into his bathroom. I showered as quickly as I could, feeling nervous because he was in the room. When I came out of the shower dressed in just his shirt, he wasn't inside. I wanted to look around for him but I felt so weak that I found myself laying on his bed.

I was almost asleep when he came back fully showered in just his sweatpants. I suddenly became awake and sat up. He smiled as he came to sit on the bed beside me. His hand moved to hold mine and I found myself kissing him. He picked me up and placed me on his thighs.

'I meant it you know,' he said.

His eyes were dark with desire and an unfathomable emotion.

'Meant what?' I asked him softly.

His hands moved to caress my face as he gazed at me.

'I do love you. I don't know how or when, all I know is I've felt it for a while now and it took my mother acting up for me to say it. I guess I didn't want to throw it at you with everything that has been happening. I have this burning urge to protect you. I miss you when you're not with me. I think about you every second. I can't stand seeing you in pain. It breaks me, Tiwa. Everything about you pulls me in.'

He kept gazing at me so lovingly that I couldn't bring myself to speak. These were words that I wouldn't mind hearing every day.

'I love you Tiwa in a way that I can't explain,' he continued.

It felt like I hadn't heard it before. If I thought I had been shocked earlier today, that was nothing compared to how elated I felt right now.

'I love you too Femi, in a way that I can't explain.'

He smiled so widely in a way that I didn't see before, but it was short-lived because he kissed me hard and I found myself giving in. I suddenly wanted to let go. I felt safe. I felt loved. I felt like I belonged.

When it came to sexual activities, I was way more sensitive than the average person. The reason was obvious, it came with endless thoughts of everything negative. It was draining and depressing. However, right then with Femi, all I could think about was that I wanted what we were doing to go further. I didn't want to stop. He dove his tongue into my mouth and I welcomed it wholeheartedly.

There was a sudden sound of lightning and heavy rain which made me yearn for him more. He stood up with his hands on my waist and placed me gently against the wall. My blood was pounding in my veins and almost as loud as the sound of the heavy rain. I could feel the budge beneath me as he pressed himself against me.

'I think we should stop now if you don't want this to go any further,' he stated as he nipped at my neck.

'I don't want to stop,' I responded, gasping when his hand moved to hold my breasts.

My nipples were hard and I felt like I was going to come undone when he pulled my shirt above my nipples because I knew what was coming. He moved away from the wall and placed me gently on the bed. His breaths were raspy and it was then that I noticed how long his eyelashes were, almost twice as long as mine.

'You're so beautiful. I could look at you all day,' he said as he stared at me from where he stood.

'I was going to tell you the same,' I said nervously, and he smiled.

I could feel him, the hardness of him, and the muscles I yearned to touch daily.

'Are you sure? I don't want to hurt…'

I shut him up with my mouth, loving the way his lips always seemed to be ready for mine. The need to be touched, taken, and given overwhelmed me.

'You won't help me get rid of the memories. Let me start afresh with you,' I uttered.

My words seemed to get rid of all his doubts because he began to touch and kiss me everywhere. All the way from my forehead to my toes, my belly, the top of my panties, and my thighs. I was hungry for him, and my clit ached in ways that they never had.

I hadn't been touched this way before. It felt as if I couldn't be close enough to him. When his lips grabbed a nipple, I felt like I was going to burst from so much sensation. His fingers moved to take off my underwear and I opened up my legs for him, eager for what was to come.

I wanted to feel him too. I moved to grab the edge of his sweatpants and he withdrew to take it off. He was naked under, his rigid length stood before me, the tip slimy with moisture and I was eager to taste it but he pushed me back to the bed, with his mouth going to my nipple. A small sound escaped me when I felt his finger inside me. It felt uncomfortable at first and he paused for seconds as if waiting for me to give him the go-ahead. I nodded and his fingers began to move. I moaned not so subtly this time as he touched my delicate, aching flesh.

He moved his fingers and I didn't have enough time to complain about the sudden loss because he replaced it with his tongue. I was haywire, and I gasped as he did wonders, feeling a bundle of sensations that I had never felt before. It didn't take too long before I found myself convulsing, my legs shaking as I came undone. His eyes moved to mine and he knew what I wanted without me having to say it but he asked anyway.

'Are you sure?'

I nodded. I had never been this certain about anything before.

'I need you,' I responded.

He kissed me softly before opening the drawer beside the bed. He picked up a condom which he handed to me. I smiled nervously.

'I've never done this before,' I expressed.

But I opened it and rolled it over his hard length. He gritted his teeth as he eased softly inside me. My clit was throbbing, but I wanted him. 'I'm sorry that it hurts' he said as he moved slowly.

I opened my legs wider hoping he would get the hint. He did and we both groaned and cried out our names as he increased his pace. It went on again and again till another rush explored through me. I felt him lose it, his eyes closing as he came.

'I love you so much, Tiwa. I do,' he whispered as his head rested on my chest.

'I love you too, Femi.'

With life, you could never get it all. At least my own life had made that clear. I was having the most memorable moment of my life. I had just made love to a man I was so in love with and it had been beautiful. But the universe was definitely not in tune with this.

'There's been an update on the case,' Femi said as he picked up his call.

The call had chosen to come at this moment to turn a memorable moment into a horrible one. I looked at Femi as he answered the call.

'What do you mean it's difficult? Commissioner Orji, I believe I have been compensating you. You don't seem to be doing enough.'

He stood up and paced around the room. His face was drawn into a thin line and I asked for him to place the call on loudspeaker but he was too agitated to notice. He was naked and even if this was the first time I would see him this way, it felt like I had always been this comfortable with him.

'This is serious. What are you insinuating? I can't believe this. Do you want me to focus my case on you instead? Then watch what you say. One week. That's all I'm going to give. No, you can't change my mind. Goodbye, commissioner Orji.'

He ended the call and ran his hands through his face.

'What's wrong?' I asked even if I could easily guess.

'He said they can't find the person. Fuck it! He said he doesn't even have a suspect.'

He sat down and I sat up, pulling the duvet to cover my chest. 'Is that why you're so mad?' I asked.

His frown deepened as he kept staring at the wall.

'The stupid man had the guts to say that you could have done it yourself because you were trying to get my attention.'

He paused for a second.

'He said that's women for you.'

I sighed not disappointed because I had no regard for the Nigerian police anyway. They had ridiculed me so much in the past already that I always expected the worst from them.

'I know you told me to not rely on them, but I just needed to. It was the right thing to do,' he said softly.

My hand instinctively moved to hold his face as I drew myself closer to him.

'Don't beat yourself about it. We will sort it out, okay? I just need to be more careful. I'm trying to find another apartment so I don't have to go to my present one. I'm scared it will give me nightmares,' I chuckled in an attempt to ease my nerves.

'You can stay here you know. I can help you get your things from there. You don't have to go back,' he said.

But I shook my head. He had done so much for me already. He gave me a job, I couldn't also rely on him for a place to stay.

'You know I'm not going to accept it,' I replied.

He sighed loudly.

'It didn't hurt to try,' he murmured and I smiled.

'But you can't stop me from helping you look for a new one,' he protested and I nodded knowing he wasn't going to take any other answer.

'Sure, I would love your help,' I responded.

He bent to kiss me softly and I kissed him back.

'Thank you for allowing me to be with you. I don't deserve it but the way I feel about you is too strong for me to let you go.'

He kept kissing my face as he spoke sweetly to me.

'I love you, Femi. You've also helped me to have a better memory of what it feels like to make love,' I responded, trying my best to not let my tears drop.

'I'm glad and may no one else take my place,' he said and I laughed.

'Never, not now at least.' I assured him keenly.

'I hope it's never because I'm here to stay and I'm not going anywhere in case you all are having ideas,' he continued, his eyes moving around the room like there were people around us.

'Femi, we're the only ones here,' I said as I giggled.

'It doesn't matter, baby' he responded sweetly.'

You know those tears I was worried about before? Well, they came at that moment, but it was fine because this time they weren't because I was sad. They were happy tears.

Chapter Twenty-seven

A Long Ride

THE FIRST TIME I EVER thought about having sex was when I was fifteen. My love for romance novels had been the source of my wild imagination then. Although I was more into the romance aspect, the feelings involved and the happiness that came with knowing that someone uncontrollably wanted you. All these didn't mean that I never wanted to be touched by a man. I was a teenager and it was only normal that I would. I only never wanted it to be taken away from me forcefully, not in that way. That was never in my plans, never in my imagination. It was the last thing I ever thought would happen to me.

Unfortunately for me, it turned off my hormones in a way that I doubted was possible for any normal living person. For the first few months, I was a shell of myself. I wished I had my own world away from every man. I had no male specie that was dear to me so that made it easier. Every male was a suspect. Every touch from them stung, it was horrible, devastating, and heart-wrenching. It still amazed me that it was beginning to change, especially when I least expected it.

The next morning was a bundle of activities. Femi had to hurry to see his mother because she had suddenly decided to leave earlier. He was hesitant to go because he didn't want to leave me after our first night together but I insisted he did. She was his mother, after all, and I already felt terrible enough about the day before.

The sun shone brightly through the windows despite them being covered by the lace curtain. It was a Sunday and it always lived up to its name. I checked the time on my phone and realised it was just past noon. I had slept back after Femi left and it had been just an hour ago. I felt a little sore from last night and this morning. Obviously, we didn't just stop last night. It was like Femi was trying to make up for all the time we took.

I was in the shower when my phone rang. I was worried it was Femi and he would need me to get into his apartment but then I remembered he took the spare keys. It had stopped ringing when I came out of the shower but then it rang again. It was an unsaved number. I contemplated between ignoring it and finding out who it was. But with recent events, that didn't seem like the best idea. When my phone rang again, I decided to pick it up.

'For someone who seemed ready to help, it's beginning to feel like you've changed your mind' Dapo's voice sounded the same on the phone.

I had genuinely forgotten that I had told him I wanted to get him and his brother together.

'I'm sorry. I've been quite busy,' I pleaded.

I was beginning to have goose bumps because the room felt too chilly from the air conditioner.

'I know Femi is on the way to the airport with our mother, so I felt this would be a good time to call,' he said as if expecting me to thank him.

All I could think about was my guilt for doing this behind Femi's back. I shouldn't be keeping this from him. I could imagine the look on his face when he finally finds out.

'Thank you for that. I'm going to save your number. I will get back to you when I'm ready,' I assured as I searched for the remote to the Air-Conditioner before my body froze to death.

'Don't take too long because I might have changed my mind by then. Bye for now,' he said as he ended the call.

I sighed loudly, feeling exhausted from everything around me. I felt as if I had too many things to do. I hadn't gotten any new threats or scary outcomes since the one in my apartment and I wasn't sure if that was a good or bad sign. Was the person giving up because they knew the police were watching? That's even if they were. Or maybe the person was waiting for the next possible time. The latter sounded more pleasant and as much as I wished that was it, I knew it wasn't.

Femi came two hours after. He said there had been heavy traffic and he had stopped to get groceries so I wouldn't be hungry. The irony was that I had already gone grocery shopping myself because the emptiness of his kitchen felt too odd. I had made his favourite soup and despite me knowing how good of a cook I was, I still felt nervous as I waited for him to taste it.

'Do you like it?' I asked as he swallowed the *poundo yam*. His wide smile was enough answer for me.

'I love it. This is going to give my mother a run for her money. How are you so good at everything?' He asked as he bit into his meat.

I rubbed his back tenderly as I watched him eat.

'I learnt from my mum,' I answered softly.

'Oh, I can imagine how much of an amazing cook she must have been. This is heaven. Come eat with me,' he said but I shook my head.

'I can serve myself. This is for you,' I responded but he shook his head as he patted the chair beside me.

'I insist'

I didn't argue anymore and decided to eat with him. I had tasted the soup and it was delicious but eating it with the *poundo yam* was something else. We engaged in pleasant conversation as we ate and it felt like everything was right in the world.

'I love being here with you. It feels like we're in our own world' Femi said.

I laid on his thigh that evening, with his hands stroking my face tenderly.

'Me too. I wish Monday wasn't so close' I groaned and he chuckled.

'We can ditch work. I'm the boss, remember? I'm not going to fire you,' he said and I sat up.

'That's even worse' I replied, especially as I was still trying to convince myself that it was okay that I was dating my boss.

'It's not. You just need to get used to the fact that you're dating your boss, babe' he smirked in that devilish way of his. 'I don't think I ever will,' I insisted.

'Then you're just torturing yourself because this is going to be a long ride,' he said as he bent to kiss me.

I kissed him back wholeheartedly, with his words ringing in my head over and over again. This was going to be a long ride.

'I guess I can try to get used to it,' I said and he laughed loudly before joining my lips with his again.

It was the fifth of November, three days before my birthday. I felt neutral as always. I hadn't celebrated my birthday since my mother died. I had no one to celebrate with and it felt too much like our tradition. She usually baked me a cake herself which we would share with the neighbours. Then she would cook me all sorts of food, most of them were meals that we hardly ate because they were expensive to make. She would make me catfish pepper soup and isi-ewu. Thinking about it made my lips water. I loved my birthdays at that point in my life, but after I lost her they made me miserable.

I hadn't told Femi yet but I didn't really want to because it wasn't necessary. Why tell him when I wasn't excited about it anyway? And I was feeling guilty because today was my meeting with Dapo. I kept pushing away the thought that this was a mistake. But I had already made the plans, so it was too late to cancel.

I hadn't moved to my new apartment yet because I hadn't found one. I was still in Femi's apartment but my plan was to move by the end of the week. That meant my birthday. It was the little thing I could do for myself. Zainab recommended me to this home agency but I was still considering if I could afford their rent. They were higher than my last one but at least they came with better security. I only needed to have a better budget. I also needed to finish my novel so I could at least get extra money from it. That is if it was even good enough.

When I got downstairs, Dapo's car was waiting for me.

'Good evening,' I said as I got into his car.

It felt so chilly inside because of the air conditioner.

'Morning, let me reduce the AC,' he offered as I strapped on my seat belt.

'So it's nice of you to do this. Where is Femi right now?' He asked as he started driving.

I felt nervous, stupidly nervous. What the hell was I doing? Why couldn't I mind my own business? This was foolish of me.

'He has a business dinner to go for. He will be back in three hours, so that's how much time we have,' I replied, hoping I didn't sound as frightened as I felt.

'That's more than enough time. But wait? How are we going to do this anyway? How do you intend to get me back with my brother?' He asked me the multi-million-dollar question.

'I just need to know the roots of the problem. I can't talk to him about it because he won't tell me anything about you both. I don't even think this is right, maybe we shouldn't' I said softly.

He shook his head as we got closer to the Cafe.

'It's too late to stop now. Let's just get it done with,' he countered and I nodded in an attempt to convince myself too.

'Aren't you going to order anything?' He asked.

I looked up from the small menu, my eyes moving to the waitress beside us. We sat in the Trinas Cafe. It was quiet because most people came here to study or have business meetings. Their menu had very limited food options which was understandable. I decided to order the first thing I saw.

'A sandwich is fine,' I said and she nodded.

'Still thinking twice about this?' Dapo asked for the third time since he picked me up.

'It's fine. Let's just continue so I don't feel like I wasted my time to come here. When did your problems start with Femi?' I asked him.

'It's been years now. We were just teenagers then,' he said fondly. 'I see, what about your sister?' I asked.

The question definitely didn't sit well with him because he suddenly became uncomfortable.

'I've not seen her in years, three to be exact. She's not a fan of mine,' he explained.

I listened attentively, trying to think of a reason why three siblings would have such a horrible relationship.

'That's sad. Why is it so bad between you three?' I queried.

He shifted uncomfortably in his seat, his eyes moving to behind me. The waitress arrived with our order. I thanked her as I collected my tuna sandwich.

'It's complicated' Dapo said as he drank from his coffee.

The steam that came from it was so visible that it amazed me how he was able to drink it so swiftly and without flinching.

'Well, isn't everything complicated? Fine, let's talk about Femi alone. Why are you both this way? It's almost like he hates you,' I said as I watched his face darken from my bluntness.

'Well, maybe not hate you but something close to that,' I added, trying to ease the sting.

'No, it's fine. He does hate me. I mean it's glaring' he chuckled sadly.

'It was nine years ago. We went to a party. Me, Femi, and our sister. She was just thirteen. I was seventeen, practically an adult. Femi was…'

'Fifteen' I said from my own calculations.

'Yes,' Dapo nodded before taking another gulp of his coffee.

'Whose party was it?' I asked.

'It was a friend of mine, my best friend then actually,' he replied, his eyes closing for a second, probably at the memory.

'I'm guessing it didn't go well?' I asked, more curious than ever before.

'Not going well is an understatement, it was horrible. I shouldn't have gone. I shouldn't have taken them there. That was the biggest mistake of my life,' he noted.

He drank another huge gulp of his coffee this time and I was almost certain the cup was almost empty.

'Why? Did anything happen?' I asked him even if the answer was pretty obvious.

'Well, I…I'm sorry I can't do this,' he said before standing up hurriedly.

He brought a huge load of cash from his pocket and dropped it on the table.

'Where are you…'

I didn't finish my question because he walked away before I could. I stared in oblivion, reliving the fact that he had just left me here at the café. I was dumbfounded.

'What just happened?' I whispered to myself.

If anything was supposed to have gone wrong, this was way out of my expectations. I looked at the one thousand naira notes on the table. This was the waitress' lucky day. I raised my hands and called her over.

'This is yours,' I said.

She looked at me with eyes so wide that I feared they would burst. She kept muttering loads of thank you that I had to leave to think of what next to do. I couldn't believe he had left me here stranded. Maybe I had gone too far, but he had appeared to be fine with my questioning. What happened must have been so horrible or did he hurt them? There were so many questions. It made me more curious. I sighed loudly as I stared at the moving cars around me. I still had an hour more because Femi wouldn't be back till nine pm. The sun had already set and it was pretty dark. I needed to get a taxi or a bike to get home before he did.

I stood for about ten minutes without seeing a taxi that wasn't full. I decided to walk a little bit more to another junction. Maybe I would find one there. I was just about to cross to the other side of the road when someone grabbed me. Not grab, it felt like my neck was being pulled out of my body. He was quiet this time.

'Please, who are you?' I pleaded but he didn't say anything.

People say bad memories cause great pain but right now it was the thought that I would have to experience that bad memory again that wrecked me. I tried to scream but no one could hear me because no sounds came out. He pulled me with him to a dark alley. No one was close by, and I suddenly wanted to throw up. In fact, I needed to, maybe that would make him leave me, at least just for a second. That was all I needed to try to flee.

'What do you want from me?' I managed to say, wishing I could see his face.

He had the same mask on and there was something familiar about him but I couldn't connect him with anyone. He pushed me closer to him, his hands had already moved to grab my right breast so forcefully that I yelled in pain. He hit my head against the wall. The pain that came from it was so overwhelming that I suddenly felt dizzy. He used his other arm to grab both my wrists.

'Please don't do this to me again,' I pleaded, my tears already falling rapidly.

He removed his hand from my breast but my relief was short-lived because he started undoing the button of my pants. As it was in the past, I was no match for his physical strength. My only chance of hurting him would be if I scratched him or had some sort of weapon but he was holding my wrist anyway.
I cried as I realised I was out of depth. I couldn't get out of this hell hole. My mind went to Femi, how would he handle this? I thought of Dapo who had left me but it wasn't his fault too. It was mine, I had this darkness that never seemed to let me be. Ever since I had been born, my own parents even had to give me away in a cowardly manner. Why was I in this life again? My wrists were burning from the tight grasp.

'Please no, not again. I'm begging you. Whatever you want, I will give. Please don't damage me any further. I wouldn't be able to handle it. It would kill me.'

I begged but it only made him more aggressive. He punched my stomach so forcefully that the impact left me breathless. I was in so much pain that moving my body felt like torture. But I couldn't just be still this time, I needed to fight back. I needed to. I could do this. He succeeded in removing the button on my pant, and he pushed his fingers inside. He must have thought I was too weak to fight back because he let go of my wrist which he held tightly with his other hand to grab my breast again. I kicked his balls so forcefully and used my nails to scratch his neck so deeply at the same time. He let out a scream as he withdrew from the impact. I didn't hesitate. I ran as quickly as I could manage, the middle part of my body feeling like lead. I was in so much pain, but I withheld.

He didn't run after me. I don't know why but it felt like a miracle to me. I ran and ran till I got to the main road. There was traffic and still no taxi. I saw a woman walking with her kids. She looked at me, her eyes opening widely as she stared at me. It was dark except for the lights that came from the passing cars.

'Please, do you know where I can get a taxi? I need to...'

The floor suddenly swayed beneath me, and the last thing I saw before the darkness overcame me was someone bending over me. When I woke up, I felt a magnitude of pain that I had not felt before. I sat upright and found myself somewhere completely unfamiliar. Everything in the room looked bathed in white, the blankets around me, and the four corner walls. The only colour around me was the blue T-shirt of the lady with her body away from me.

'Zainab?' I managed to say and she turned around so suddenly, her eyes swollen from tears.

'You're awake. I was scared. Thank God! Oh my God, I need to call Femi. He's been worried sick about you. How are you feeling? Does your head hurt? Of course, it does' She kept muttering her eyes moving all over me as if trying to confirm it herself.

'It hurts but I'm okay. How did I get here? Where's Femi?' I asked, the horrible memory coming in full.

My tears flew rapidly as I hugged Zainab tightly.

'It almost happened again. It almost did, Zainab' I explained as I sobbed.

She held me softly, her hands patting my back.

'I know. I'm so sorry, Tiwa. You don't deserve this,' she whispered.

'Let me call Femi,' Zainab said as she stood up to get her phone.

'Where is he?' I asked her.

I was wondering how he would feel if I told him I was with Dapo when this happened. I shouldn't have gone out with him, this was the universe punishing me.

'He's been in the hospital all day. He didn't leave your side, not once, he only left when the police called him about updates. He left with Dayo,' she explained.

I smiled at her happy at what this meant.

'You called him, does that mean it's going well between you guys?' I asked.

'Tiwa!'

We both jumped at Femi's loud voice as he entered the room. The pain that came from moving my body rapidly was so severe that I tried to contain myself. He walked to hug me so tightly as if he forgot my body had just gone through a terrible ordeal. I yelped in pain which had Femi gasping,

'My God, are you okay, Baby? Where's the doctor? Why isn't he here? What the hell is wrong with this hospital? Is everyone so incompetent?' He kept yelling furiously, his eyes dark with fury.

'Just calm down okay? I'm fine, I'm okay. God, must you be so extra?' I asked him softly and he shook his head.

'This is me only being worried about my girlfriend. What the hell happened? I'm such a fool. I should have been with you. I knew I shouldn't have gone for that party. I knew it. It was boring anyway without you. I'm so sorry, Tiwa. I'm…'

'It's not your fault, baby. I'm sorry too for leaving without telling you' I said, knowing the question that would come next.

'Where did you go to? When I got the call from you and heard a strange woman's voice, I was confused but when she said she called the first emergency number she saw, I drove like a madman here. I don't think I've ever been that frightened. I don't want to ever go through that again,' he said as he placed his forehead on top of mine.

'Who was it? Who hurt you? Did you see him?' He asked and I shook my head, my tears falling rapidly.

'I wish I did, but I didn't. It was him, from my past, I'm so sure' I said.

He pulled me tightly, his arms engulfing me more softly this time.

'Where were you?' He asked.

I was about to answer when Dayo walked in with a tray of bottled water.

'Zainab said you needed water,' he said softly.

I didn't say it but I definitely did. I was just about to drink it when the doctor entered.

'How is my patient doing?' He asked as he came in with a nurse who held a tray of injections, plasters, and other things I couldn't name.

'I'm not the best but do I have to take those?'

Femi withdrew from me as I stared at the injections. The doctor smiled kindly as he checked my pulse.

'You need them, but I promise they won't hurt' He responded softly.

'Are you going to tell me where you were?' Femi asked but his expression was soft this time. He was just genuinely worried.

'She was with me.'

We both turned around but my jaw dropped at who we saw. It was Dapo. He stood behind the doctor, his face sombre. I could feel Femi's fury from the way his face changed rapidly. Who told Dapo I was here anyway?

Chapter Twenty-eight

My Whole Being Is Yours

THE TENSION IN THE ROOM increased a thousand folds. Dapo walked further into the room and for someone who left me alone at a restaurant, he looked quite sober. Almost as if he cared about me.

'What are you doing here?' Femi asked, his deep voice stern.

'I needed to check if she was okay,' he replied, not relenting.

'Are you going to tell me why you were with my girlfriend? I mean I've always been so against you coming near her and it seemed like I was just being ridiculous. But the one time you both are together, see what happens. She gets bloody assaulted. She's hurt, Dapo. I don't know what else could have happened if she hadn't been able to escape so fast,' he said angrily.

'I know. I feel guilty about that, okay. I shouldn't have left her there. That was my mistake' Dapo responded.

Zainab kept watching the scene unfold with Dayo by her side. I felt sorry that they had to witness this.

'You know one thing you're fond of? Making mistakes. It's your specialty, your disease, and don't you dare make another one with the girl I love. I don't care if you're my brother, I don't bloody care what it takes but I will…'

'Femi, for heaven's sake, this is not the same thing. Don't compare these two incidents, don't do that. Do you think I've been able to move past it? Do you think you're the only one still hurting? You have no idea how difficult it is to accept that everything was my fault,' he countered.

I watched Dayo place his hand on his shoulder in a quest to calm him. These two brothers had something going on. I wanted to know and didn't want to at the same time.

'I'm sorry but this is a hospital, we have other patients,' the doctor said kindly.

We had all forgotten that he and the nurse were here. Their expressions looked too normal as if they were used to hospital dramas already. I guess being a doctor could be entertaining after all. You get to watch free unedited dramas.

'I'm sorry, Doc! Could you come back later, please? Just give us a few minutes' I asked and he nodded, walking away so quickly like I had just saved him.

'I'm sorry, Tiwa. I shouldn't have left you alone. I guess that ends our meetings. I will see you whenever I see you again,' Dapo uttered as the doctor left.

'What meetings? You won't be seeing her anytime soon,' Femi responded as Dayo walked away, his shoulders had been no longer visible when I spoke.

'You shouldn't have been so mean? Why did you react that way?' I asked Femi.

His expression held so much pain I hadn't noticed. Maybe I had but not in this high voltage. It was heart-wrenching and I wanted him to open up to me.

'What meetings, Tiwa? What were you doing with him?' Femi asked sternly.

'I think we will be leaving now' Dayo said as his hand moved to Zainab's shoulder.

I smiled softly as I witnessed this beautiful sight. At least one good thing was right in the world.

'Thank you so much for coming, I'm grateful,' I said.

Zainab walked over to hug me, at least she was better at remembering that I could only do soft hugs for now.

'Call me if you need anything, okay? I love you so much' She kissed my forehead before also saying goodbye to Femi.

'I hope you get well soon. I will see you at work, boss' Dayo said to Femi who nodded, his eyes not leaving mine.

'Do you want to talk about it?' I asked Femi as they left but he shook his head.

'Not now, I just want you to be okay. The doctor should be…'

'Coming now,' I completed his statement as I watched the doctor and a different nurse come inside.

'Ready now?' He asked and I nodded as Femi sat down on the couch at the other end of the room.

I was discharged way earlier than I expected to be. I was happy because I dreaded hospitals. I had been here so much when my mother was sick that being in one then had brought up so many emotions that I usually loved hiding. It was my luck that they had let me go only a few hours after Zainab and Dayo had left. Femi had asked the doctor a hundred times about his decision to let me go home. The doctor had kept reassuring him that I was fine, I just needed to take my drugs and come back to check on my bruises if they got worse.

Femi carried me all the way upstairs. My eyes were heavy and I felt pain all over. He dropped me on the very soft comfortable king-sized bed and set very comfortable pillows behind my back so I could sit upright.

'You need to eat something. I ordered food for you on our way here because the maid isn't coming over today,' he noted as he watched me tenderly.

'That's fine, thank you,' I replied and he smiled sadly.

The bell rang and I watched him go get the food. Eating the hot pepper soup and rice wasn't so easy. I loved it but as I chewed, my stomach felt like I was being constantly punched. He fed me and didn't complain as I ate very slowly. After I had enough, I drank some water as he held the mug for me.

'I want to shower,' my voice croaked after he had dropped the tray of food.

'I need to clean up you know, wash his hands away. I can feel him all over me,' I whispered and Femi nodded rapidly as he stood up.

He lifted me in his arms and carried me tenderly into the huge bathroom, setting me down slowly before turning on the shower. I was still fully dressed, he held his hands out to help me.

'Let me help you take this off,' he offered as he untied the strings that held my top together.

He had never undressed me before, not like this. I felt self-conscious because of the new scars all over my body. After removing the strings he turned around

'I don't know if you are comfortable with me doing this. I can get you something to wear. You just had a terrible ordeal with another man,' he said softly.

'If you need anything, call me.'

He kissed me softly before walking and closing the door.

'Thank you,' I said feeling grateful.

I needed to wash this myself. I felt insecure and I needed to be alone, even if it was for just a few minutes. I stepped into the shower after shrugging my top and skirt off. The warm water helped my aching muscles and body despite the stings that came from my bruises. There were various soaps and I picked just anyone. The one I chose smelt heavenly, just like Femi and I inhaled it embracing the very familiar scent. It was a breath of fresh air. I washed my body as hardly and softly as I could. Satisfied with how

I felt, I turned off the water and put on a clean white towel, then I heard a knock on the door.

'My Femi' I thought to myself.

He had obviously been waiting at the door in case I needed him, tending to my every need.

'Come in,' I said.

He held up pieces of underwear and a big shirt. I smiled wondering where he got them from.

'I heard the tap go off. Here, which one do you want?' He asked.

He showed me various colours - blue, white, black, red, and pink. I pointed at the black one.

'Where did you get them from?' I asked and he smiled softly.

'My sister had them delivered from her store here. I called her and I asked Zainab for your size.'

I thanked his sister even though I had never met her yet.

'Tell her I said thanks,' I replied.

He nodded before dropping them on a shelf above us, and then he pulled out a new toothbrush from the vanity drawer.

'Here!'

He watched me brush as he stood by the door and I didn't feel uncomfortable. When I finished, he helped me take off my shower cap.

'Let's get you dressed,' he offered.

He brought me the shirt. It was his, I could tell from how big it was. I brought you this very big one so it would be easier to get it past your head.

'You don't have to take your towel off as I help you, it's fine,' he said but I smiled warmly at him.

He had seen the whole of me already but he was trying so much to be understanding that all I wanted was to tell him how much I adored him. I nodded and he helped me wear the shirt which fitted so comfortably. I removed the towel and he grabbed it before handing me my underwear.

'I will turn around so you can wear them,' he said, his lips curved in a smile. He turned around and I found myself grinning too.

'I know this is fun to you,' I teased and he shook his head.

'Nope, just being at your service. I love taking care of you,' he retorted.

I smiled more as my heart melted. I wore the underwear as quickly as I could despite the aching pain in my belly.

'You can turn around now,' I said and he smiled as he stared at my stomach which had my hand on it.

'It hurts really badly, doesn't it?' He asked his face turning more worried.

'It's okay, it will heal,' I assured but he moved closer.

'Can I see the bruises? I just want to look,' he said.

I nodded, swallowing as he raised the shirt, revealing my thighs and panties. I watched his frown deepen as he ran his hands through my stomach.

'I'm sorry I wasn't… I wish… I'm sorry I wasn't with you,' he said clearly struggling.

'Don't blame yourself, it's good you weren't. What if he harmed both of us?' I said teasingly and he chuckled.

'You really have no faith in my fighting skills,' he alleged as he moved to carry me into the bedroom.

'You're not carrying me, it's just steps away.' I protested.

I walked ahead of him. I sat on the bed and realised we were actually in his room. I hadn't paid attention when we first got in.

'I will sleep on the couch,' he said as he walked towards it but I shook my head.

'No, stay with me. Come to bed' I replied.

He smiled before moving towards the bed, his heavenly smell drawing me in. He turned off the lights beside us as I placed my head on his chest.

'Don't think I've forgotten that you were with Dapo. You still have lots of explaining to do when you're better, of course' he said and I sighed.

He obviously wouldn't let it go.

'I haven't forgotten, thank you for being mine,' I rejoined and he kissed my forehead.

'All I want to be is yours and for you,' he said as my eyes drifted close. 'I love the way you care for me,' I responded and he patted my hair softly.

'Get used to it, baby. I'm going to do it always.'

He kissed my forehead again and I snuggled closer to him, feeling at peace now.

'Goodnight, Tiwa. I love you so much. My whole being is yours.'

The next few days involved Femi fawning over me despite me telling him I felt better. It was typical Femi but that didn't make everything easier. Our lives were at risk as long as whoever attacked me was out there. Femi was definitely worried which explained the new security measures he placed in his apartment. He also insisted I never leave the house without him. This wasn't how I wanted to live. Was life really worth it if I continued to live in fear? I couldn't go outside without looking behind me. Going out late felt like putting myself in danger. I was frightened and my anxiety kept me awake.

Femi noticed and I could see how affected he was but I needed him to understand that this wasn't his fault. There was nothing he could do. I had brought this upon him and I would never forgive myself if anything ever happened to him.
It was a Saturday morning, the day of Zainab's sister's wedding. After a mini argument, Femi reluctantly allowed me to sleep over at Zainab's place. He felt it was me exposing myself but he needed to understand that he couldn't watch me every second. Besides, I wanted to experience this. It felt like they were my siblings and I had never been involved in a wedding before. The venue was Coroba Hall, an extremely popular event centre in the State. It had been decorated by the Oribidi wedding planners. It involved four sisters who took over their late mother's business of event planning. She would definitely be proud because they had done a wonderful job. The hall was dazzling with the matching centre pieces. There were beautiful petals and bouquets scattered around the hall.

The wedding involved a small group of family and friends. During the introduction, they told me their names but I could only remember Aisha because of how much of a talker she was. And I meant that in a good way. I was shy when I met new people but she spoke so much that I didn't have to stress myself about what to say next. To me, that was a gem that you hardly came by. The bridesmaids were dressed in purple and white lace. Everyone's dress was the same. I was one of them and I felt like an achiever because this was the closest I had ever been to wedding preparation.

'I'm glad to see you're doing fine.'

I turned around to the very familiar voice behind me. Dapo looked handsome in his three-piece dapper suit. His beard looked fuller than I remembered and his eyes held more depth. He looked like he had aged five years more, not because he wasn't handsome but just because of the visible pain in those eyes of his.

'Thank you, I'm sorry about Femi. He's very protective of me,' I said thankful that Femi had gotten an emergency call which kept him from seeing Dapo talking to me right now.

'As he should be. You really are in danger,' he said and I smiled despite my nerves.

'This isn't the place to be talking about that now, is it?' I replied trying to convince myself as well.

'Baby girl, it's time' Zainab said as she pulled me from Dapo murmuring apologies to him.

'I hope I don't mess this up,' I said as I joined the beautiful ladies at the entrance of the hall.

'You can't mess this up, it's just to walk and dance,' she said.

But her eyes weren't focused on me. They were focused on Dayo her boyfriend. It brought me so much joy to me that two people I cared about were together. They had only started dating a week after Dayo said he couldn't keep his feelings for her away anymore.

'Go meet him' I said to her and she chuckled.

'Don't look at me like that especially when yours is literally on his way to you.'

I turned around and saw Femi walking in fast strides to me, his dark suit making him look like a Greek god. This beautiful man cared for me and loved me and I hoped we get to celebrate our wedding one day.

'Have I told you how stunning you look?' He said as he waved at Zainab who went to meet her boyfriend.

'Yes, but I don't mind hearing it again' I said as I moved to kiss him wholeheartedly.

The music started and I quickly wriggled from Femi, eager to get this wedding started. Zainab's sister looked beautiful in her wedding dress. It was very conservative but beautiful. Her new husband was Christian and she said it had been her choice to have a white wedding because she loved the concept. I couldn't blame her though, it was beyond beautiful.
The reception was amazing with lots of food to eat. I had only drank little wine but I felt lightheaded.

'It was pretty obvious you would be a light head. I know them when I see them,' Femi chuckled as he carried me to his Mercedes Benz at the parking lot.

'I feel fine, just very tired. That's all!' I insisted but he laughed.

'Tomorrow morning will be the judge of that,' he teased as he bent to kiss me and dropped me on the passenger seat.

'Is she okay?' I heard Dayo ask as he handed Femi his phone. My eyes were closed from exhaustion but they must have assumed I was asleep.

'You left your phones with Z,' he said.

'Oh, thank you. She's a little tipsy but she will be fine,' Femi replied.

'I'm glad. Any leads on the culprit?' He asked.

I could feel the alcohol wearing off little by little.

'Not exactly but the police said they're close. I'm just worried about her. He seems really desperate,' Femi said frustratingly

'He must be for him to have done what he did. I hope you find him. Oh, by the way, I saw Dapo talking to your woman. I don't trust him one bit,' Dayo continued.

I was instantly annoyed. Why was everyone against Dapo and who gave him the right to report me to my boyfriend as if I was a child?

'Thanks for letting me know. I need to go now.'

I could hear the anger in Femi's voice and I was so tempted to yell at Dayo for overstepping his boundaries but I also wasn't ready for Femi's scolding.

'I know you're awake,' he said as he started the car.
My eyes opened and moved to his.

'Dapo only wanted to be sure that I was doing good. It wasn't in Dayo's place to tell you what was going on,' I said as I sat up.

'I don't want you talking to him. He could be a danger to you' he warned, as he drove out of the gate.

'Why? I'm not going to stop talking to him until you tell me why,' I protested but he wouldn't relent.

Dapo had told me part of the story but I needed to hear it from Femi's point of view.

'You don't need to know,' he said but I wasn't going to let this go.

'Well, I guess he's my new best friend,' I said stubbornly.

'I'm still not going to tell you.'

'No? Okay then. Don't you dare tell me not to talk to him again! I'm going to talk to him and please don't…'

'He knows who raped our sister,' he yelled as the car almost hit a truck that was right in front of us.

'What?' I said my heart contrasting in my chest. 'Your sister? Are you sure?' I asked him, tears filling my eyes.

'Of course, I am. I didn't find out until two years ago that he knows which of his friends did it which makes me wonder why he kept quiet all this while. For so many years, he watched our sister become a shell of herself. She never wanted to say who raped her but as her brothers, we are supposed to fight for her. Even my mother doesn't talk about it. It's like everyone wants it to be secret but I'm never forgiving him until he tells me who raped her. The person must pay no matter who it is.'

'Oh no. I'm so sorry. Do you think there might be a reason why he hasn't said anything? Have you tried to get your sister to talk? Does she hold the same resentment towards him?' I asked but he shook his head.

'She doesn't seem to but that's just how she is. She says she understands why he can't say anything. But you know what? I've had enough. I need to get to the root of this.'

He turned his car around so quickly that my heart skipped.

'Where are we going to?' I asked him.

'Dapo's house,' he said.

Chapter Twenty-nine

Truth Uncovered

THE DRIVE TO DAPO'S HOUSE took us only thirty minutes. The area was neat and fancy, so Femi had no problem parking his car outside the gate. There was less risk of his car getting vandalised in this area. We had just come out of the car when I spotted another lady getting into Femi's gate. She turned around and I recognised her immediately. She was Femi's sister and the expression on Femi's face at the sight of her was bittersweet.

'What are you doing here?' He asked as she walked closer to us.

She looked beautiful in her grey pants and her expensive-looking white blazer. Her black bone straight fell all the way to the end of her waist and all I could think about was the strength this young lady possessed.

'Femi, I was going to come to see you,' she said as she hugged her brother tightly.

The hug was long, a signal of how long they hadn't seen each other.

'I've missed you so much. I'm hurt you decided to see Dapo before I did,' he protested but her eyes had turned towards my direction.

'Hey, beautiful. I've heard so much about you, the girl who has got my brother star-struck,' she said as she hugged me too.

'It's nice to meet you and thank you for the underwear,' I replied cheerfully and she smiled softly, her hands putting away a lock of her hair.

'It's fine, I'm so sorry you got hurt. Men like that deserve to be locked forever,' she expressed and I could hear the pain in her voice.

'Does Dapo know you are here?' Femi asked gruffly.

'He does,' she nodded.

And as if on cue, Dapo came outside. His eyes widened as he turned to me and then to his brother,

'I wasn't expecting you,' he said to his brother, and as they stood side by side, I saw how physically alike they were.

'We have something to discuss. I'm glad you are here,' he focused on his sister.

Without waiting for Dapo to let us in, Femi entered the gate and everyone followed him. The house was painted white. It was magnificent, a three-storey building. It looked like where royalty would live. I wondered how he was able to get such a huge place for someone who had just recently moved to the country. Well, in Nigeria there was nothing money couldn't do. The gateman greeted us and there was a lady who was dressed in a uniform waiting at the entrance for us.

'Welcome, sir and mas,' she greeted as she opened the door.

For someone who hardly came to his brother's home, he seemed very familiar.

'You still haven't told me what you are doing here,' Dapo remarked.

'I'm not going to waste your time, tell me who raped our sister,' Femi said bluntly and my breath cut.

My eyes went to Kikelomo who looked dumbfounded. She sat down and dropped her bag on the floor.

'Femi, what is this?' She asked, her tears beginning to pour out.

'I need to know. The fellow needs to be punished. I'm tired of seeing you this way. I know you're strong but ever since then, you've had a shell around you. You're no longer the same. Everyone has learnt to live with it but I can't. This is for you. You need closure, sis,' he expressed.

I suddenly felt like I shouldn't be here as this was family business.
'I already told you I can't say. She asked me not to.'

Dapo moved to his mini bar to get a drink. This was my cue,

'I think I should leave. This is a family matter.'

'Stay,' she demanded, her tears already very visible.

'I guess it's time for me to open up. You're right, Femi. I'm not okay. I'm struggling. If only you knew, if only mum allowed me.'

'What do you mean if mum allowed you?' Femi cut in and Dapo looked interested too as if he knew nothing about this.

'Explain further,' he said, as he dropped the glass on the centre table.

'She told me not to speak. She said I was going to destroy the family. She said no one would be able to provide for us if I spoke. I couldn't let that happen. I couldn't let it affect you guys.'

She was crying now and I moved up to sit beside her. I understood her pain. This wasn't easy, it was difficult, and no one may really understand how difficult it was to talk about this. It felt like opening a wound and placing pepper all over it.

'What? Do you mean she knew? All these years and our mother knew? I can't believe this,' Dapo said.

Femi's anger was so visible on his face that I felt sorry for his mother.

'Who was it?' He asked.

I honestly didn't want to hear this part. It seemed as if it would make everything different.

'It was daddy,' she confessed and the air went thick.

I cried with her because to me this was worse. Her father, someone Femi looked up to, how could he do this to his daughter? How in the world could a father rape his daughter? I heard stories about this, and saw it on the news but witnessing this first-hand was earth-shattering.

'My God!' Femi exclaimed as he sat on the floor. Dapo went to get more drink and I held their sister as she wailed.

'It was before we went to the party. I had already been raped before we went and I ran to tell mum but she immediately told me Dapo was taking us to a party and that I should go with you guys. She said if I really needed to say I was raped, I should say someone raped me at the party. I was only 13. I felt helpless. She was my mother. I didn't know what else to do, so I lied. I told you it was Dapo's friend but I never told him who it was because I couldn't put an innocent person in trouble. And because you were so insistent Femi, I begged Dapo to act like he knew who it was. He only agreed to take the blame because I threatened to kill myself,' she explained.

'What kind of parents do we have? I can't believe it. I honestly… God! I'm so sorry for not protecting you then. I kept begging you to come home not knowing you were running away from our horrible parents,' Femi said helplessly.

I watched his eyes move to his brother.

'You should have told me you had no idea. I saw you as a coward who chose his friend over his sister. I thought you knew who raped her but refused to say it. I can't believe I hated you over nothing,' Femi struggled with his words.

Dapo kept drinking. It seemed to be his way to handle all this pain. 'I couldn't blame you then and I don't blame you now either. If the tables were turned, I would have felt the same way. What are we going to do now? Father can't get away with this, he can't,' Dapo uttered but their sister shook her head.

'Do nothing! I'm relieved to have opened up for the first time since it happened. You don't have to do anything to him. I hate daddy so much but I still love him at the same time. I hate mother the most, though. She knew but chose the family name instead. She knew how much I suffered, but kept reminding me that I did the right thing by not speaking up. Daddy, on the other hand, never spoke about it anymore as if it didn't happen at all. If not for how scarred I was from what happened it would have been like that night didn't happen at all,' she lamented.

'Well, it happened and he's not going to get away with it. We never know, he could have more victims,' Femi replied.

After much convincing, their sister still wasn't ready to confront their parents. But Femi said he would do it because he couldn't pretend. We were in bed now and not many words had been spoken since we left Dapo with her.

'Do you want to talk about it?' I asked him softly, my head on his chest.

'Not really, what I need is to know who hurt you too so I can send everyone to jail at once,' he replied and my eyes filled with tears again.

'I just hope your sister is okay,' I said. He rubbed my back softly before turning my head to face his.

'She's not but I will make sure she is eventually,' he said softly.

The next day was even worse, Zainab had called to inform me that she and Dayo had a bad argument and he wasn't answering her calls. Femi, Dapo, and their sister had travelled to Lagos. She had finally decided to confront their parents and despite her saying it was okay for me to come, I knew I shouldn't. This wasn't my place and I had work to do here. I couldn't neglect work just because Femi was my boyfriend. This was the only time Femi and I had been apart since my attack. He made sure to leave me with a bodyguard who was a nuisance because he practically followed me everywhere. His name was Sonny and he had a thick Hausa accent although he didn't talk much. He drove me to work in Femi's BMW and on our way home after work, I realised there was nothing to eat at home.

After getting groceries, Sonny dropped me at home and I was able to convince him to leave me for a few hours because I needed my privacy. It wasn't long before I heard a knock on the door. I dropped my cutlery knowing fully well that Sonny had probably come back. But it wasn't Sonny I saw when I looked through the hole at the door. It was Dayo. I felt so relieved to see him. Judging from the grim expression on his face, it was obvious that he had probably come to talk to me about his fight with Zainab.

'Hi Dayo.'

I took a step to hug him but he immediately pushed me inside and closed the door. I gasped because that push was familiar; the level of aggressiveness, the strong fingers that held my shoulders tightly that I could already feel the blood draining out of them.

'Dayo, what's going on? I don't understand, Dayo don't...'

'Shh,' he murmured as he grinned widely.

'You should know who I am. I kept waiting for you to figure it out but I guess you were not as smart as I assumed you would be,' he said mockingly, my eyes going to the gun he held. He moved to lock the door and turned to me.

'Don't you dare scream or I will blow your brain out.' I'm here to finish what I started. I should have killed you after raping you all those years ago. I would have but you tasted so good that I knew I had to have you again.'

'I don't understand. How could it be you? My God, I even pushed you to my best friend. Please tell me you did not hurt her, Dayo.' I managed to say those words as I thought of him doing the same thing to Zainab.

He laughed as he removed the very familiar mask from his pocket. I had been going crazy wondering who it was not knowing he was with me all along.

'How did I end up in the same company as you? It could not have been a coincidence...' I asked him as he moved closer to me.

'Of course, it wasn't. I was responsible for advertising the new position that was available in the company. I knew you were looking for a job. I know everything about you, every single thing, Tiwa. It was not difficult for me to tell your Lagos friend, Chioma, about a vacancy in the company. I had to get close to her to know what you were up to. You didn't tell her everything but the little you did was enough for me to work my magic,' he laughed as he pulled me closer to him.

I moved to push down his collar and I saw the scar I gave him.

'Oh my God, you mean Chioma. She told me she heard from a friend about the job vacancy. I thought it was a sign that I needed to leave. I assumed…'

'Shh,' he said as he licked my neck.

His gun was pressed against my stomach and I knew all he needed was one hand movement and I would be gone.

'Why're you doing this? What did I ever do to you?' I asked and a low jeering laugh rumbled from him.

'What didn't you do, you mean?' He said.

The hand holding the gun snaking down to the front of my body, rubbing against the swell of my dress.

'It's because of you I don't have a mother. It's because of you I grew up on the streets. My mother abandoned me but was eager to raise you as a stranger. I watched her cater to you from afar. Do you know how that felt? Knowing how much I was suffering but she acted like I didn't exist. You deserved everything I did, you deserve even worse, both of you. Her death wasn't enough, I should have stabbed her instead,' he said distastefully.

Never in my life had I seen such naked smothering hatred, and my tears were overflowing as he grabbed my breast with his other hand.

'Don't tell me you killed her. She was sick. I found her on her bed in the morning.'

He shook his head, his eyes holding so much hatred that it was a shock that he hadn't killed me already.

'It was easy to get in your little house when you weren't around. She deserved it, all it took was a pillow. I couldn't let her die of natural causes,' he paused to laugh.

'You know what made me angrier? She begged me not to harm you even when her son was right in front of her. She pleaded with me to leave you alone. I couldn't take it, I killed her instantly.'

Fury clutched at me and it took all my willpower to not give in to the feral instinct calling me to attack him, gun or no gun. He was crying now and I could see a young boy who only wanted a mother's love, but that didn't justify what he did. He had been merciless, a liar, a murderer and I needed to find a way to escape.

'But why? I'm sure she didn't mean to abandon you. She told me about a child then but she said she never found you' I gasped as he pushed me towards the couch.

'She gave up easily. Immediately she found you, she forgot all about me. I had to go through hell from strangers who treated me like dirt. I slept hungry almost every night in those early years. It was horrible. I wanted to die but not without revenge on you. Do you know why? You are the reason why she gave up on me. You took my mother away from me.'

Someone suddenly knocked on the door and I sighed in relief believing that it must have been Sonny or Femi that had come to my rescue. Dayo held his gun towards me as he walked backwards to peep through the small hole in the door before opening it. My fear grew when Zainab entered. She was going to get into trouble because of me.

'Zainab, you need to leave. Dayo raped me, it was him. I'm so sorry I pushed you towards him. Zainab leave,' I implored but she stood still and her face was expressionless.

'You are such an idiot, who do you think helped me with my plan? Your friend is my partner in crime.'

My heart rate dropped as I looked at Zainab waiting for her to shake her head in refusal, but she only stared at me with her arms crossed. She looked too comfortable for someone that should be scared.

'Zainab? What's going on?' I asked her, my voice breaking but she turned to look at me, her eyes were cold that I found myself shivering at the intensity.

'He's telling you the truth. I've been helping him all along. Who do you think kept those notes in your locker? I mean are you that gullible to think that I would be so nice to someone that I just met? Well, I can't blame you because you are used to getting so much attention,' she snickered as she moved to sit on the black couch by the TV.

I sat on the floor because my legs had become weak from shock.

'Please, tell me you are lying. I opened up to you. I trusted you. You were my best friend,' I said tearfully but she looked at Dayo who looked bored at what was going on.

'Enough with this drama. It won't be long before your useless bodyguard comes back, so I need to finish what I came here to do,' he blurted as he dragged me by my wrist and lifted me.

'I need to know, why did you do this? What did I ever do to you?' I asked her as she watched Dayo forcefully remove my top.

'I would do anything for the man I love,' she replied sarcastically.

Where was Sonny when I suddenly needed him? I instinctively moved for the glass cup on the centre table but he punched my head before I could even try.

'Don't you dare,' he warned as he ripped up my shirt and straddled me. He pulled my shirt above my head and his hand moved under my jeans.

'I'm going to have you and kill you,' he said and no matter how much I struggled, he was stronger.

My head filled with the thought that Zainab was okay with watching this happen. She was okay with him raping me, and she was fine with him killing me. I thought of the first moment I met her, so all that had been an act. She had known I was coming. There were so many questions and so many holes that I needed to fill. I yelped loudly as Dayo pulled my hair aggressively.

'Look at me,' he said.

But I couldn't. If he was going to kill me, the last thing I wanted to remember was his face. I was out of my depth. I closed my eyes in withdrawal when I heard a loud banging.

'Get off her right now,' Femi yelled.

Sonny and some policemen barged into the room, and I was so exhausted that I didn't care that my breasts were open for them to see. At this point, I was done. Dayo pointed the gun toward my head, as he pulled me up with him.

'Don't come close or I will shoot her,' he cautioned and I saw the fear in Femi's eyes.

Dapo stood beside him and it was then that I saw the police grabbing Zainab who looked more scared for Dayo than herself.

'Please, don't hurt him,' she cried out as she tried to wriggle free from the policeman's grasp.

'It's all your fault. Everything is your fault, Tiwa. I hate you so much, I… '

'Take her away,' Femi yelled out as the policeman with the help of another took her out of the room.

'Everyone quiet,' Dayo said loudly, his arm was around my neck.

He pulled me closer to him but I was in so much shock from everything that had just happened that I felt numb. All I could think about was that it had all been a lie. Zainab hated me. She knew everything. I let her into my home. God, I let her in more than I had ever let a friend in. I trusted her. Was this what betrayal felt like? It was horrible.

'Drop the gun,' a tall dark skinned policeman commanded as he held his gun towards Dayo whose heavy breath I could feel through my neck.

'Please,' Femi pleaded.

I could feel the anger through his gaze, fright mixed with fear, his eyes locked with mine and I knew what he was saying even in the silence. He was trying to reassure me, he wanted me to know that everything would be fine but would it really be? I didn't think so.

'I'm not leaving here without her. You can try to kill me but I only have to pull the trigger, and boom she's gone,' he boasted.

His arms were sweaty, and I thought of fighting back but it felt almost impossible.

'You are putting yourself in more trouble by holding on to her. Let her go,' the same policeman said again.

It was then I felt Dayo's hand loosen. It was only for a second but it was enough for me to move forward a little and kick back with all my strength. It was then that I heard the gunshot, only that this time I found myself falling back helplessly.

Chapter Thirty

The Survivor

THE THING IS, I WAS no stranger to pain. I had felt it in varying degrees. I never welcomed pain but it came after me without any warning. I had flashes of consciousness which only featured more blinding light that was occasionally disturbed by dark blurry shades. I tried to listen to the humming sounds around me in an attempt to pick out the words of the familiar voices that I could hear.

I tried to focus on the moving shapes, straining to make out the hazy features of a face but I was incapable of making an adequate sketch. The day came when I was ready to give up. I got tired of fighting but as my breath shortened, I heard an anguished familiar voice of someone repeatedly calling my name and telling me all kinds of things that would only want to make a woman stay, so I decided I was going to stay. I must have unconsciously won the battle with my weak body because I was suddenly back in that sea of light again.

'Tiwa!'

The white light cleared as my vision started to fill with sharper details. I was in a hospital room, and light brown eyes stricken with fear were gazing at me.

'Femi?' I muttered.

'I'm here, baby,' he cooed with frantic gentleness as he moved his fingers to entwine mine.

'What h…happened? I managed to say.

The helplessness in Femi's voice was quickly extinguished by a dark, furious look that reminded me of thunderstorms that came out of nowhere.

'You got shot, Tiwa. We need to stop this game of you being in the hospital and me having to wait for you to wake up because I don't think I will survive the shock if anything like this happens again. I love you so much,' he said, his lips so thin and lightly pressed together.

I giggled or tried to, judging from the unfamiliar sound that came from my mouth.

'I love you too. Tell me what happened,' I demanded and he shook his head as if the memory made him shudder.

'One of the cops shot Dayo when it became obvious that he was going to kill you, but it was too late because he was able to shoot you before we got closer to get the gun from him,' he explained as I tried to recollect the memory of everything that had happened.

'Where?' I asked.

'Your left shoulder,' he answered as his eyes moved down to where my injury must have been under the layers of bed sheets covering me.

'There was too much blood when I got to you,' his face pinched with the torture of someone relieving a very traumatic experience.

'You were unconscious, and it took a long while for the ambulance to come. No one would tell me that you were going to be fine, that it wasn't as serious as it looked,' he added as he dragged a trembling hand down his face.

'They worked on you for days and it felt like an eternity of misery,' he sighed loudly as he ran his fingers through my face.

'At a point, the doctor said it would be a miracle if you survived because you had already lost a lot of blood.'

He looked up at me with those brown eyes of his. I had never seen eyes that looked as haunted as his before.

'If I have to go through the fear of losing you again, I swear to you I will become an absolute madman, Tiwa.'

I smiled as I used my little strength to hold onto his fingers. 'That doesn't sound like a bad idea if I get to see your madman face,' I replied teasingly.

'It's not funny,' he muttered, giving me a withering stare.

'Is Dayo dead?' I asked him and he nodded in affirmation.

But instead of feeling so much relief, I felt pain because I had loved him as my friend but I hated him for killing my mother and raping me. I wished he had survived so I could ask him more questions to know why he would do such horrible things but maybe it was better this way. This way, I would be able to close this painful chapter in my life and it was then that I remembered Zainab. I suddenly felt a bundle of emotions that I could not put into words as memories of the event that had happened overwhelmed me.

'What about Zainab?' I managed to ask and he nodded as he ran his hands through my hair.

'She is in jail currently. She admitted to everything because apparently, her life had been dedicated to Dayo.'

I shook my head still in disbelief. It felt like I was dreaming or in an alien world where only ridiculous things happened.

'I need to talk to her, Femi. I need to know why. Did she not care about me at all? I just… I can't believe it, Femi. I…'

'Shh, just rest. You need it. Don't worry about Zainab for now. You've been through so much. Other people who care about you are here to see you. I sent everyone away earlier. I told them they needed to keep their problems away from you,' he said sternly.

'But now I think you can see them just so you are reminded of how loved you are,' he continued.

'Who? Who came to see me?' I asked him not feeling overly eager to see anyone. Not after finding out that two of my friends were my worst enemies.

'You will see them for yourself. Guess who's also here,' he asked and I smiled.

'Who could that be? I asked.

'An old friend of yours and my aunt, arrived a few minutes ago. She was worried when she heard about everything that had happened. She also wants to meet the girl that won my heart,' he said as he leaned close and bruised a soft kiss on my cheek.

'Tiwa!'

I turned towards the door at the sound of Dapo's voice. Beside him stood Kikelomo as well as Isaac who had his arms around an elderly-looking woman who I remembered vividly from my first day in Femi's company, but it was when I saw Chioma that the tears left my eyes.

'Chioma, what are you doing here?' I asked as my eyes went to Femi.

'She contacted me when the news came up about Dayo and told me about how she was close to him. She has also been helping us with the investigation,' he explained.

'For how long have I been here?' I asked because it seemed like so much had happened for it to be just a day.
'It will be two weeks tomorrow,' Femi replied.

I winced thinking of how difficult it must have been for Femi to wait for me to wake up for so long. I wept as I watched Chioma walk towards me.

'I'm so sorry, Tiwa. I had no idea I was leading you towards the lion's den when I told you about the job. I hate the fact that I played a part in everything that has happened to you,' she expressed but I shook my head as I hugged her tightly.

'I should be sorry. I never called you after I left. I tried so hard to start afresh and forget about my past that it only ended up hurting me. You were truly a good friend to me and I should have called. I'm so sorry,' I pleaded and she nodded as she held me tighter making me yelp in pain.

'Be careful with her,' Femi said worriedly and everyone in the room laughed.

'You are such a mother hen,' Kike said as she walked towards my hospital bed.

'I'm so sorry about everything you've been through. Please know that I understand your pain and I'm always ready to talk when you are,' she offered.

'Thank you for that,' I replied as I noticed that Isaac was watching us closely.

'Are you and him together?' I asked her.

'No, but we were together a few years ago,' she said, a hint of pain flashed in her eyes which told me that there was so much more to their story.

'Oh,' was what I managed to say.

That kind of explained the tension between Femi and Isaac. Femi's tendency to be protective also played a part.

'We will talk about it more when you get off this bed, so please get well as soon as possible,' she said as she moved to hug me again.

Hours later, I had gotten more information from Femi about what happened while I was unconscious. Zainab had been Dayo's accomplice. She had been responsible for placing those threatening notes on my worktable. She had also been eavesdropping on my conversations whenever she could to get more information about my whereabouts. She and Dayo had also hired the person that broke into Femi's apartment to place my picture there because Dayo could not have done it himself as it was too risky. The same person had also been responsible for placing the dead snake in my house. I shuddered as I remembered that day vividly.

Zainab had sounded so worried as if she genuinely cared about me. I called her to tell her what happened not knowing she knew about it in the first place. I needed to see her even if Femi was against it. It was for me. She was currently in jail after she had pleaded guilty to everything. I felt sick at the thought of someone hating me so much that they would do anything to hurt me. She had been in love with Dayo and had been willing to do anything to get him to love her. I thought of her family, I hadn't heard from any of them. Were they as shocked as I was?

I also spoke to everyone that came to see me at the hospital even Isaac and I knew he was also affected by this because of his friendship with Zainab.

'I'm sorry. I know how much you cared about her,' I said to Isaac but he shook his head in response.

'It's not even that, it's the fact that I thought I knew her when, in fact, I did not,' he replied with a sigh, his eyes going to Kike who from the way her hand rested on Femi's shoulder seemed to be having an emotional conversation with him.

'Do you love her?' I asked without thinking.

'I thought I stopped but seeing her again after all these years is proof that I still do, maybe even more than I did before. I know I tried to be with you, Tiwa. Trust me, everything I felt was genuine. I thought I wouldn't be able to feel anything again for anyone after her but when I saw you that day at the party with Zainab, I felt intrigued. I don't know to explain it but it's like you ignited something in me that I thought was forever locked away. So, when I knew you and Femi were together, I chose to respect that because he didn't deserve that, not after what happened between his sister and me.'

I wanted to know more but I could tell that it took him a lot to say these words so I chose to respect that. 'Well, I do hope you get her back,' I said softly, my eyes going to Femi who was walking towards us.

Corinne and Sam had come to see me while I was unconscious. Corinne had also sent me an email earlier.

'I know you are aware that I'm not really a fan of you but I don't wish to see you dead. Get well soon.'

It was weird but this was Corrine. Life could be shocking, isn't it? The people you expect to care do not give a damn while the ones that seem to not care actually do. I also spoke to Mrs Bello, Femi's aunty. She had been the sweetest woman and she made sure to tease Femi about how he would have sent the love of his life away if he had let me go without giving me the job. She also mentioned that she was ready to be a grandmother, so we should hurry to get married before she died.

As much as I wanted to get married to Femi, I knew that he needed time to get over everything with his parents. His father had been arrested after Kike finally agreed to press charges and many other women had opened up about how they were his victims as well, including his mother who apparently had been begging Femi and his siblings for forgiveness, but he said he needed time before he could bring himself to talk to her. These were enough reasons for Femi to not be thinking about marriage. For now, we could just be together and heal from everything that had hurt us.

Epilogue

Love and Thunderstorms

THE MONTHS FOLLOWING MY GETTING discharged from the hospital were eventful. After trying to summon the courage, I finally got a chance to visit Zainab in jail but she refused to talk to me. I went three more times but to no avail. Mustapha, her brother, had called me to apologise on behalf of his family. I was grateful the conversation was over the phone because I wept all through. He said she refused to talk about it to them as well. It was as if she had locked us out of her life. Everything had become non-existent to her because Dayo had died. After trying three more times with no success, I finally listened to Femi and stopped. I had to live with the fact that she would never give me answers. Maybe there was still a chance that she would call me one day to talk, but I chose to not hold on to that hope because I had more to risk if she decided to ever call me. So why not focus on the answers that I did have, on the people that never left me doubting, on the matters that I could handle, on the more books that I could write and the better things that life had to offer, dreams yet to be fulfilled?

I woke up on the morning of my wedding day to find the sunshine winking at the window of the magnificent room I had slept in with Kike and Chioma. The June breeze was frolicking with the curtains and I could not stop myself from smiling at the fact that I would be Femi's wife in a few hours. One year had passed since I got shot, and Femi had proposed to me on our first vacation together in Spain. Everything that happened must have given me such a good writer's flow because I finally finished my book and published it. I kept having back-to-back interviews because of how well-read my book was. Femi had forgiven his mother and had invited her to the wedding but she said she didn't deserve to be there. His father, on the other hand, was in jail and would be there for the next thirty years. It had been difficult for Femi and his siblings to accept the fate of their parents but they were happy now. Kikelomo and Isaac had gotten closer but she kept saying that it was nothing serious.

'The bride is awake.'

I heard Kike say as she opened the door. She was wearing a beautiful purple robe that we had chosen and she held huge and beautiful roses which she handed to me.

'From your soon-to-be husband. It has a note inside,' she said and I sat up to collect it excitedly.

'Read it out loud,' Chioma requested from where she stood behind Kike.

'Yes please,' Kike seconded from where she sat at the other end of the room.

'To the love of my life, Tiwa. I love you endlessly. I've been unable to sleep because I can't get over the happiness that I feel because you are getting married to me. Thank you for coming into my life when you came, and thank you for teaching me what true love is. It's 9 hours, twelve minutes, and 20 seconds till you become my wife and I honestly can't wait. I hope you slept well because you are not getting any sleep when we leave for our honeymoon. I love you, babe. See you soon.'

'Gosh, he's so romantic. I need my own Femi,' Chioma said as she sighed loudly.

'Me too,' Kike also chorused.

We both turned to look at her ridiculously.

'You have Isaac. You just need to give him a chance,' I stated but she shook her head.

'Today is about you, not me. Let's get you ready so you are not late and my brother develops a heart attack thinking you are not coming. I'm going to go check on the makeup artists,' she said as she left the room.

Chioma and I both looked at each other before laughing loudly. The thought that Zainab should have been here ran through my head but I constantly reminded myself that life didn't always go as planned. I had given too much power to the people that had hurt me in the past and I wouldn't anymore. I needed to focus on the good people around me, especially my soon to be husband.

My wedding dress was ivory white with the silhouette of a ball gown. It was strapless with a sweetheart neckline. The bodice was strong around my breasts and waist. It was designed with white silk petals that spread out down the turtle skirt of the dress. I had diamond pearls on that had a splash of pink that had been gifted to me by Femi. I was also wearing the diamond necklace that he had first given me. It was an amazing coincidence that they matched my dress even without planning it and I couldn't wait to see the smile on Femi's face when he noticed them on me. My wrists were sheathed in a pair of fingerless gloves that extended right up to my elbows. My makeup was flawless and, for once, I noticed that my eyes were bright and joyful. There was no trace of pain in them and anyone that would see me now would assume that my past had been a joyful one.

'Wow,' Kike gushed as she sniffled.

'Just wow,' Chioma said softly.

'I can't wait for him to see you,' Kike continued and I laughed nervously.

Kike had become the sister I never had. Our relationship had blossomed so much and I could not be more grateful for this set of people around me.

'Femi is calling,' Chioma said and I hurriedly collected my phone from her.

'Couldn't you wait for one more hour?' I asked him teasingly and he laughed.

'I just needed to confirm that you were still coming,' he replied nervously and I smiled.

'I'm wearing a very heavy wedding dress and I've sat through three and half hours of hair and makeup just for you,' I responded dryly.

'Oh,' he said sheepishly.

'Are you really in your wedding dress?' He continued and I smiled as I imagined the excited look on his face.

'Yes, and if you want me to be early, I need to start leaving,' I noted.

'True! I will see you in church,' he said as he ended the call.

Our wedding was exactly as I had dreamed of as a child. It was in a church in Italy and when he told me that he remembered those words that I had told him the first day we almost kissed by the lake, I felt overwhelming love for him. Our honeymoon would also involve touring my dream countries - the Maldives, Morocco, and Paris. He had planned everything and it was way beyond my expectations. Slow music played as I started to walk down the aisle on Isaac's arm. My eyes focused on the dark tall man in a black suit standing by the altar next to Dapo, his best man. Femi's vows were as beautiful as I imagined them to be. When it was time for us to kiss, everyone applauded as he kissed me heartily. We were now truly married and I was now Mrs Tiwalade Hope Adebanjo.

During the reception, I was having so much fun that my legs were beginning to hurt badly.

'Are you okay?' Femi asked worriedly and I pointed at my feet.

'My shoes are killing me, so don't be surprised if I fall flat on my face,' I explained with a groan.

He grinned as he held my hands and led me towards our table. I scrunched my face as he suddenly knelt and removed my heels through the heavy layers of my skirt only to rub my aching feet slightly before he slipped new white Nike sneakers over my feet.

'I can't believe you remembered,' I said as my heart clenched. He chuckled.

'I wanted you to believe that things like this do happen,' he said as he tied my shoelaces.

I had told him that same night by the lake that I had watched a movie where the bride got away with wearing sneakers at her wedding and that I had found it cool. I didn't think he would make my dreams come true anymore than he already had.

'Have I told you how much I love you?' I asked him and he kissed me softly.

'Yes, but I never get tired of hearing it. Let's go back to dancing, Mrs Adebanjo,' he requested as he stood up.

I grinned as I placed my hand over his, and everyone paved the way for us to take over the dance floor. That exact moment as we danced was when I got the inspiration for my next book and I mean this book, the one you're reading right now. I needed everyone to know that sometimes you don't get closure and that's okay.

There will always be unanswered questions. There will be holes you cannot fill. There will be losses that have the capacity to break you. You will meet people, some are only there during dawn, some while the sun sets, and the ones for you will stay both during the dawn and when the sun sets. That's life.

Life can be perilous but despite all the pain and havoc, happiness can be found. Therefore, I needed everyone to know that my mother was right. I did get my happy ending. I deserved to be loved and so does everyone else, every victim out there, no matter how dark it might seem, no matter how overwhelming the pain may be.

You only need to keep fighting. You're not alone and one day, when God thinks that the time is right and you are able to summon all the strength you have, you will be able to let go of the ghost of the past and claim what everyone should for themselves - a happy ending.

The end.

ABOUT THE AUTHOR

Bridget Akanbiemu was born in Nigeria, she is a first-class law graduate from the University of Liverpool and is currently doing her LLM and LPC at the University of Law, London. She loves talking to God, she enjoys writing, acting and is a sucker for a good romance and Oreos ice cream. When she isn't reading or writing romance stories, she's spending time with her family and friends. This is her first novel, and she is open to her readers contacting her.

@adubri @adubri bridgoakanbiemu17@gmail.com

Printed in Great Britain
by Amazon